Maryneal 1962

BY

ABIGAIL F. TAYLOR

A Wild Ink Publishing Original

wild-ink-publishing.com

Edited by Brittany McMunn

Cover Design by Kate McLain

Layout Design by Abigail Wild

ISBN Print: 978-1-964885-25-4

ISBN Epub: 978-1-964885-26-1

"As you're pretty, so be wise. Wolves may lurk in every guise... Now, as then, 'tis simple truth: sweetest tongue has sharpest tooth." - Charles Perrault

Chapter One

I try to ignore Kitty as she mutters to herself about the outfit she wants to wear. For her, fashion comes easily. Our town, small as it is, sometimes feels like we're stuck in a time warp. Kitty, with her finger on the pulse of the larger cities, stands out with her forward trends. Before today, she'd never second guessed an outfit, so I know her nervous energy must be because of a boy. If I ignore her, I can fake ignorance if Dad asks me about Kitty's dating life.

This is the first year we've been allowed to go to the carnival without Dad. When he told us we could go, a rush of responsibility swelled in my lungs along with a sense of pride that comes with being the responsible older daughter. Now, I'm not so sure. Out of the corner of my eye, I see her stuff tissue down the front of her new cotton brassiere. Kitty only started wearing one a few months ago and she uses it as a weapon.

The twinge of guilt that comes with suspecting Kitty's plans plucks against my lungs and I focus on cutting out pictures of Paul Anka from my magazine. Kitty twirls in front of our floor length mirror and presses her long hands over the waist of a green nylon dress. Only moments before she paraded around in a pink paisley top and white capris.

"I like the dress," I say as I flick the picture over and dab the back of it with a glue brush.

Paul Anka joins my collage of other starlets and crooners like James Darren, Ann Margret, Marilyn Monroe, Chuck Berry, and The Mills Brothers. Dad doesn't mind what music we listen to, even though it's so radical from his own. It's one of the reasons he's so cool, despite being a cop.

Kitty's side of the room pops with much more color. She has a few pictures of her favorite celebrities, but her wall is dominated by swatches of fabrics and dress patterns cut out from fashion magazines. Recently, she added pictures of Standard Poodles, but Dad says the breed isn't a suitable match for our ponies. I don't know if that's true, and Kitty doesn't believe him either. She's done her reading. Poodles are hunting dogs, and they would do well on a small ranch like ours. We suspect Dad just thinks they're ugly.

"Oh, what do you know?" she says with an irritated twist of her lips.

This is understandable. Tall as I am, I prefer overalls or slacks. That way I know I'm fully covered if I bend over.

"It looks good on you, that's all," I say with a shrug.

I run my thumb over Paul Anka's profile, pressing out the bubble of air that has settled between the paper and the blond, speckled wood of my wall. My fingers pass from him to the faded paper along the far end of the wall where my collage starts. Ingrid Bergman stands there. She's my own angel of inspiration; a reminder that tall women can be beautiful, too. Dad cut her out of a magazine article on the evolution of film and gave it to me. I think that if I should ever get married, I'd like my wedding dress to be identical to the white, capped sleeve dress that she wears in this picture.

Kitty gives herself another twirl before deciding on the green nylon dress. That settled, she begins to carefully comb through her small makeup collection, taking each powder and lipstick into serious consideration. She looks up at me, very much a doe-eyed starlet in her own right. Her soft brown eyelashes brush against her round cheeks when she glances down, and the curl of her bangs remains unmoved despite her insistent spinning.

"Come here, will you?"

I fold my magazine and lay it neatly on my bedside table and go to Kitty.

"Are you wearing that tonight?"

I look down at my faded jeans and the nice, buttoned blouse I've worn all afternoon. "I was thinking of putting on a different top."

"The yellow one," she says nodding. "With the pleated front."

I change into it while she looks through her makeup box again and then I stand in front of her and twirl, mimicking her. I bat my eyelashes and make kissing sounds at my own reflection.

"Ha-ha," she says humorlessly. "Bend down, you sasquatch."

She takes up a golden tube of lipstick and taps it gently to my lower lip, which is considerably larger than the top. So is Kitty's, but she styles her mouth in such a way that it looks like an eager heart, ready to press against someone else.

"I'm sorry," I say.

"For what?" she asks, pressing her lips together and rolling them around, silently instructing me to do the same.

"For not knowing how to do all this."

"I didn't know you were supposed to. Suzie's mom taught us."

There are things I know I'm supposed to do as a sister because we are rudderless without a mother of our own. Dad taught me, without shame, about personal hygiene and how to wear a sanitary napkin. He bought my first rubber slip and brassiere, too. But it is my responsibility to teach Kitty these things. I can help her navigate around the chaffing wool and the nonabsorbent cotton of the sanitary napkins, show her how to sew and cook, but she is ahead of me on other things that girls ought to know. Social etiquette, fashion, and charm are her strengths. She's come by them so naturally that I never expected anyone to have shown her.

"Look up," she instructs before brushing my eyelashes with mascara. Then she wiggles her nose. She does this whenever she needs to build up courage to say what's on her mind. "I think Manny Lawrence likes you."

"How do you know that?"

"Bobby Davis told me. He overheard it in the locker rooms after gym one day. Manny and Slick were talking."

Manny Lawrence and Slick James were two of the best-looking boys in my year and I squirm uncomfortably at the idea of them discussing me. I wonder in how much detail. Did they evaluate each part of me or was it just a passing comment?

You know Delah.

Sure...

She's alright, don't you think?

I've never thought about it.

I wonder if boys undress the same way girls do, if they take careful, appraising steps out of their clothing while they talk among themselves, or if they stare straight ahead at the locker room's stained walls. All last summer, Manny dated Lauren Willoby. She dropped him after a session of serious necking at Starry Night Theater left her covered in runny black makeup. Manny claims it was mustache wax but the little hairs on his upper lip are not as prominent as they once were and now everyone on the wrestling team calls him Manny Maybelline.

"I think Slick is much cuter," I say, even though I've never thought to compare the two.

"Slick is easily the cutest," agrees Kitty. "Then Hardy. Manny's not bad to look at but he is very nice." She pinches my cheeks to give them an extra bit of glow and waves me off. "Okay! You're pretty. My turn!"

"Duh! I've always been pretty. You're the one who has to wear makeup to look moderately human."

Kitty playfully sticks out her tongue. I catch a glimpse of my face in her vanity. Despite my tight curly hair flying away from my face, bits of hay still stuck in it from today's chores in the barn, Kitty has made me stunning. I press my lips together again, caught up in the magic of how I can look the same and, somehow, remarkably different all at once. Kitty smirks as I lean in closer to the mirror and touch my nose where she's made the pores vanish with powder.

"Suzie's mother says makeup is for men, so that we can attract the best of the group and live happy lives as happy wives," she informs me as she outlines her eyes with a flourish. "But I'm starting to think that's not true. I wear it because I like it. Maybe that's just me but I feel special dressed up. So, why not feel special every day?"

She is much more detailed to her face than she was with mine but I'm grateful she didn't paint me past my comfort zone.

"You're meeting Suzie at the carnival, right? Or is she coming here, too?" I ask, taking up a hair pick to get out the tangles in my curls without frizzing them into a puffy and unmanageable mass.

"There. By the gates."

We fall into a silence only shared in comfort with people you've lived with. There isn't much to do but idle away the time until my friends, Barbie and Sandra-Lee, get here. Our house is the second furthest away from the town square but for whatever reason, it has always been the meet up place for us.

Kitty, done with her face and hair, moves away from her vanity and picks through our collection of records. Dad bought us an aqua-marine Dansette record player for Christmas and whenever we've found a chance to make it out to Sweetwater or take day trips to Abilene, Kitty and I blow our allowance on new albums. She puts on Paul Anka and does a little two step, her Mary Jane Straps click against the floorboards, and she mocks dancing with a tall partner. I formally bow to her, and she performs a sweeping courtesy.

"Leave enough room for the Holy Spirit," I say, imitating Preacher John's serious tone and Kitty snorts. We dance with our hands on our shoulders, our arms outstretched. Kitty's face turns serious as we sway awkwardly around our bedroom.

"Have you ever kissed a boy?"

"No," I say, blushing violently. I don't want to have this conversation with Kitty. It was bad enough having it with Dad. He talked only about the mechanics involved with being married and having babies. He used his hobby of breeding ponies as an example of the biology but he never told me how it would *feel*.

The needle passes over the scratchy surface of our well used album and ticks off the seconds before it hits the grooves of the next song. I let go of Kitty and walk over to the window to see if I can spot Sandra-Lee and Barbie coming up and over the crest of our dirt road. The sun is low and turns the sky blue-gray and pink. In the far distance, I can see the lights of the Ferris Wheel flicker and chase each other in pops of yellow.

"I'm practically the only one in my year who hasn't," I add bitterly, turning back to Kitty. "Why? Have you?"

She shrugs and then shakes her head. "I don't mean on the cheek. What do you think it feels like?"

"Barbie says it's wet," I say. "She says you're supposed to open your mouth some but not all the way."

Kitty lets out an excited gasp. "Who has she kissed?"

"I'm not telling!"

"Who?"

"Ask her yourself."

Kitty tilts her head to one side, her plucked eyebrows pinching together, and I know she's thinking of pushing the issue or working her way through the tidbits of school gossip she keeps in a corner of her brain. The truth is, Barbie turned real cagey when Sandra-Lee and I asked, so I don't know who she kissed. I think it was somebody un-popular and she doesn't want anyone to know about it. Kitty decides not to ask again.

"What about if he wants to put his tongue in my mouth?"

"Gross! Who would do that?"

She touches her lips thoughtfully, taking up her tube of lipstick and tucking it away into the pearl-pink clutch purse she plans on bringing to the carnival. "Suzie says that's how real women do it. Says she saw it in a movie."

"Well... what are you supposed to do with your tongue if his is in your mouth?"

"I don't know. Maybe it's not so bad."

"It's as bad as spit."

I'm acutely aware of how red my face has turned. The idea of kissing like that seems too personal. I think of how it might taste or the slickness of a tongue on top of mine. I picture Manny and his painted mustache leaning into me and parting his lips. It fills me with a sudden, brief repulsion. At the same time, I don't want Kitty knowing what a kiss feels like before I do. Not just because I'm older and I'm supposed to know these things, but because I don't want her changing. I don't want her to grow up and do things *real* women are supposed to do.

"If Bobby tries to kiss you and you decide you don't want to do it, you don't have to," I say. "Don't let him make you feel like you owe him."

She nods and turns back to the vanity to check that her hair did not stray while we danced. I'm secretly impressed she doesn't bother denying her intentions for the night. "I want to kiss him. I think I do."

"Okay, then," I say but Kitty looks at me, unsure of how to take my response.

"Is there anyone you want to kiss?" she asks.

Again, I think of Manny. Then of Slick, and Hardy who lives in the last house on our dirt road. I've known all of them my entire life. They're the cutest boys in my year and all the girls, even the ones going steady with other boys, have opinions on which of the trio is the best looking. Although I know they're attractive, I've never actually pictured myself touching their skin with any part of mine. I haven't even thought about what it might be like to share a kiss until Kitty asked me.

"I dunno," I admit.

The edges of Kitty's soft brown eyes crinkle but she doesn't push. I grab a fist of my tight curly hair and braid it so I can hide my face from her. Whenever Kitty wants to talk, she has a static heat that spreads out from her and tickles the back of my neck. I'm anticipating the next question she's about to ask, but Dad saves me, calling to us from the bottom of the steps.

"The girls are here! Y'all ready?"

"Yes!" we shout back in unison.

Kitty holds out her arms for me to give a final inspection as Barbie and Sandra-Lee's footsteps ricochet through the house as they race up to our attic room.

"There's lipstick on your teeth," I tell her, and she licks her smile clean.

Barbie, first through the bedroom door, squeals, "Oh my God! Kitty, you're so cute!"

"So, are y'all ready or what?" asks Sandra-Lee, popping her bubble gum. She bends at the knees to check her reflection in the vanity and pats the perfect arch of her twelve-foot blonde bouffant. Sure, her hair isn't really that tall, but it seems that way when sitting behind her in math class. Halfway into the hall, our progress is derailed by an argument. Should we bring purses or keep our money in our pockets? Kitty and I both have new beaded clutches Dad bought for our most recent birthdays.

Since I don't take mine to school like Kitty does, I want to take advantage of the outing to the carnival to use it. I attach the thin shoulder strap before looping it across my body. Barbie, long and willowy in all her movements, dips her hand into the pockets of her tight pants and pulls out a few folded bills. She sticks them into my purse and for that brief instant I am sharply aware of the dynamic energy of her closeness. I pray she doesn't see me blush.

Finally, we descend to the lower levels of the house, chattering in excitement about our chaperone-free evening. Dad waits for us in the entryway, his hand on the front door's brass knob. Clearly he's ready for a few peaceful hours alone.

"Y'all act like you've been away from each other for years!" he chuckles. His voice, a little gruff around the edges, is paired with an easy grin.

We all pause mid-sentence, pat our hair, and smooth down our blouses. Sandra-Lee cups her hand and waves it in mild swoops. She's learned this from Grace Kelly's royal wedding. The whole town had gone to watch the event at the Andersons'. They have a television that picks up signals from Sweetwater and Roscoe. Ever since then, Sandra-Lee has tried to cultivate the delicate charm and beauty of the new Princess of Monaco.

We all follow Sandra-Lee in a promenade of waving to our adoring public. Barbie presents her hand, knuckles up, to Dad. He gathers her fingers and gives them a little shake.

"I want y'all home before dark. Say 'yes, sir'."

"Yes, sir!" we chant back.

"I mean it," he says, thin eyebrows pinching as Sandra-Lee and Barbie run to collect their pink and yellow bicycles, which they've left lying beside the front garden. Kitty stands on her toes and pecks Dad on the cheek before bounding down the porch steps.

"Yes, sir," I say again.

Dad nods and runs a toughened hand over his clean, square jaw. He has a ruddy-cheeked agelessness to him. I'm convinced it's a childlike quality which has molded him into a patient father. Only the crinkles around his greenish-brown eyes and the flecks of gray that have started to appear in his curly brown hair hint at his age.

"I know Bobby Davis is good people but he's still a teenage boy," Dad says calmly.

Blood drains from my face. We live in a small town, barely two hundred people, and I'm embarrassed I thought I could keep something from him. Everybody knows everybody's business, why did I think this time would be different?

Dad waves away my unspoken apology and presses on, "If you see him get out of line, you set him right."

"I will," I promise.

His smile returns and he pushes me toward the others.

Kitty doesn't have a bicycle, but she is content to sit on the handlebars of my powder blue Schwinn Starlet. Dad stands on the porch and watches us disappear around the dirt road's steep curve and out of sight.

The wheels of our bicycles bounce in the ruts made by old, heavy Fords and over the curbs of tall grass that survive in little strips along the path. We pass a few other houses along the way. Mr. Yeats' farm, where Dad's busted a handful of cock fights. The Burnel's blue Queen Anne, which is tumbling down now that Jeb Burnel is too old to take care of the house's bones. We pass Wilma and Martha Anderson tanning in lawn chairs. To them, going to the carnival in the middle of the day is totally square's-ville and they won't make an appearance until evening. Wilma waves to us as we pass, and Barbie, leading us with a casual speed, rings the tiny bell on the left handle of her bike. Our dirt road turns to tarmac and straightens out to a neat, long arrow into Main Street.

The land unfolds around Maryneal like a starched, yellow-green blanket. It is an endless yawn: the town that doesn't die, where men are expected to be men and women are expected to play their part.

A cement plant scars the drawn-out solitude, sticking out like a crooked tooth on the horizon. It keeps the town afloat with steady work. Still, Dad says Maryneal is starting to shrink because the cement plant isn't enough. There is too much of the world and young people can't stand to sit still long enough and appreciate the simple beauty of a quiet town.

For all its shortcomings, Maryneal has a gentle quality that makes me want to stay. I've never thought to live anywhere else but here and I can't imagine what a larger town might be like. How can anyone want to live in a place so big you don't know who your neighbors are? Or a place so loud you can't hear the bullfrogs at night or ponies whickering in their stalls?

True, there's not much in the way of entertainment except for Starry Night Theater, where I work in the summer and on weekends during the school year. Other than that, the only options are church socials, loitering around the square, and sneaking out to the old graveyard to smoke reefer and drink beer. Best of all, at the start of summer, when the ground is soft enough for tent stakes and the nights are still cool, the carnival comes through.

People from all over Nolan County come in to take dates, spend money to earn a prize, or buy tickets to ride the Tilt-a-Whirl. There are fun houses with mirrors that stretch and pull and mash you together until you're nothing more than a spread of color. There's eating contests and sideshows with men and women covered in tattoos, barking out their feats of strength and death-defying stunts.

Livestock is presented near the carnival grounds, too. Some years ago, people who sat on Nolan County's committee decided it would be more convenient to host the Stock Show at the same time and it's done a lot of good for the communities. Last year, Dad sold off three ponies and used some of that money to buy our newest mare off of an Indian down in Bitter Creek.

In the evenings, visitors from neighboring towns swarm to the square. Diggs' Pharmacy is packed with folk buying ice cream or finding any old excuse to stand near the air conditioning unit that turns the store into an ice box, even when temperatures reach over 110 degrees. Buzzy's Diner gets almost too much business for the short-order cook to keep up with. The sticky, humid air permeates with the smell of grease and hard clashes of laughter. Buzzy allows blacks to eat in the main room and the diner becomes its own sideshow. Blacks watching us watching them eat, each group trying to figure out what makes us so uniquely separate. Maryneal is fully white. A few families, like the Anderson, hire black or Hispanic help, but we usually don't see entire families coming into Maryneal unless the carnival is in town.

If we follow the road directly, we'll wind up at the church. Instead, Barbie veers to the right and we pass behind Diggs' Pharmacy, Lone Apple Bank, and Burnel's Goods. It's a quick ride through the back of the shops but I have to pedal slower with Kitty on the handles. Barbie and Sandra-Lee get too far ahead of us. They stop in the field between the square and the Starry Night Theater. Threads of bent yellow grass weave across the field, marking others who have ridden their bike through. Sandra-Lee takes a small flask from the basket hanging off the front of her bike and the silver catches the light as she shakes it, urging me to hurry. Barbie laughs at some unsaid joke, her tangle of bronze hair caught up in the wind. She combs her fingers through it and a few strands stick to her lip gloss.

"What is it?" Kitty asks when I finally reach them. She hops off the handlebars and rubs her sore bottom with the backs of her hands.

"Butterscotch Schnapps." Sandra-Lee removes the lid of her flask and holds it out for us to smell.

It reminds me of the hard candies old ladies like to suck on during Preacher John's long services so they don't disrupt by coughing.

Barbie takes the first, tentative sip. "Yuck! It's like medicine and syrup."

"Can I try?" asks Kitty.

We all exchange glances. I nod. "Just the one."

She tries it, swishes the thick liquid around her mouth, and swallows. "I kinda like it. It doesn't taste like booze."

"I know! Sometimes Mom puts it in her evening coffee." Sandra-Lee nods and drinks, then she offers it to me.

I take the flask and sniff again. Not only is Kitty about to be kissed before me but she's now had a drink, too. I'm surprised by the bitterness of my thought and take two drinks just to prove I'm as cool as my little sister. It tastes the way it smells; sticky and hardened with sweetness. It coats my tongue before the flavor settles on the back of my throat, and I hand the flask back to Sandra-Lee.

"I'm with Barbie on this one. It's gross."

"More for me then," says Sandra-Lee with a shrug.

We all take another sip, and when I gag, Barbie throws her head back with an infectious laugh. Her loose hair catches again in the wind. Sandra-Lee tightens the lid and tucks the flask back into the bottom of her basket.

We push our bikes over the last crest of the hill and park them behind Starry Night Theater's concessions stand. Mrs. Dunne complains every year about how close the carnival lot is to the theater. She's always saying she loses business when it comes through town, but I honestly don't think that's true. I think Mrs. Dunne is at the age where she likes to hear herself complain about something.

During these months, when people all over Nelson County flood into the carnival, they end up coming to the drive-in, too. Last year, we ran out of popcorn there were so many people. It wasn't just locals either. I sold tickets to *Creature from the Haunted Sea* to a few geeks and tattooed buskers who stayed in the back on the bleachers with a lot of the blacks where they wouldn't be bothered. A woman the size of a toddler came in with them. I'd never seen anyone like her, flat nosed and bulging in all the wrong places. She was very polite, and I wanted to see her act at the carnival, but I'm not old enough to go to any of the tent shows without Dad. He hates how the geeks are forced to display their oddities, so I've never been.

The carnival is as unchanged as it's ever been. Every year long lines surround the ticket booths and stands selling beer, lemonade, and salted almonds. The fun houses and rides are in the back with arcade games and photo booths lining the littered paths. It smells of fried food and hot metal and grease. Barkers shout and taunt. There's so much laughter it comes in waves after the metallic plinks and clangs of penny whistle music. Just a little way beyond the fun houses are the tents where, for a few cents a head, the exotics of the world are relieved: bearded women, limbless men, feather dancers, and sword swallowers.

Kitty's friends wait by the ticket booth, but I stop her from running to them. Not far from them are the boys from the JV football team, Bobby Davis among them.

"What?"

"Do you have enough money?"

She holds up her clutch purse but knows better than to flash the cash around in front of all these strangers. Dad always tells us to respect the carnival workers but be mindful of where they are. He says they're Travelers and their ways are very different from ours. Stealing is not a crime but an opportunity.

"Okay, just keep it in front of you."

"Obviously."

Sandra-Lee nudges my arm and gives Kitty a wink. "Delah, she knows how to handle herself. Let's just go."

"Amen!" says Barbie. "I want to go to the fun houses!"

"Okay! Okay! Just... I don't know... meet us at the Tilt-a-Whirl by eight-thirty."

Kitty nods in quick little jerks and shouts over her shoulder as she darts through the clusters of families still waiting to purchase tickets. "Sure. See you later!"

We pick the shortest line and wait our turn to buy the entry pass and tickets for food and rides.

"Oh my gosh!" Barbie grabs onto my wrist as we pass through the gates. "Look! There's Hardy. Isn't he just the cutest?"

"Yeah, he's swell," I roll my eyes. Sandra-Lee smirks.

"Whatever!" Barbie's smile spreads wide. "If the two of you get lost in the hall of mirrors, I bet you wouldn't complain."

Barbie giggles again. "Never mind Hardy. There's someone else checking you out Sandra-Lee!"

"Who?" Her head jerks over to the group of boys, round cheeks burning.

"Act casual!" says Barbie, playfully slapping Sandra-Lee's arm. "But it's Slick."

I look in the direction Barbie nods her head. Slick leans against the corn dog stand, chewing on the edge of a stick, a tan Stetson tilted back on his high forehead. He mumbles something to Manny and Hardy beside him, but his eyes keep flickering over to us. His flannel shirt is tucked into his Wranglers so everyone can see the belt buckle awarded to him from last year's Ag competition.

"Gosh, he *knows* how to wear a pair of jeans," Sandra-Lee whispers and a deep blush spreads down her neck.

"Do we want to go over there?" I ask.

The boys are all on the wrestling team, and therefore, the most popular in our year. Barbie and Sandra-Lee could easily fit with their crowd but I'm too quiet for them.

"Just follow my lead," says Barbie.

Sandra-Lee mimics the way she sways her hips. I've never managed to master that particular sashay, so I keep to my own, quick pace. I end up at the corn dog stand before them. The boys expect me to say something, but I can't think of anything. I open my mouth and only a wordless stammer escapes. I turn to the cashier and order a Nehi. It's handed to me with the cap still on and I look around the outside of the booth for a bottle opener.

"Let me get that for ya," Slick mumbles. He casually takes the bottle away from me and uses his belt buckle to snap the tin cap away from the glass.

"That's quite a trick you have," says Barbie, batting her eyes.

"Yeah?" asks Slick as though it were nothing, handing the soda back to me.

"Yeah," agrees Sandra-Lee and the color in her cheeks has given her an attractive glow.

Slick straightens from his oh-so-careless lean against the stand and the cashier looks relieved to be rid of him at last. He gives Sandra-Lee a once over and says, "Honey, I'm going to win you a bear! C'mon!"

She takes his hand, and they stroll off without looking back. Manny whistles low and his puckered lips bend his mustache wax awkwardly until the skin around his mouth looks like a cat's anus.

"Smooth," he says.

"Y'all want to keep us company?" asks Barbie. "We're going over to the fun houses."

"Sure, that's where we're headed. Right, Hardy?"

"I guess y'all can tag along," says Hardy with a grin.

I swallow a mouthful of the Nehi but it reminds me too much of the Butterscotch Schnapps. Into the trashcan it goes, where it clanks loudly before settling onto crumpled paper and half eaten nachos.

Chapter Two

It's warm inside the fun houses, especially where the mirrors catch the late afternoon sun, and it smells of plastic and cotton candy. Some paces ahead of us, a little girl laughs as a mirror warps her mother's face into an egg and then into an hourglass. Barbie crashes into a dead end she thought was another path out of the maze and the way she laughs at herself makes me laugh, too.

Hardy stops to look at his expanded self in one of the mirrors. "I look like my dad! Come see!"

We stumble over to him through the mirror maze. Both Manny and I get lost in another wrong turn and have to double back. It's surprising at how vast the fun house is on the inside. From the line, it didn't look all that impressive. Manny threads his fingers into mine and leads me the other direction. His skin is warm and dry against mine and I'm not exactly sure when I should let go. I don't know if I mind him holding my hand but all I can think about is Kitty saying Manny is interested in me. Does his holding my hand mean something more? Then another thought hits me as we turn down the next path to follow the echoing laughter of our friends; holding Manny's hand feels so much different than holding Barbie's. For a flash, I wish it was her with me instead of him. There is a comfort in her familiarity I can't find in Manny, no matter how much he smiles at me.

We finally reach the others. Hardy turns himself sideways and puffs out his cheeks. "I've seen the horrible future! Quick, somebody, knock on wood so it doesn't happen!"

Manny lets go of me and taps his fist against his own crotch. I tighten my lips and try not to laugh at the crude meaning. He winks and a little titter escapes me. Barbie waves me over to another mirror. She leans into it and her face expands like a bull frog's. The mirror stretches me out like saltwater taffy. I shift for a better look, and I'm suddenly squeezed together. We giggle as we make fish faces and continue to warp ourselves.

Hardy sighs. "It only made you taller. Damn! Why can't I have your luck?"

"I'll trade you a few inches any day," I say.

I'm six feet tall and it's never really bothered me. I like the fact I can reach the higher shelves, work around with heavy equipment in Dad's barn. Best of all, I like it when my teachers can't look down their noses at me. Before tonight, I haven't thought about what it would be like to date somebody shorter.

Manny, decidedly bored with the mirrors, darts ahead to the next part of the fun house. He shouts, "These steps move!"

"They did that last year!" Hardy shouts back, rolling his eyes at Barbie and me.

"Yeah, but I forgot!"

Barbie shrugs as Hardy hurries to catch up with Manny. We work our way more slowly through the maze until we make it to the shifting stairs, then through a rolling barrel, and back down a set of stairs that don't move but are surrounded by surreal paintings of men and women turning into animals. These stairs spit us out onto the paper-strewn carnival grounds.

"Let's check out that one!" Barbie says, pointing to another fun house with Sunny, Cher, and The Partridge Family painted on the front.

"I bet it's not any different than this one," says Manny with exasperation. "Besides, there's hardly any line for the roto jets!"

"Heck no!" says Hardy. "I'm not getting on that with you. Last time you lost your lunch!"

"I did not. In fact, I bet I could eat three hot dogs *and* drink a large coke and not vomit."

"Make it six hot dogs and you got a bet," says Hardy.

Manny considers this. The roto jets clank up a candy-striped pole and spin clockwise as the arms shift up and down, causing the seats to shake. "Okay, but you gotta do it, too."

They spit into their hands and shake on it.

Barbie tosses her hands up in the air with mock defeat. "I'm not going to subject myself to this. Let's go see what trouble Sandra-Lee is getting into."

For a second it looks as though Hardy is going to convince us to tag along but Manny is tugging him to the hot dog stand. With a frown, Hardy looks to Barbie and then me. "Catch you later?"

"Sure," I say. "By the games?"

"Dude! Let's get a move on before the line gets long!" Manny moans with another tug on Hardy's Letterman's jacket.

Barbie and I march off in the other direction, trying to figure out where Slick and Barbie might have wandered off to. We walk up and down the sawdust rows, pausing to admire the goldfish in tiny glass bowls offered up as prizes, or the delicate clouds of pink cotton candy piled up on paper cones. A little black boy runs ahead of us, nearly knocking Barbie down, and not long after, a young woman speeds after him. One of her hands holds onto her pretty, blue velvet hat while the other stretches out like a claw, ready to snatch him by the overalls. She shouts an apology as she passes us. The little boy spins and hides behind a trash bag, thinking he's only playing a game, unable to see the agitation on his mother's face.

We reach the end of the main attractions. Up ahead is a makeshift archway staked into the ground. Over the top reads **Oddities!**

Barbie threads her fingers through her hair and looks around. "Well, let's head on back to the games. I guess maybe we missed them."

"Wait! Can I just look at the show list? I want to see if there's a knife throwing contest like last year."

Since Dad has always been against these types of sideshows, neither Kitty nor I have ever been allowed to go. This year is different because I'm old enough to go without a chaperone and I don't want to miss out on anything.

"Sure," says Barbie. "That could be fun to watch."

We pick our way through the breezeway, littered with peanut shells and wrappers the warm wind kicks this way and that toward the small red tents at the back of the lot.

One of the barkers sees us and shouts, "First show starts at ten o'clock! Hurry and get your tickets now! Seats are limited!"

"Are there any shows that start before eight?" I ask.

The barker rolls his curly mustache around his thumb and looks down the row of tents, considering. "Nope! Earliest show is ten o'clock."

My insides deflate into nothing. So much for trying to see a show without Dad hovering to tell me off.

"You should come and see our strong man! He can lift five hundred pounds with one hand!"

"I don't even know what five hundred pounds looks like!" says Barbie, breathlessly, as she looks at the painted poster of a man wearing only a leopard spotted loin cloth.

"Well come to the show and see it for yourself!" He flashes a wide smile, the brim of his straw hat cuts a shadow attractively across his pointed, bronzed face, and I'm reminded of a coyote.

Barbie looks at me, wide, hazel eyes shining with the same excitement I felt seconds before I realized I wouldn't be able to see any of the shows because of my curfew. "Maybe you can sneak out?"

The thought didn't occur to me, and I think of Dad's face knitting together when he realizes I disobeyed him. "I don't know... maybe."

"Live a little, why don't you?" says Barbie and she fishes out her pocket money for a ticket. "I bet Sandra-Lee would love to see it, too! We can say you're spending the night at my house. My parents won't care if we stay out late."

I chew on my lip. I've never done *anything* bad before. If I stay out past dark, just the once, it wouldn't be so awful. Besides, it's just a strong show, and if I make sure Kitty is home safe when she's supposed to be, that's even better. The barker wiggles his thin eyebrows and holds a second ticket in the air. It's like he's read my mind.

"Okay! Why not!"

"That's the ticket!" He plucks my money out of my fingers with a flourish. "See you both at ten! Now, why not go entertain yourselves with Madam Lulu and her palm reading?"

He gestures down the row of tents with an open hand. At the far end sits a wooden wagon painted in pastel greens and yellows. A little step ladder leads to a rounded door with *Madam Lulu* painted in white, joined-up writing.

"Fortunes told! Lucky charms! Mystic magic love potions? She's got it all!"

This time it's Barbie who hesitates. "That's evil. You know Preacher John says that's the Devil at work."

"Oh, it's just a load of hooey!" I tell her, waving my hand in the air. "It's all an act, isn't it?"

I look to the barker for confirmation, but he only shrugs and curls his fingers around the long hair on his chin. "Gotta find out for yourself."

With a burst of sudden determination, I pocket my ticket for the late show and hurry down the path to the Traveler's wagon. Barbie pants behind me, her shoes slapping the soft earth as she catches up.

"What do we do?" she asks, clutching her purse. "Do we go up and open the door or knock?"

I look behind us to see if the barker is still there but he's vanished and when I turn back the round wooden door swings open and a rasping voice shakes out of the wagon. "Enter."

"Oh, Delah, no!" Barbie shivers.

The heat of her hand slides against my wrist but I'm already walking up the small set of steps. The entrance to the wagon is so small that even someone shorter than me would have to duck to avoid getting hit over the head with the brass bells hanging from the arch. Despite herself, Barbie follows me up the creaking, painted steps.

A bony and frail woman sits on a pile of cushions facing the entryway to her wagon. In front of her is a low, circular table made of unfinished wood and painted to look like the constellations. Her hands flick through a red painted card deck. A fat, silky scarf hides her hair, and she doesn't have any eyebrows, not even drawn in to distinguish her forehead from the rest of her. Free of makeup or perfume, her freckled skin has the texture and color of new leather. Long, bare feet stick out from billowing green gauchos and a black halter top with long sleeves slashed to reveal pointy, freckled shoulders. She is the most oddly beautiful person I've ever seen.

"Sit," commands Madam Lulu in that same rough voice and gestures to a pile of cushions at the side of the table closest to me.

"Do I need to take off my shoes or something?" I ask.

Barbie hovers outside the door, her head dipping in and out of the darkened space, curiosity betraying her.

Madam Lulu has beautiful silk fabrics draped over the lamps and woven carpets lining the floor of her wagon. Behind her is a little kitchenette with cabinets painted in the same yellow as the exterior and I've only just realized she probably lives and sleeps here when she's not traveling with the carnival.

"Thank you for asking," she says and the skin above her large, nut-brown eyes crinkles in amusement. "But you may leave them on if that is more comfortable to you."

I look behind me. Barbie returns a nervous glance. The air shifts, the quiet denseness of something unearthly and I understand Barbie's fear. I think of Preacher John's damnation of things ungodly.

Madam Lulu lets out a gentle sound that is trapped somewhere between a chuckle and a sigh. "Your friend may listen by the door, or she can come and sit with you. I don't bite."

Barbie stays where she is. "Th-thank you. I'm okay."

Madam Lulu nods to the cushions in front of her and I take a seat, crossing my legs. The pillows are full of down and fluff up at my sides. Little bits of feather poke into me. I ask, "What do I need to do?"

"Would you prefer the tarot, or your palm read?" She gestures to the cards she was shuffling before I came in.

"What's tarot?" I've seen crystal ball gazing in the movies and palm reading, too, but I've never seen cards used.

Madam Lulu picks up the deck and shuffles them quickly through her long fingers. "You will pick seven cards in silence, and I will flip them over and explain their meanings. You take from it whichever calls out to you. For example, if you pick the Seven Arrows, it could mean you are about to gain the upper hand in a struggle or that you need to prepare yourself for a task that is suddenly presented to you. If one of those interpretations sparks a memory or thought we can discuss how it relates to the next card. Sometimes a card will not mean anything to you and that is fine as well. It doesn't have to have a meaning at all."

"That could be fun," I say.

"Yes, it is very interesting," she agrees.

I'm curious if I will ever get tired of hearing the way she speaks. Her voice is almost too deep and rough edged to belong to someone so frail. There is no accent, but a weird melding of vowels.

"Okay. I'll give that one a try."

She hands me the deck of cards. "Shuffle them face down and try not to think of anything in particular or your energy will direct the reading to that specific thing."

I take the cards, which are tattered and worn, and shuffle them as best as I can. I've never managed to do the bridge with cards the way Dad can. I stop, wondering if I've already ruined the reading because I thought of him.

"Are you finished?"

"Let me try again."

I shuffle the deck again, determinedly focusing on their deep purple backing and the pale cracks running through the paint. I hand them back to Madam Lulu. Then my thoughts travel to Barbie and how much she can see from where she stands. I turn to give her an encouraging grin, but I can't see her face now because much of the sunlight is behind her.

Madam Lulu fans the deck out on the low table between us so all of them are available for me to access. "Pick out seven. Take your time."

I'm slower in the selection considering moments ago I was adamant this was all just a magic trick. Picking the cards has suddenly become a very important process, and I hover over a few before drawing out one after the other. Once I'm done, Madam Lulu swipes her hand over the remaining cards and puts them back into a neat stack. She flips over one card at a time and explains them to me.

She pauses over the fourth card and her fingers tremble as they touch the purple backing. She doesn't say anything at first but shifts her hand back across the other three, as though testing the heat off them, before finally flicking over the fourth. The image is of a man lying face, blood and dirt surround him with ten swords standing out of his exposed back. Madam Lulu doesn't explain to me what it means. Instead, she begins frantically flipping over the rest and a deep rumble escapes her throat. There is a tower being struck by lightning, the twisted body of a man with a mangy head of a dog, and an upside-down heart suspended in the air with three knives.

"What is it?" I ask, confused by the sudden change in her attitude. Before the fourth card, she had stayed perfectly neutral. "Is this part of the routine?"

"Routine? Routine?" she mumbles. The word comes deep from inside of her. She takes more cards from the deck and flicks them over the cards I've already selected. "No. No. I was safe from this! I paid attention to all the signs!"

Madam Lulu scrambles to her feet and moves around her tiny wagon, shifting through the cabinets where mason jars and misshapen bottles clank together. My shoulders curl in, and I watch her in my own silent panic. Should I run or wait?

Behind me, Barbie hisses, "Delah! Delah, let's go!"

I slowly uncross my feet and begin to crab walk backward to the round door but Madam Lulu spins on her heels and screams, "Wait!"

I stop and so does she. There is a wild and wet-eyed fear that crumbles the skin around her bony face. Her hand reaches out to me with the demand before it drops to swing loosely beside her. "Wait," she says again, softly this time. The ridges of her throat move up and down as she swallows. She returns to rummaging the cabinets and mutters to herself. "I can't find it... I can't..."

"What can't you find?" I whisper.

"This will have to do for now."

She takes down a small glass jar filled with an amber liquid and hands it to me.

"I'm not paying for that."

"No charge! It is aconite and holy oil. Dip your finger into this and make the sign of the cross. On your door. Each window of your house! I'm sorry. I'm sorry! I've brought a danger to this town, and you've crossed hairs with it! I don't know how, but you are in its sights! Please, do as I've instructed. Guard yourself. Pray to your Jesus! *Please!*"

"Okay," I say, and I take the jar.

"Go home right now while the light is still strong. Go home and lock the door behind you and tell your father you are scared! Tell him whatever you must so that he will protect you and your sister!"

"How do you know I have a sister?"

She grabs my jar-filled hand and pushes it into my chest. "Promise you will do this!"

Barbie hoists me up by the armpits and frees me from Madam Lulu. "She promises! Okay?"

"Go. Go now!"

Madam Lulu shoves past us and we fall off the stairs and into the sawdust. She ignores our grunts of shock and shoves the steps inside the wooden frame of the wagon. She bolts the round door shut and at a near run moves around the wagon to hop into a mini-bus the wagon is hitched to.

I help Barbie up to her feet and we step back to watch Madam Lulu make short work of driving away from the lot and out of the carnival.

Barbie and I exchange nervous glances then burst out laughing. We swat at each other's legs, freeing our clothes of the sawdust we landed in. The molten glow of the sunset has spread over the steppes, scrub brush, and desert spoons. I can still see the wagon bounce over the kicked-up dust.

"That was a bit much," I say once our laughter has died out. My hands continue to shake. "You think she meant to head off to Bitter Creek?"

"I don't know." Barbie runs her fingers through her long hair and plucks a bit of yellow straw free from her bronze tangles. "She didn't even take any money from you. Maybe we should just go."

"But it's not even close to eight. Let's just find Sandra-Lee and see what she wants to do."

"But what about that holy oil?" She takes it from me and holds it up to catch the sun. "Looks kinda like pee."

"Eww. I hope it's not." I take it from her and stick it in my purse. "I'll take it home with me. If I hear someone outside, I'll put it on my window like she says."

Barbie glances around uncertainly. Barkers and performers in heavy cloaks and sequenced costumes hurry between tents, setting up for the late-night shows, but a few stop when they see Madam Lulu's space has become suddenly vacant.

"Where'd she go?" a man with his face covered in bright tattoos asks us. Barbie gives a tiny yelp at his appearance.

"I dunno," I say and point westward. "She went that way."

"Damn," he says. His tongue is forked like a snake's. "Must have a good reason, huh?"

"I dunno," I say again.

The man shrugs and continues on to his tent. Barbie and I look at each other in silence. Then the whirring and plinking of arcade games and musical rides swells again and we are reminded where we are.

Barbie throws her head back in another burst of trilling laughter, tears running down her face. Her wide mouth sucks in air with momentum until she finally manages to wheeze out, "Oh my Gosh! Oh my Gosh! I was so freaked!"

"I was, too!" I admit and I'm laughing because Barbie has to hold onto me to keep from sliding into the soft grass. "What a weird person!"

"Sandra-Lee is going to scream when she hears this!" she says as she regains some composure. We walk back down the Barkers' gauntlet, and I steal another glance over my shoulder. The man who told us about Madam Lulu is nowhere to be found and there's a dark niggling in the pit of my stomach. I'm starting to doubt how much of that card reading was just for show, but I'm glad Barbie is beside me. I'd hate to be standing here alone with the weight of the reading pressing in on me.

We find Sandra-Lee and Slick waiting in line at The High Striker. Wilma and Martha Anderson are hanging around, too. They're wearing similar rayon polka-dot dresses. Martha's is lilac with white dots and Wilma's is white with lilac dots. Their matching blonde bobs curl underneath their ears. Wilma has a daisy clipped in her hair. They have always liked dressing this way, adding an extra flair to the fact they are the only set of twins in the entire county.

"Hey!" says Barbie and she gives each twin a side hug. "Y'all finally decided to join us!"

"Well… we're here at any rate," says Martha smoothly.

I've never liked Martha. Wilma might be the biggest gossip in school, but Martha is petty and stupid.

"I'm sure someone *must* be happy to see you in public," I respond and Sandra-Lee tucks her face into Slick's big shoulder so Martha can't see her laughing. Slick, on the other hand, doesn't care that Martha sees him approve of my comment. He gives me a wink and Martha's peppermint-red lips curl in a silent sneer.

"Did you see Lauren Willoby? She's here with that *senior.* Roger Landis." Wilma says, attempting to smooth over the static between me and her sister. Her thinly plucked eyebrows wiggle dramatically. "And I heard they were caught kissing behind the ring toss booth by Sheriff Muller!"

"No!" says Barbie.

Sandra-Lee says nothing, but her eyes briefly flicker to Slick's as though she likes the idea of getting caught behind the ring toss with him.

"Did you see them kissing?" I ask.

"Well… no," Wilma admits. "But I saw them over by the popcorn stand and Roger's lips are all red."

"Maybe he had a cherry ice pop?"

"Oh, Delah! You're no fun!" Wilma says lightly and flicks her hand at me.

It's Slick's turn to try and ring the bell on The High Striker and the barker takes his money, then steps aside to reveal the hammer Slick is meant to use.

"You get three turns!" the barker announces. "See if you can win a prize for the lucky lady!"

Slick tilts his Stetson backward, his enormous arms flexing against the surprising weight of the hammer. His shirt strains across his chest and arms until all the wrinkles have vanished and Sandra-Lee ex-changes a guilty look of pleasure with me and Barbie. Embarrassed I'm caught looking, my cheeks burn.

Barbie examines him the same way she did with the poster of the Strong Man. Slick flexes his fingers around the smooth wooden handle and swings it in a wide arc. The silver head slams down, and a small metal ball shoots upward. It clanks loudly against the bell at the top.

The barker watches the ball slide back down to the base of the game. "Three outta three wins you a live goldfish!"

Slick turns to Sandra-Lee whose face turns a deeper shade of pink. "What do ya say? Your daddy gonna let you have a goldfish?"

"Sure," she squeaks.

Slick nods once and slings the hammer again and again. Each time the metal ball hits the bell with a deafening clang.

"Whooo-weee!" exclaims the barker to the small crowd that's gath-ered to watch Slick wield the hammer. "This must be the son of Thor! Anyone else think that they can master the High Striker? Step on up! Win your girl a prize!"

He disappears behind the game and returns with a small bowl with a bright orange and white fish swimming inside. Slick takes it from him and shows it to Sandra-Lee, his hard face becomes softer as he grins wide. "Is it okay if you're my girl now?"

"I'll be your girl," Sandra-Lee says. Now her whole face is red. She takes the fish from Slick and holds it close to her so it isn't jostled around.

"Oh, Slick! That's the sweetest thing I've ever heard," coos Wilma. "Isn't it the sweetest?"

"Sure is," says Martha, rolling her eyes. "Look! There's Hardy! Let's go over and say hey."

The six of us walk across the littered lot and Hardy waves at us. At first, I think he's alone, but Manny appears out of the bushes, wiping his mouth with the back of his hand.

"Let me guess who won," I say and Hardy points at himself with both thumbs.

"Dag, Maybelline!" chuckles Slick, roping his arm around Sandra-Lee's narrow shoulders, mindful of her bouffant. "How many times I gotta tell you? Don't go tryin' to out eat Hardy! He'll win every time!"

"It wasn't an eating contest," I tell Slick. "It was a 'who can hold six dogs down and ride the roto jets without hurling' contest."

"And a large coke!" adds Hardy.

"And a large coke," I say.

Manny's cheeks expand and he disappears behind the bushes again.

"Dag!" says Slick again. He looks at Sandra-Lee. "Say, you want to ride those roto jets or the Ferris Wheel?"

"Uhm…" she looks down at her goldfish.

"I bet the conductor of the ride wouldn't mind babysitting your pet. I bet they're used to watchin' peoples' things."

"What time is it?" I ask Hardy.

He checks the new wristwatch his father gave him for his birthday last month. "Just after eight. Why? Gotta date?"

"Yeah with the Jolly Green Giant. He's really swell."

We all laugh, even Manny, but Martha tries to dig at me. "Only a Giant would be interested in you."

"At least I'm interesting," I say with a shrug. Hardy barks out a laugh and slaps me on the back. Manny struggles out of the bushes again.

"What's so funny?" he asks.

"Nuthin'," says Slick. "You missed it."

"Your mother," says Hardy.

"Watch it!" says Manny and he holds up two fists.

"We've got time for a ride. Don't we?" Barbie asks me. "If the lines aren't long?"

"Wait… do you really have a date?" asks Hardy, surprised and serious.

"Dad wants me and Kitty home by dark. We're going to meet her at the Tilt-a-Whirl soon."

"Well, hell!" says Slick. "I could ride that thing all day! Let's head thataway."

"But Wilma and I haven't even gone to the fun houses yet!" Martha simpers. She pouts her lips, batting her eyes at Hardy and Manny. "Don't you boys want to go?"

"Why?" asks Manny. "We've already seen them. They're the same as last year."

"Are they? Pooh," says Wilma. "I guess we can do those later. I don't mind going on the Tilt-a-Whirl, but it makes Martha sick. Maybe you can watch Sandra-Lee's fish?" she adds hopefully.

"I will not!" Martha stamps her foot and storms off toward the fun houses.

Wilma looks to us and shrugs. "I don't know what has gotten into her. Maybe I'll have a talk, and we can catch up later?"

"Sure," says Hardy. "You know where we'll be."

Wilma waves to us and then darts after Martha, shouting her name as she weaves her way through the clusters of families. The rest of us head on over to the Tilt-a-Whirl and line up behind some older kids from our school and a few from Roscoe. While we wait, Barbie tells everyone about Madam Lulu, the tattooed man with the snake tongue, and how we were pushed off the wagon before Madam Lulu drove it off. She's an excellent storyteller and describes everything without exaggeration, except for how her hands flap around as she talks.

"Dag," says Slick when Barbie finishes. "What y'all do?"

"Nothing," I shrug. My hand presses against the outer lining of my purse. I'm glad Barbie didn't mention the oil. I like having something kept secret. "She just... I dunno. She looked at some cards with pictures on them and then got real upset."

"You shouldn't be messing around with that stuff," says Manny. "Preacher warns us all the time about the Devil's influence."

"Hog wash!" says Hardy. He slips his hands into his back pockets and watches the Tilt-a-Whirl spin and jerk around at an unsteady rhythm. His eyebrows pinch, but whatever he's thinking about, he keeps it to himself.

"Well... anyway," I continue, after a beat of awkward silence. "She didn't even read my whole fortune! She just gave me this holy oil and told me to make crosses on the windows with it."

I stare at my feet, wishing I hadn't felt pushed into sharing about my jar of holy oil but the last thing I want is for rumors to spread that I've been doing witchcraft. I don't want Dad upset at me or Preacher John frowning down at me from the pew on Sunday just because I was interested in a magic trick.

Manny offers an understanding shrug. "My mama had an old injun come by the house one time when Maria was sick with pneumonia. I had to drive Dad's truck all the way to Bitter Creek and heck if she ain't the only breathing thing left out there! And she come shufflin' out of that sad house with a jar of holy oil like that. But she did her thing around our house and put the oil on the windows and all. Next day, Maria's fever dropped like she'd never been touched with the sickness."

"How's that different than Madam Lulu?" I ask. "Or does your mama tell you it's not the Devil's work just because it was an old injun who did it?"

"It ain't the Devil's work if'n you're praying to Jesus."

"Y'all hush and give this man some tickets." Slick breaks into our argument. He gives the ride operator three orange tickets and loops his arm around Sandra-Lee's shoulders, leading her off to the far side of the ride.

I push my way past Manny and follow Hardy to a seat. Barbie follows and we sit opposite of him. Our feet touch his and he grins at us. Whatever troubled him has vanished from his soft, handsome face.

"What?" asks Barbie. She grabs a hunk of her long brown hair and studies it, looking for a rogue piece of cotton candy or mustard or something the boys might have slipped in.

"Switch seats," he says to us, "or Delah will crush you."

"Maybe *I* don't want to crush *Delah.*"

I nudge Barbie out of the chair and into Hardy's side, reminding her, "I've got an unfair advantage over you."

We switch seats moments before the ride kicks off and into the air. Barbie's side slams into Hardy's and she squeals with delight. I hold tight against the blue-painted metal sides of the seat. Without a partner beside me, I'm jostled from one end of the bench to the other. Across the axle, Sandra-Lee and Slick rise into the air. The wind dents her hair, but she doesn't seem to mind, and Slick flexes his arm some as she grips his bicep. His free hand is pressed down onto his Stetson. Sitting in the bench opposite them is Manny and a black girl who lives in Roscoe. Both look miserable and sick. Then the ride shifts, and I feel myself levitate off the seat. My fingers tighten around the bar in front of us and an involuntary whoop comes out of me as I'm dropped and pushed into the back of the thin cushions.

When the ride comes to a complete stop, Barbie lifts the latch and slides out limp and dizzy. My center of gravity pulls down, and I mourn the loss of those sensational minutes where I was flying and weightless. Hardy grins at me as he hops down from his seat, and I blush.

"So girls," he asks. "Ready for round two?"

"Absolutely!" Barbie shouts, punching the air with a fist. She looks at me with hopeful eyes. She'll have another chance to press up against him.

"I can't stay," I remind them.

Kitty waits for me by the exit with two paper cones of pink and blue cotton candy. Half of the blue is gone, her lips frosted with a deep stain. "We have a curfew."

"Oh, that's too bad!" says Barbie. She turns to Hardy. "I'm game if you are?"

"Well okay... as long as you don't feel left out or nuthin?"

"I don't." I give Barbie a wink. "I just wish we could stay longer but you know how my dad is." I turn to wave at Sandra-Lee. "Bye! We're going!"

"Okay!" she shouts. She and Slick haven't even bothered to climb down from their seats.

"Want me to take your goldfish home for you?" Hoping my voice carries over the new surge of music coming from the ride's multicol-ored center. Now that the sun has set, the lights illuminate everyone into pinks, yellows, and greens.

"Nope! I'll get him! Thanks!"

Kitty holds out the pink cloud of cotton candy for me once I finally make my way toward her. Her wheat-blonde hair has lost some of the luster from earlier in the afternoon. With a small huff, she says, "I'm ready to go."

"That bad, huh?"

She shrugs and peels away a strand of candy and lets it dissolve around her fingers before putting the rest of it onto her tongue. I know she'll talk when she's ready and that I need to be quiet so she can tell me everything that happened with Bobby Davis, but I'm itching to tell her about Madam Lulu.

We cut across the carnival field in silence, occasionally pointing out rides or games we didn't get a chance to look at or which ones we want to visit again after church tomorrow.

Darkness surrounds us as we step away from the threshold of the carnival's technicolor glow. The smell of burnt popcorn and roasting pecans linger. We pick our way back toward Starry Night Theater using the lamplight of the concessions stand as a lighthouse in our ocean of grass. Now that the sun has set, the warm breeze has turned into chilly night. Thin wisps of cloud that proceed the rolling in of a thunderstorm dart across the sky, silvering in the light of an expanded moon.

Kitty stops and her small fingers reach out, connecting with the soft inside of my wrist. "What is it?"

"What's what?"

"That," Kitty says, tugging on my sleeve. Her eyes are wide and wet urging me to keep walking, but I stand still to listen. Heavy and slow movements shake the tall grass and shift the rocky soil. I can feel it, step by step, vibrating up my spine.

"Maybe a 'dillo or a coon? Keep walking and it'll scamper."

"Doesn't sound small enough to be that," whispers Kitty. "Maybe it's a bobcat or a ky-ote?"

"They don't get this close," I say but we stop walking and listen again. Whatever it is, it's tracking us. A heavy, wet breathing followed closely by a low growl. "It must be somebody's dog. Mr. Dunne let out old Reda again. Go on, git! Go on home!"

"It's not old Reda," mutters Kitty.

"So walk faster," I say. A dry, cold fear rolls down my spine and my grip tightens on Kitty's hand, keeping my eyes forward. Just a few minutes and we'll be safely inside the drive in.

We're almost across the field when a hollow cry carves itself into our bones. Whatever animal is out in the dark, it's coming right toward us.

"Run, Kitty!" I shout and propel her forward with a shove.

Kitty stumbles toward Starry Night. I'm close behind but trip over my shoelace. My knees land on a sharpened rock with a resounding thunk.

"Delah!" Kitty turns and reaches out for me. "Delah! Are you okay?"

"I think so."

We don't make it another two feet before a black and grizzled force yanks Kitty to the ground. I hear the wind knock out of her followed by a little, wet gasp. I scream, shattering my vocal chords as I sprint toward the massive thing. My fingers curl into a tangle of matted fur as I attempt to pull it backward but my hands might as well be noodles. My grasp is weak and slides away from the undulating, unearthly muscles. There is a slick pop and Kitty screams.

Her cries explode through the field but are drowned out by the zinging pops and clanks of the carnival. The beast throws itself forward and flings me off. With a wild snarl and another empty, long howl, it turns on me. The yellow of things that see in the night swims in its eyes.

Kitty sucks in air, rolls onto her stomach, and scrambles back toward the crowds and the bright lights. She hasn't stopped screaming. The beast turns its attention back to her for a second time. It is too quick and before I stand it's on top of Kitty again.

"No!"

There are silhouettes of people running toward us.

"Help!"

Kitty's shrieks become thin and fade into the dark. One of the people breaks from the group and dart's back toward the carnival. Another yell for help is drowned out by a crunch of bone. I dive on top of the beast again and yank it away from Kitty. It twists its neck around to sink a set of massive teeth into whatever bit of me it can reach. Somewhere behind I hear the breathless screams of Barbie and Sandra-Lee, but their voices are drowned by the rasping heat of the creature that now descends upon me.

Hardy slams into it, pushing me back to the hard earth. He yelps out in pain as the beast's uneven teeth latch onto his exposed skin. He staggers backward, a hand pressed against his neck. Blood seeps through his fingers, staining the collar of his Letterman jacket. The beast rears its ugly head and swipes a massive paw, long and curved as a man's twisted hand.

A shot is fired into the chaos and the beast collapses.

"What the fuck!" Slick shouts.

From behind the rustling of dry grass and the hurried shuffle of the Dunnes' old dog, Reda, and Mrs. Dunne come into view. "What's happened?" she asks, swinging her flashlight over us. "We heard a commotion. I told Mr. Dunne it was the movie, but he said it... he ...oh."

I look in the direction from where the shot fired. The heavily tattooed man with the forked tongue lowers his shotgun from squinting eyes. He crosses himself and marches toward the naked body of a man lying beside Hardy. I can only see the naked man's feet, thick and blackened with callouses. Hardy sways, sinking into Slick and Manny. Manny takes off his shirt and presses it into the right side of Hardy's mangled face.

I roll onto my bleeding knees and crawl toward Kitty.

"No, Delah!" Slick's voice is a long way away. "Don't look!"

But I'm already there, beside Kitty's lacerated body. There's nothing left of her face and her hair has turned red and tacky from the crack in her skull. I reach forward and cover her cotton brassiere with a swatch of fabric and the skin that has been torn from her. The tattooed man takes off his jacket and covers my sister's remains. Everything blurs. Mrs. Dunne drops her flashlight and collects me in her fleshy arms, filling my nostrils with the scent of mothballs and melted butter. My teeth grind together and lips mold into a shapeless mass with the sudden inability to speak.

Chapter Three

A soft and steady warm glow leaks into our bedroom. Dawn comes through the curtains and threads around the tidy floor, a box of tissues, and the unmade bed across from me. On the white-washed vanity, a tube of red lipstick is sentinel and ready to be used. A powder poof sits off-kilter beside it. The curved side of the mirror glitters from hairspray that hasn't been wiped clean of the glass. Dust angels lift from the doll house that hasn't been touched in years but leans against the far wall. Another relic of another memory.

My hands fold around a ragged piece of tissue. Little torn bits drift across my lap. The pantyhose I'm forced to wear itches my hips and legs. My black Sunday only shoes are too tight. My skin is too tight. Everything hurts. My ribs are folding inward, squeezing my lungs, fighting hard to make me into powdered nothing.

Dad shuffles slowly up the stairs. The soles of his shoes scrape against the wood and then soften as he passes over the tasseled rug outside our bedroom door. My door. He knocks softly and waits. I don't know what to say. He knocks again.

"I'm dressed."

The door is pushed open and the hinges cough rudely into the quiet. Dad wears his black suit that's supposed to be only worn for special occasions. This isn't special. It's the most painful thing in the world and if I had the energy I might try and rip it off of him. I can't even breathe. So, I sit there, facing Kitty's bed.

"You look lovely," he says, and the words hang themselves. He isn't supposed to say those things. Not today.

"Thanks."

"It's time."

His eyes are red, but he's given himself a clean shave. After two days of drifting listlessly through the house, he's finally showered. Underneath the scented soap and mouthwash, there lingers the harsh whiff of beer. I look up into those giant hazel eyes. They're the same as Kitty's. I'll never see her with laugh lines like Dad's.

"Do I have to go?"

He looks at me as though he's only just now realized there is another option. "No. Of course you don't."

I nod and finally stand.

The front door seems a long way off and it's overrun by wreaths, roses and baby's breath, and bundles of carnations held together with ribbons that express the sender's grief. We pick our way through the flowers and turn left to head to the graveyard that hasn't been used in fifty years. Dad asked that Kitty be buried there. His petition to Preacher John echoed through the ammonia-stained halls of the hospital and bounced off the cold title like gentle footsteps.

"The ground's not good there, Daniel. You know that."

"I don't care."

"Daniel—"

"She's only a little girl. She shouldn't... she shouldn't be so far from her daddy."

Someone has cleared away the graffiti, beer bottles, and blunts. Little yellow flowers spring from long grasses and sway in the air.

There aren't any clouds, and the heavy old oaks give plenty of coverage. It took some work finding a plot available that wasn't overtaken by the thick roots of the trees. A small blue sits beyond the oldest, crumbling stones. Chairs are unfolded for me and Dad and for the old ones who don't wish to stand through the entire graveside service.

The casket is white with gilded handles, but it is closed and covered by a huge spray of pink roses. There isn't enough of Kitty left to view. Dad spent his sleepless nights combing through photographs to put on display beside the casket. The largest one is from this year's class photo. Her eyes are bright and shining and the dimple on the right side of her cheek is deep. She'd spent a long time making sure her pigtail braids were perfectly even and that the bows at the ends matched the color of her lipstick. I can't stop looking at the photograph. Kitty is a perfect blend of our parents. I wonder if Mom is waiting for her in heaven, if she would recognize her, or if it even matters.

Preacher John wrote a good sermon, but the words fall out of my ears as they come. He calls her Katelyn several times, for professionalism, and because every time he says Kitty his voice breaks, and he loses his place in his notes. Beside me, Dad's shallow breath comes in a steady rhythm. Preacher John ends in a prayer and during the prayer he asks for forgiveness because he doesn't understand why God would want to take Kitty from us in such a violent way.

We're meant to sit and shake the hands of everyone who comes to pay their last respects. My hands are red and numb from how fiercely they seem to hold onto me. Dad mumbles and nods. His knuckles turn pale and tight. I don't know what I'm supposed to say except, "Thank you."

No one expects anything more.

Then Preacher John removes the casket bouquet and steps aside. Two burly men from the Nolan County Funeral Home begin to move the casket over the hole. There is a dull thunk as Kitty's body shifts against the velvet-trimmed walls.

"Noooo!"

Dad catapults off his folding chair and wraps himself around the casket. He gulps down great gusts of sorrow that rattle his body. From the back of the tent, Mr. Diggs and Sheriff Muller run forward to lift Dad off. He collapses into Sheriff Muller's thin arms, hands covering his face.

"My baby girl! My sweet, little girl!"

"It's alright Daniel. It's alright. Shhhh."

I hang my head and press a corner of single-ply tissue paper to my eyes and wait for the crowd and the casket to disappear. The wind sings softly through the trees, the tent wrinkles against itself and gathers the sun's heat so I feel it burn down my neck and back.

"Delah?" Preacher John rests his cool, dry hand on my shoulder. In the other is a hand shovel with dirt. "Do you want to perform the ritual?"

My hands shake as I walk over to the edge of the grave site. Clods of dirt plop against the casket's shining surface and slide off the sides. It's over and I am empty. I don't know where Dad is. There's no one left but me and Preacher John. Hardy waits at the wrought iron gate at the far end of the yard.

"Will you be okay?" asks Preacher John. He has a young face, but his eyes are ancient.

"Yes. Thank you, Preacher."

"If you ever need to talk," he says. "You know where to find me."

Hardy straightens as I get closer. Both sides of his face are swollen and blackish-purple. His right eye is bloodshot, and his neck is covered in bandages. What remains of his ear is stitched together and his arm is in a sling. The bandages on his arm and neck need changing and he smells strongly of antibiotics and aftershave.

"Is it okay if I walk you home?" he asks, staring at his feet.

"Yes."

He holds out his left hand, which is swollen with deep scratches but not severe enough to need stitches. I hesitate before slipping my fingers around his.

"At least wrestling season's over."

We both try to grin and fail miserably.

"Delah... I'm so sorry."

"Don't."

"I should've done more."

"You did more than anyone. Are you okay?"

"I'm fine. Are you? I know you're not but... well... you know what I mean. Maybe you don't."

"I know what you mean."

"I'm sorry. I don't know what to say."

We're back at my house and the soles of his boots scratch against our wraparound porch. I hold onto his hand for a little while longer. "I don't think you're supposed to say anything."

"But I want to!" Hardy slaps the porch railing with his good hand. "I want to because if I say the right thing it'll be better."

I bite my lip and stare across the wide, windswept field between here and the barn. I can't look at Hardy's ruined face and pretend I'm glad he's here when it should be Kitty. "Preacher said plenty of right things and it didn't help at all."

"Oh." His defeated tone catches me.

I wish my words hadn't sounded so harsh. I clear my throat and try again. "Thank you for walking me home but I think I want to be alone now. If that's alright?"

He takes a step back but keeps his gaze on mine. I thought I had run out of tears, but a new swell springs from my guts, and I tilt my eyes upward to stop them from leaking out. It doesn't work and Hardy's arm is suddenly around my shoulders. He pulls me into him. I gag into his dress shirt, ashamed of the snot that comes with it. Hardy doesn't say anything because there is a wet heat from him against my neck. His torso trembles against mine. He wipes his eyes with the back of his hand and nods once before stepping off the porch and taking the lonely walk back to his house up on the hill.

Dad isn't home and I don't know what to do with all the flowers, so I leave them by the front door. The stairs stretch out again and it seems to take forever to get to the attic. I strip out of my stiff, black dress and pantyhose only to leave them in a puddle on the floor before collapsing into bed without bothering to put on my pajamas. Sleep comes in fitful waves.

Later, when the house has grown dark and heavy, the sound of glass shattering startles me awake. I wrap myself in a fluffy, blue bathrobe and pick up the baseball bat leaning against my bed. A second forceful breaking has me hesitate at the top of the stairs. The first-floor glows under the lamplight. All the flowers are turned over and destroyed.

Dad sits with his legs crossed in the entryway, holding the broken piece of a vase he had apparently smashed against the wooden floor. He looks up at me, bleary-eyed. "I didn't mean to wake you. I'm sorry."

I don't say anything and go to the kitchen to grab the broom and dustpan.

"Leave it," he says. "I'll get it tomorrow."

He opens his arms to me, and I sink into them. Neither of us cry but we rock silently against the weight that has come crashing down upon us.

Chapter Four

The days pass in slow churns and I hardly do anything but sleep. I miss waking to the sound of Kitty's records crackling in the predawn. I miss the smell of her shampoo and hairspray. I miss the bundle of clothes on her unmade bed. I miss talking to her in the night, her voice a pleasant exchange for the nickering ponies, cicadas, and bullfrogs.

I can't face going into the square and seeing her friends float around like ghosts or accidentally bumping into Bobby Davis only to be reminded of that missed opportunity of first love. I don't want Sandra-Lee asking if I'm alright with each sigh that comes, unwelcome, from me. I don't want Barbie to cover her laughter or her natural brightness because she thinks she shouldn't be happy around me. I don't want to see Hardy because I'll be reminded of how he cried on my shoulder and didn't save my sister.

Dad doesn't force me to leave the house. When he goes to work, I'm still in bed, and when he comes home, sometimes I've managed to make it to the living room sofa. I don't want to leave our bedroom. I want to stay in here until the last of Kitty's fingerprints fade from the furniture, until it only smells like me: alfalfa and sandalwood.

My ribs crack against my lungs. When I exhale a heavy release, the pressure always comes back. Kitty visits me in my dreams. We watch a midnight special at Starry Night Theater and she's in front of me on one of the swings at the playground below the big screen. She turns to me, laughing as I push her high and fast. Her smile stretches and there is lipstick on her teeth. I burst with the undiluted joy that escapes her as she soars skyward, into the glow of the screen. The swing returns without her but I can still hear her laughing.

A week has passed.

I roll out from underneath my blankets, only to cradle my head in my hands. Across the room comes a quiet snuffling that immediately startles me. At first I think the last seven days have been just one large, horrific nightmare because there is a human-shaped lump in Kitty's bed.

I stand and creep closer, fingers stretched out to touch Kitty's fine hair that flutters across her cheek... but it's only Dad. Surprise flares in my cold cheeks and I drop my hand, swaying with a new wave of grief. He's curled under her soft yellow and pink duvet. It's too short to cover his socked feet from where he's tried to pull it up around his shoulders. There is a line down the center of his forehead that I've grown accustomed to that hadn't existed before... He is as ashen and frail on the outside as I feel on the inside. I nearly reach out to shake him awake but I can't bring myself to do it.

Instead, I creep across to my wardrobe to pull out a pair of clean overalls and slip them over my pajamas. I bundle my hair back into a ponytail, wash my face, and brush my teeth. It takes a lot more energy than I thought it would. Each ritual is a labor of survival. Downstairs, I tug on my mucking boots and cross the acres between the house and the stables where we keep our ponies. Mist rises from the ground, snaking around the post oaks and tall grass like a veil. Very quickly my boots and the cuffs of my overalls become slick with dew. It is a surprisingly damp start to summer.

Dad breeds ponies as a hobby. It's how he coped when mom died and I'm curious as to what new project he'll adopt now that Kitty is gone. He might end up getting a new stallion. Ambition, our black overo stud, is starting to get bored in his old age and isn't much interested in our three mares. Tessie Western Spark is the only one pregnant from last breeding season. She sways uncomfortably in her stall, whiskery lips roll around in her sleep.

Ambition trots up and sticks his head over the half door of his stall. I push my hand against his muzzle and up to his ears. He shakes his head and turns sideways, wanting me to scratch his stiff withers. I understand why Dad likes the ponies so much. Everything in this space is uncomplicated and plain. Even the sweet, rich scent of manure is a strange comfort.

Bonnie Wee Dancer hears Ambition moving around and she sticks her brown and white head out of the opposite stall. I open their gates and lead them to the paddock. Tessie is upset when I wake her but then slowly trots to join the others. Navajo Blue is our newest addition. She's still shy and takes some extra coaxing to get her out.

I'm halfway finished mucking the stalls when the sun starts to creep along the horizon, taking the veil of mist with it. The Andersons' rooster lets out a warning squawk before bursting into a full crow.

"Are you alone?"

The flat metal end of my shovel scrapes roughly against the floor as I jerk upright. The motion puts a renewed ache in my bruised ribs, and I suck in, teeth clenched. Standing in the open barn door is Madam Lulu. She adjusts a gossamer-blue shawl around her narrow shoulders and glances around the stables before stepping in.

"How did you find me?" I keep the shovel close, ready to swing it at her alien perfect skull.

"I heard your sister was attacked. I'm sorry for your loss."

"Thanks."

Energy floods away from me and I lower the shovel to lean against it. I don't want this woman to see me cry. I want to blame her for Kitty. She told me to go home immediately, while it was still daylight, and I didn't. I know it's my fault more than hers, but I want to hate her just the same. Maybe if I had never gone to get my fortune told, Kitty would still be alive.

"Were you bitten?" she asks.

Her deep, rasping voice is barely louder than a whisper. I shake my head, and she turns to look back toward the house. A light flickers on in my attic window and Madam Lulu shifts into the shadow of the barn door so she won't be seen. "Was anyone bitten?"

"Sheriff Muller says it was that barker, the one with the curly beard, who attacked her. The tattooed man shot him through the neck."

"That was no man!" she hisses. "Was anyone else bitten?"

My knuckles whiten around my shovel as she steps across the stables toward me. Her voice shakes and there is a renewed wildness in her eyes, the same that appeared after she read my fortune.

"My friend Hardy is cut up pretty bad," I admit.

She gasps and her thin hands dip into the folds of her shawl, then along the edges of her blouse, and into her skirt pockets.

"Do you have the oil?"

"What?"

"The anointed oil I gave you?" She doesn't look up while she continues to search her body and clothes for something. Dread creeps into the space between my skin and bones.

"Yes."

"Bless the house with it! Draw a cross on each window and pray! Please! It is vital you do these things!"

"Lady! You're psychotic. Get out before I call my dad!"

She doesn't listen. Instead she yanks a braided loop of leather out of a hidden pocket and stretches out her arm. Tied to the leather is a bullet.

"You must kill Hardy with this."

"I'm not—Get away from me!"

The ponies grunt and begin galloping back and forth in their paddock, excited by the commotion. Madam Lulu thrusts the necklace at me, but I don't reach for it. I raise my shovel, and she lets it fall in the hay strewn between us.

"You *won't* have a choice! It's the only thing that can truly kill him. The only thing that will break the curse!"

"DAD! HELP!"

Madam Lulu glances over her shoulder as our screen door bangs open. She says, "Your sister won't be the last."

Dad, in nothing but his socks and whities, sprints across the field. Madam Lulu runs out of the stables, back to her wagon she parked behind our property. She climbs over the fence and stumbles down the other side. Dad reaches out for her and tugs at the shawl around her shoulders. He misses but it snags on a fence post. She doesn't stop and snakes her way out of the tangle of fabric. Before Dad can clear the fence, Madam Lulu dives into the station wagon, shifts gears, and disappears into the west.

I pray to God she doesn't return.

Dad clutches the shawl and his shoulders droop. He slowly makes his way to me. Still some distance away from the barn, he calls out, "Who was that?"

I wait until he's level with me to answer because I need some time to think about how much I ought to tell him. "It was this crazy woman from the carnival. She told me it wasn't a man who killed Kitty."

"Bitch," he whispers, and he abruptly slings the pale blue fabric from his hands like it's poisoned snakeskin. His round eyes flicker in the direction of the graveyard and thumbs the skin around his nose. "Who is she to talk about my daughter?" His shoulders square and he turns back to me. "If she ever comes back, and I mean *ever*, you smack the snot out of her with that shovel. Clear?"

"Yessir."

Behind me, Ambition huffs wetly and shakes his thick mane.

Chapter Five

I wake early the next morning and sneak out to the stables. The humidity clings to my skin and makes my hair frizz into a giant puff. There is a promise of rain in the low gunmetal clouds. The braided leather with the bullet stayed hidden among the loose hay and I want it. Not as protection but as a keepsake. The traveling carnival was the last thing Kitty and I ever shared.

Tessie is the only pony awake, and she greets me with a snort before running her lips around her bucket of water which hangs in the corner of her stall. I push away the hay in the area where Madam Lulu dropped the necklace, and when I don't find it immediately, my pulse quickens. My first thought is Dad picked it up and put it in his desk drawer or in the mudroom where he keeps boxes of spare ammo. My second thought is more absurd: Did it disappear like the bearded barker who pointed me in Madam Lulu's direction? Then I see the clasp glinting from the string of lights hanging between the barn rafters. I scoop it up and tuck it into the bib of my overalls.

As I walk back across the field, a golden rectangle of light from the kitchen flickers on. It stretches out and across the front garden and over the irises Kitty loved so much. I don't want to go back to the house just yet. So, I sit on the stairs beside the flowerbed. The porch needs to be repainted, but we never get around to it. I like how it looks. The green paint peeling on the handrail from where Kitty and I jettison off of it whenever we're running late for school. The stains of spilled cocoa and nail polish. The burn mark where we tried to smoke one of Dad's cigarettes and were caught in the act.

Dad, half dressed in his deputy uniform, comes out with two mugs. He sits down beside me and passes over a mug full of hot cocoa overloaded with marshmallows. It's how I've always liked it, but we've never been allowed cocoa in the morning. His flat brows pinch together over deep set eyes, but he gives me a small smile. I notice the hair at his temples has finally started to silver.

"I think you should keep the beard," I say.

He runs his hand over chin and cheek. "You think? It doesn't look unprofessional?"

"Unprofessional? Look at where we live."

He looks across our acreage and down the dirt road. Freckles of sunlight break through the clouds and sweep across the rolling grasses. His smile deepens and he leans into his coffee. "It's beautiful, isn't it?"

Dad is the rare breed of person who molds himself into his surroundings and becomes content with how things are. Except, some of his easy confidence is now buried with Kitty and there are mornings where I see a spark of desperate hate when he looks to the old graveyard.

"I'm going to go to Sandra-Lee's today," I say, staring into the foamy swirl of sugar clinging to the sides of my mug.

"Yeah? That's good... that's real good." He puts his hand on my back and his warmth spreads along my spine. "I'll drive you."

Dad uses his legs to push himself off the low steps and retreats back into the house. I stay out on the porch, drinking my warm cocoa, and wait for the rain. It comes slowly with fat plink-plinks against the eaves. Then it turns quick and cold, and the country road is hidden in sweeping curtains. The glass wind-chimes Kitty and I made last summer sway together, a harmony in the storm.

I think I'm ready to push forward. Today is a test and the dreary weather feels like an extension of myself, as though the last bit of pain rushes out of me and through the plains.

Chapter Six

Mud spatters against the sides of Dad's brown police car from the nameless dirt roads and the windshield wipers click in the silence. He parks in front of Sandra-Lee's house. We stare out of the windshield at the washed-out cottage. For the first time, I realize I'm doing something without Kitty, and it petrifies me into a stillness. Dad waits for me to tell him to take me back home.

"Okay. Have a good day patrolling," I say with a smile that becomes almost genuine.

Dad reaches over and puts his hand at the back of my neck. He kisses my hairline. "Take your time," he says. "No one expects anything from you."

"Okay."

Mrs. Goodwin stands on the porch, her thin red hair held down by a plastic bonnet. She waves to Dad and steps cautiously down the slick stairs to meet us. "Hiya, Daniel. Strong weather's coming in. Might hail."

"Thanks, Nina. I'll park if it turns."

She nods, opens my door for me, and pulls me into a warm hug. The plastic sticks to my cheek. "Sandra-Lee's in her room. Y'all be quiet now. Daddy did the night shift at the plant. He's only just gotten to sleep."

"See you, Dad," I say, and I offer another encouraging smile before heading inside.

Mrs. Goodwin slides into my vacated spot and closes the door to have a more private chat with Dad. I'm not too curious. I'm sure she wants to talk about Kitty.

Sandra-Lee sits on her bed cutting out paper dolls, but she drops her scissors when she sees me and yanks me into a fleshy hug. "How are you? Do you want something to drink? Mom made sweet tea."

She keeps her voice low, her parents' room is just next door, and I can hear Mr. Goodwin snoring into his pillow. I shake my head and sit down on the edge of her bed, my hand expands over the chenille duvet. "Can I help you cut out the clothes?"

"Sure!" she squeaks. "I'll get the spare scissors from mom's sewing kit."

I stare around Sandra-Lee's room while I wait for her to return. Mrs. Goodwin designed it in pastels. The muted tones of teal and pink are soothing and well organized throughout the room. Nothing is out of place. Not even the prize goldfish swimming lazily on Sandra-Lee's windowsill. At the head of her bed is a white felt bear I've never seen before. Its button eyes are blue and so is the bow around its neck.

"Did Slick get you that?" I ask when Sandra-Lee comes back with a second pair of sharpened scissors.

Sandra-Lee nods and sighs. "He's so wonderful. I didn't think anyone could be so sweet! Least of all, Slick James!"

Slick is our wrestling team's heavyweight champion, and I don't think anyone imagined him to have a soft bone in his body. She hands me the scissors and I begin cutting out a selection of evening gowns. If her dad hadn't taken on the night shift, we'd listen to her collection of Elvis records or call Barbie on the rotary phone and press our ears together, swapping dirty jokes or digging up the latest gossip in town.

"So have you kissed, yet?" I ask. "Like how Barbie says? With tongue."

Sandra-Lee's cheeks brighten, and her polished nails run over the dimple in her chin as though she's imagining Slick's stubble scrapping against her. "Maybe a little... I was so nervous that my nose bumped into his."

"What's it feel like?"

"Hot. Like he's breathing into my mouth, and it tasted a little like his dip."

"Gross!"

"It really wasn't all that bad. You'll like it." She drops her voice and shifts closer to me, the secret rolling around her mouth like a pearl. "It gives me a feeling behind my belly button. Like I need to go to the bathroom, even though I don't. It's a good feeling. Kinda tickles."

"Really?" I imagine what being tickled while having to pee must feel like.

Her face deepens before the color fades and she turns somber. "I'm sorry. That's rude of me. What you must be going through right now."

"No! It's okay. I like hearing about what's going on. It makes everything seem almost normal."

"I saw Miss Hawthorne yesterday at Diggs' Pharmacy," says Sandra-Lee, selecting a ball gown and folding the little tabs over her paper model. "She's real upset about... everything."

Miss Hawthorne was easily Kitty's favorite teacher, mostly because they shared such a passion for literature and Kitty was already reading at a college level. Miss Hawthorne was supposed to tutor her over the summer to prepare Kitty in the event she might skip a grade.

"Oh," I say. I pick up another page of outfits and begin to cut.

The rain stops right around the time we both start to feel hungry. Mrs. Goodwin packs us paper lunches and sends us out. We walk the mile down to the town square, mindful of our shoes sticking into thick mud. Main Street isn't nearly as busy as it would be on a cloudless day but there are still noontime shoppers drifting around. I realize the carnival has left early because Buzzy's and Diggs' Pharmacy are emptier than they ought be. A strange void scoops out the space between my lungs and I feel guilty for all the people of Nolan County. Their summer is ruined because my sister died, and no one understands it's okay to go about business as usual.

Sandra-Lee leads the way into Diggs' and a blast of cold air slings the sweat off my face and neck. We sit on the benches at the counter and Mrs. Diggs appears out of the stock room, carrying a box underneath one arm. She's much older than our other friends' moms and has a fleshy middle and thin arms and legs, like a spider almost in the way she's proportioned. Even though she's one of the nicest people in Maryneal, her face has a sour, pinched look to it.

When she sees me she drops her box and bottles of Aspirin roll around the floor. "Oh, Delah! Sweet pea!"

"Thank you for the casserole Mrs. Diggs," I mumble into her shoulder as she pulls me down for a hug. "How's Hardy doing?"

"Fine. He's fine. He'll be here in just a little while to help with the inventory. How's Daniel? He's not come to Buzzy's for his coffee yet."

"I guess he's okay... all things considered."

"Of course he's not. But he will be. If there's anything. Anything at all."

"Thank you."

Sandra-Lee and I bend down to help her pick up all the Aspirin. Sandra-Lee asks, "Can I use your phone? I just want to call Barbie."

"Of course," says Mrs. Diggs, waving her hand to the booth by the back door. Sandra-Lee weaves her way through the medicine aisle and stops by the magazine rack before continuing. To me, Mrs. Diggs asks, "How's your sleeping? If you're having trouble, I can find you something that'll help. Chamomile."

"I've been sleeping too much."

"No such thing when it comes to... your body needs rest." She clears her throat and starts to shelve the bottles.

"Mrs. Diggs, I don't know if you realize, but Hardy wasn't just caught up in what happened out there. He tried to save her. He really did."

She turns to look at me, small eyes watering, and presses her hand against my face. "Thank you for telling me. He hasn't talked much about it. I think he's still rattled. We all are. Who would have thought such a thing could happen?"

Sandra-Lee returns. "She's meeting us in the gazebo. Thanks, Mrs. Diggs."

"Sure, sure. I'll tell Hardy you're out there."

Chapter Seven

The benches under the gazebo are mostly dry. Sandra-Lee and I unwrap the lunch her mother made for us. An apple. Peanut butter and banana sandwich. Corn pone. A box of raisins.

Now that the sun has crept out from behind the clouds, the square is starting to fill up again. Preacher John makes his way into Buzzy's Diner, and he stops in front of the gazebo to offer me and Sandra-Lee an awkward hello. Barbie comes gliding in on her bicycle, the wheels flecking mud around her bare ankles. She's wearing a halter top and no bra. It's a scandal to reveal so much skin but she assures us that this is everyday wear along the west coast. I'm so happy to see her that I choke back my pone with a little cry. For a glittering moment everything is fine in the world. Barbie on my left and Sandra-Lee on my right. A normal picnic with the girls while Kitty is off with... no one. Reality slams back into me and tears fall freely mixed with short hiccups that taste like buttered cornmeal.

Sandra-Lee puts her arm around me and rubs her hand against my shoulder.

"What just happened?" asks Barbie.

"N-nothing! I'm just so happy for both of you and I wish—" I can't finish my thought and thankfully I don't have to.

Barbie pulls out a square bit of tartan fabric and dabs my cheeks dry. Then she holds my hand and squeezes. I haven't cried this much since waiting for Dad to come pick me up in Sweetwater's hospital. The pressure on my ribs lifts away, evaporating into Barbie's warm hands and Sandra-Lee's well-meaning hug. From across the square, Manny waves at us.

"How's things?" he asks, straddling the gazebo wall and frowning at my puffy eyes and swollen, snotty nose. "Trade you my Nehi for your raisins."

"Okay, I guess. Weird," I answer honestly.

Barbie pats my eyes with her handkerchief again. I hand Manny my box of raisins and let him keep his Nehi. It reminds me of sharing Schnapps with Kitty.

Across from me, Hardy slides gingerly out of Slick's apple green Chevy. Slick steps out with much more grace and removes his Stetson, placing it briefly over his broad chest. "Heya, Delah. Good to see you out an' about."

"Thanks, Slick."

Both of them sit on the bench opposite us. The bruising around Hardy's neck and face is healing remarkably well. He's no longer wearing an arm sling, but his neck is still thickly wrapped in gauze. The stitches have been removed from his mangled ear. I can see where the scarring of his neck and earlobe will meet once it's fully healed. The tightened skin pulls Hardy's mouth into a permanent grimace. He lays out several fried spam sandwiches, a soup thermos, several bananas, and a carton of buttermilk. We all hear his stomach growl with hunger as he tears into his first sandwich.

"Dag! You trying to jump into my weight class or what?" laughs Slick before he swipes one of Hardy's bananas and peels it with one hand.

Hardy shrugs and mumbles around a mouthful. "I'm hittin' a growth spurt or something. Nothin's touches the sides, you know?"

Slick snorts and nods. "I'll tell ya. Mama got so sore with me last night. I ate the entire meatloaf by myself."

"So," says Barbie, gathering her hair into a loose ponytail. "We have another Church Social coming up! I want to enlist all of you for decorations."

I look up from picking apart my sandwich and she gives me a wink. I love that she is keeping our friends' attention away from Kitty's profound absence. She turns to Hardy and grins all ivory and straight lines. "I want you to get all the boys on the wrestling team to clear away all that heavy shit from behind the church."

"Kay," he mumbles, biting into a thick hunk of fried spam. A slice of tomato and mayonnaise ooze out the back end of the crust-less bread.

"Slick, could you see if your mother will share her punch recipe? Also, if she can get a list of the ladies at the church who are willing to help chaperone?"

"Yeah-yeah, sure," Slick laughs as he playfully paws at Sandra-Lee's green-knitted cardigan. "She'll love an excuse to keep the Holy Ghost between us!"

"Stop! Stop, you!" Sandra-Lee giggles and leans in for a kiss.

"What about me?" asks Manny.

Barbie considers him and nibbles an apple slice from Sandra-Lee's abandoned sack lunch. "Just make sure your mustache wax doesn't get all over your date's face."

"Dag!" Slick's deep rumble breaks him free of Sandra-Lee's lips and he slaps the table with the flat of his hand.

Manny pales. "Jeez-Louise, Barbie! It wasn't like Willoby complained about my kissin'."

"So you say."

"So she says!"

"Hey," says Hardy to me. "You gonna eat your apple?"

I shake my head and hand it to him. I'm struck with a sudden desire to run away from them all, screaming and waving my hands like a lunatic. I inhale slowly and somehow maintain my sanity. "I think I'm going to go home now. Is that okay?"

Sandra-Lee straightens her top and untangles herself completely from Slick. The mood shifts in the gazebo, and I hate that it's because of me.

Sandra-Lee says, "Of course it's okay! Why wouldn't it be?"

"Want company?" asks Barbie.

"I don't know. No... it's okay. I just want to walk for a bit."

I try to keep cheerful as I wave goodbye to them, then I head up the path toward home before I decide to turn down the alley and walk toward Starry Night Theater. I make my way slowly to the metal carousel. Jewels of rainwater cover the seats, and I swipe at them until it's dry enough to sit. The rusting gears squeak and I push off with the toe of my shoe. I'm too tall to sit comfortably without having a leg dangle off the end.

I like how the drive-in looks before the shows start and the lots fill with cars. Rows of speakers hang from their crosses and the parking spaces are free of debris and folding chairs, free of children running between cars. Free of crows picking at the fallen popcorn. The emptiness is like the heavy velvet curtains that rise just before the start of a play.

I'm vaguely aware of Mr. and Mrs. Dunne peeping at me through their apartment window above the concession stand. They're most likely debating on coming down to talk to me, but I don't want anyone else telling me how sorry they are. Sorry doesn't bring Kitty back.

Mr. and Mrs. Dunne don't bother me but there are footsteps just the same. Light and cautious. I don't turn to see who it is, and I think I might be imagining it until Barbie speaks up. My heart skips and I twist around, nearly smiling at the surprise.

"It's going to be okay," she says sitting down beside me, ignoring the drops of water. She smooths her hands over her knees and examines the weeds poking through the wooden slats of the carousel's base.

Is she thinking of those final moments and what she was doing before Kitty's screams shattered the dark? I do. Every night when I stare across my empty room, always expecting to see a small lump curled underneath the blankets in Kitty's bed. I think about how her eyes turned from fear into a blank nothing. How her body no longer belonged to her. How her spirit vanished.

"How will it?"

Barbie's answer comes slow and thoughtful, "I don't know, but it will."

She nudges the carousel, pushing me faster and faster until a genuine smile cracks through the tired skin around my mouth. Sunlight shifts through the thick clouds, pollinating us with a clean warmth.

Mrs. Dunne descends the creaky wooden steps of her apartment. I haven't seen her since the funeral. Reda, the old fat beagle, galumphs down each step in front of her.

"We're opening soon," she calls out to us.

Mrs. Dunne normally radiates a sort of secret pleasure she keeps tucked in the pocket of her gums, only for her to taste, but today her expression is pulled at the corners. A bitterness touches the tongue. She is wiped from my vision, and I am pushed unwillingly into memory. The sweep of her flashlight. Red liquid pumping into the soil, moving slower. Losing rhythm.

I break out in a clammy sweat and Barbie puts her hand on my bare arm to steady me. Reda pushes her snout between my legs and rolls her head sideways to look up at me, willing me to scratch her behind a scabby ear.

"Did you want to stay for the picture?" Mrs. Dunne asks kindly.

"I just wanted to sit here for a bit while it was quiet," I say. "Can I come back to work on Wednesday?"

"If you feel up for it, sure. We'll put you in the box office." She turns back to the concession stand to grab the large popper she'd heated up for the night.

Barbie hops off the carousel and arches her back in a long stretch. Her lower ribs push against skin, already beginning to tan. She walks home with me, and I wish Sandra-Lee was with us, bouncing around theme ideas for the next Church Social instead of in some hidden corner of Maryneal where she and Slick tangle in a private embrace.

Barbie picks wildflowers along the way and threads them into a crown. "Manny's going to ask you to the Social," she says.

"How do you know?"

She shrugs and adds a Black-Eyed Susan to the mix of dandelions. "Because he asked me if he had a chance."

"Oh," I say and quicken my pace a little as we approach the incline of the dirt road that leads toward my house.

"Well?" she asks.

"What?"

"Does he have a chance?"

I snort angrily. "I dunno! It's not something I ever thought about. I don't want to think about it right now. It's hard to think about anything else but... I dunno."

Barbie rolls the crown around in her hand, examining the pockets of green leaf where she might stick another flower. "Who would you want to go with? Hardy?"

"Sure. I dunno. At least with Hardy I wouldn't get mascara all over my mouth."

We both laugh and stop just before my gate. I'm grateful she's distracted me with the trivial interest of boys. As annoying as it is, the alternative is Kitty. I'm tired of thinking about her and I hate myself for it.

"Can't I just go with you?" I ask Barbie.

She doesn't look at me. Her dark, round eyes are fixed on the crown, and she spins it around her long fingers. My insides flutter with a snap of dread. What if she asks me why? I hardly know the answer myself.

She reaches up and places the makeshift crown on my head. The pointed leaves tickle my forehead, the tight coils of my hair push against the delicate petal as though protesting having to share an already crowded space.

"Sure. We'll go together," she says. Then she steps back a few paces and brings her forefingers and thumbs together, creating a frame around me. She makes a clicking sound and winks. "We'll be the belles of the ball!"

Chapter Eight

In the summers, Starry Night Theater opens at seven in the evening but the first movie on the large screen doesn't start until eight-thirty. The second screen, opposite and stationed slightly off to the right, won't start until nine. The drive-in is designed this way so people can't watch both movies simultaneously, though I can't imagine it would be enjoyable to watch one, without sound, and through the rear-view mirror.

Roger Landis and Parker Armstrong, two seniors, usually work the concession stands in the summer and on weekends during the school year, but since I arrive early for my shift in the box office, I help Mr. Dunne get the popper going and lay the hot dogs out on the rolling grill. Mr. Dunne is silent and rusted over. He has the odor and the weatherbeaten appearance of a person who spent most of his life roughing it in the wilds and certainly prefers the company of animals to people. He's much older than Mrs. Dunne, too. He has an infectious gap-toothed smile but rarely shares why he's grinning.

Purlie, Preacher John's only son, comes down from the booth and rolls a cigarette while he talks to us. He's brawny like Slick but taller. His jawline is smudged with dark, rust colored stubble. He knows a heck of a lot because he lived in New York and studied religion and law in college. When he left Maryneal, none of us ever expected to see him again. Purlie has radical ideas and Nolan County was too small for him to stretch. But, he came back in November and nobody, not even Wilma Anderson and her predilection for gossip, knew why.

"Say, Reg," he says to Mr. Dunne, squinting his small blue eyes as smoke rolls up his face. "Is it true we're going to get *Birdman of Alcatraz*? Same as everyone else?"

Mr. Dunne drops a heavy sack of popcorn kernels and wipes his brow with a printed cloth. His glasses slide down to the end of his nose as he nods. "Yep. Poster just arrived if you want to put it up by the ticket booth?"

It's unusual for Mr. and Mrs. Dunne to receive a movie on time. Usually they wait until it's been out in the big cities for a few weeks, when the rights are cheaper to buy. We just got *Blue Hawaii* and *Bachelor Flat,* and both have been out for several months now.

"Who's in it?" I ask.

"Burt Lancaster."

"I like him. He does a lot of interesting movies."

"He's alright," Purlie says, rolling the cigarette from one corner of his mouth to the other. I think I imagine him standing a little straighter. "Better than Elvis, anyway. I swear if I hear Ku-UI-po one more time, I'll blow my top!"

He swings his hips from side to side and does a pretty good impression.

"Watch it, kid," says Mr. Dunne lightly. "Man's a war hero."

He dumps two cups of kernels into the popper and adds oil. Two pumps instead of one for that extra golden color.

Purlie leans back in a stretch and then drops a hip against the counter. "Way things are going, I'll be one, too."

"All I'm saying is there's more to a man's mettle than his physical prowess."

I look at them but neither explain what they're talking about. "What do you mean you'll be a war hero?"

Purlie shrugs and reaches out to muss my hair like I'm still a kid. "Aw, heck! It's just conflict. Cuba... The far east. Someone's got a bone to pick with someone else."

"I don't want political talk here. Work's not the place for this type of serious matter and it ain't worth the trouble trying to keep up with Washington."

"I was only yammerin'," mumbles Purlie and he flicks the end of his cigarette into an empty trash bin. "I don't mean anything by it."

Mr. Dunne grunts. "Way I see it, we got enough trouble on our own soil without you bringing in your east coast philosophies."

Purlie looks at me again, his small blue eyes flicker as he takes in all of me. "I'm real sorry about your sister."

"What good is that?" I snap. "She's still flat on her back, feeding the tree."

Mr. Dunne wipes his wrinkled forehead again and turns to pull the metal lever of the popper, dumping out steaming, golden popcorn. He starts up a second batch. Purlie kicks at a bit of dust on the floor. I chew on my thumbnail, not wanting to apologize, but not knowing what else to say.

"Is it okay if I read after I sell the tickets?" I ask.

"Course it is," says Mr. Dunne. "Both of you best set up. Gate's about to open."

I hurry off to the box office before my embarrassment forces me in proximity to Purlie again. I know he was only trying to be kind but it just isn't good enough anymore. Nothing helps, really, but I'd rather have nothing than kind and useless words.

I pass Mrs. Dunne on the way to my booth. Her well-built arms are full of poster tubes and a can of glue. Reda shuffles behind her, searching for stray food. She gives me a wink and shouts over her shoulder, "I'll check on you in an hour!"

I get situated in my booth and flick on the neon green *OPEN* sign. Ford trucks, chipped and rusted, and slightly used luxury cars and vans cough up fumes and roll through at a snail's pace. Slick's apple green Chevy is unmistakable toward the back of the line. I smile as he pulls to a stop. He tilts his Stetson back and Sandra-Lee leans across the bench seat, and his lap, so she can talk to me through his window.

"Hey! I didn't know you were working tonight."

"Yeah. Didn't feel like being at home."

"You could've joined us! We asked Barbie to come along but she's caught up with organizing decorations for the Social."

"You need a ride home?" Slick asks, blowing away Sandra-Lee's stiff hair because it's brushing against his nose, tempting him to sneeze. "I don't like the idea of you on your bike after dark."

"Dad's picking me up," I say but a gush of gratitude makes me want to stretch out of my booth and hug them both. "Thanks though! You're one of a kind."

"That's good, then," says Slick. A car horn beeps politely at the end of the line. Slick shifts so he can get his wallet out of his back pocket, and he hands me a dollar. "You see *Blue Hawaii* yet?"

"No, but it's Elvis," I say. "What's not to like?"

The car horn beeps again, this time with more aggression, and others join in. I hand Slick his tickets and he touches the brim of his Stetson before driving off. Sandra-Lee turns to wave at me through the back window.

When I've sold out of tickets, I click off the *OPEN* sign and step out of the booth to stretch my legs. I don't walk far, just around the perimeter of the box office. Twilight has turned the sky a dusty lavender and pink along the horizon. Thin strands of cloud blister the growing dark and high above me is a growing moon. I marvel at its pure whiteness, how it hangs like a loose grin.

Gravel crunches beneath the wheels of the last remaining cars still searching for places to park. I feel the weight of myself as I move around. The ground beneath me is separate and distant than the chorus of the families I pass by. The Hoopers wave to me from an elevated picnic bench, baby Gertrude latched eagerly to Mrs. Hooper's small breast. Mr. Hooper returns from his raid of the concessions. He teaches biology and chemistry at our school, but there's talk he's going to transfer to Roscoe or Sweetwater because it's offered him better pay.

Roger Landis and Parker Armstrong take turns shouting, "Fresh Popcorn!" Both wear candy-striped aprons and paper hats at jaunty angles. Lauren Willoby passes by with Wilma and Martha Anderson. We exchange hellos but they don't stick around. It's clear that Lauren wants to get to the concessions before her movie starts but she doesn't have popcorn on the brain.

Purlie waves at me from the top of the metal staircase that leads to his crow's nest. Another rolled cigarette dangles from his lips. Tendrils of smoke slink around the glow coming from the first projector. An advertisement for Jr. Mints dance across the screen before *Blue Hawaii* begins. It is followed by a cartoon where a bag of popcorn juggles kernels and a hot dog performs flips while its bun idly watches.

I wave back and return to my box office. Not long after the opening song, the whirl of the second projector is heard, and the opening credits for *Bachelor Flat* appear on the second, smaller, whitewashed board.

I take out my copy of *Othello*. It's the first book we're going to read in Miss Hawthorne's senior class, but Shakespeare confuses me.

I figure if I start reading now, I might be able to understand it by the time school starts again. My copy has underlined words that seemed important to the previous reader. Anything is better than allowing my thoughts to drift back to the, now vacant, carnival field and moon hanging over it.

"Whatcha reading?" Purlie pops up on the other side of the box office.

"Shit!"

"I didn't think that word had three syllables. Want a Cracker Jack?"

He tilts the open box in my direction, and I pick out a candied peanut. Purlie shakes the box and fishes out the prize: a small brass ring. He slips it on his pinky, and it won't fit past the first knuckle. "Sorry about earlier."

"It is what it is. Thanks for trying to make me feel better."

"Didn't think you'd grow up so strong, if I'm honest."

"I didn't think so either."

"So, what's the book?" He pops Cracker Jack into his mouth and turns his attention briefly back to the projection booth, checking that the reels haven't caught fire.

"*Othello* but I don't get it."

"What's to get? A black man marries a white woman, and even though he's got clout, it upsets a lot of people. She allegedly cheats on him with his best friend and then—"

"Wait! I haven't gotten that far! I'm only at the beginning."

"Sorry," he says and offers the box again. He's left the peanuts for me. "I'll see if we have a copy of the Orson Welles version. I bet you'll get it once you see the movie."

"Would that ever happen? In real life?" I ask, flicking through the pages and wishing I could soak in the whole story by just touching the paper. "A negro man and a white woman?"

"The whole world is changing, Delah! You can't see it stuck in this place."

"I'm not stuck! I like it here."

"That's because you don't know any better."

"I know more than some."

Purlie glances across the field and his head angles like a dog's, considering an unshared thought. Luckily, I'm saved from Purlie expanding on his life theories by Sandra-Lee. She trots toward me in quick, small steps. Despite her speed, that blonde hair of hers doesn't move.

"Well if it isn't little Sandra-Lee Goodwin!" says Purlie and he pushes himself off the booth's counter. "I don't think you've grown an inch since I saw you last summer."

"You have... just not vertically," she responds with a sly grin.

"Ouch." He melodramatically clutches his heart. "I think I'll get outta your hair before you two hens peck me to death."

He strolls back up to the projection booth and swings his feet over the ledge, getting comfortable to watch *Bachelor Flat*.

"He's not grown," I say, squinting at his outlined form.

"Sure, but boys have fragile egos. They just hide them better than we can," she says with a superior nod. "Gosh! Just the other day I told Slick his shave was patchy and he wouldn't stop touching his face."

"Oh," I say. I fold the corner of my book down and slip it back into my purse.

"Won't you come and watch the movie with us?" asks Sandra-Lee.

"I should probably see if Parker and Roger need my help."

"Okay," The corners of her red lips turn down. "I just... I feel like I'm losing you. Is it because I'm dating Slick? No, that's not it. That's stupid. I'm sorry. I know the reason. I know it's not anything I can fix or change, but I wish I could. Gosh, I'm just sick all the time! It's all anyone ever talks about, you know? Of course you do! But we were *there,* and I can't talk about it. I don't know how I'm supposed to feel."

"I don't think you're supposed to do anything or feel a particular way."

"I still..." Sandra-Lee pauses and searches around her clutch for a napkin. Tears streak down her face and she quickly dabs them away before her mascara smears. "Sometimes I wake up. I hear her screaming."

I rub my nose with the back of my hand. "I wish you wouldn't tell me this."

"Sorry. No, I'm not. We're *all* hurting, Delah. Not as bad as you or Mr. Nix! Not even close!" She rushes her speech, seeing the blood drain out of me. What does she know of grief like this? What does anyone? "But everybody loved Kitty. We all wish she was back."

Sandra-Lee presses the edges of her fingers against her tear ducts again and bats her eyes. I know she's not trying to make me angry but I'm starting to lose my nerve. I think if one more person says anything about Kitty, I'm going to throw the first thing I can get my hands on and aim for that person's face.

"Don't you think Slick is missing you?"

"Yeah," she hiccups. "I just wanted to come by."

"Thanks," but I don't mean it and she knows it.

Sandra-Lee turns, hugging her thin cardigan around her narrow shoulders, head hanging. I wish I could wind back the clock and go back to yesterday when we were cutting paper dolls and pretending like everything was how it used to be. Or better yet, wind it all the way back to before the sun set on Kitty's life. It was so bright that night, the moon so heavy with a pure white glow. The shape of the beast. The blistered feet of the man. Five diagonal cuts across Hardy's neck.

"Wait! Sandra-Lee!"

She turns and looks at me with an inhale of hope. "Yes?"

"Did you see what did it?"

"I don't... it was a..." her plucked eyebrows pinch together. "It wasn't a man. I know that's who the tattooed man shot but the thing I saw... it was on all fours."

"No joke?" I ask. My mouth is filled with cotton.

Sandra-Lee thinks on this again and then gives me a slow nod. "It was an animal. Unless you've seen a person run on their hands and feet?"

I think of the times, as children, Kitty and I would thread our legs through the sleeves of Dad's old shirts and race each other in the backyard, hunched over like gremlins. I want to laugh and turn bitter with endless tears. The memory hurts too much. I will keep getting older and Kitty will remain, thirteen and brazen. I have the oyster of our childhood but who can I share my middle years with? Or the infinite expanse between now and old age?

"No. I can't think of anyone who would run like that," I say.

"Sandra-Lee! Where've you run off?" Slick swaggers through the row of cars and trucks facing *Blue Hawaii*.

"Over here!" Sandra-Lee waves her hand in quick dainty flicks of her wrist. "We're just catching up!"

"Honey, maybe let Elvis do the talkin' for a change. That's what I paid for. Hey, Delah. Much change in the last hour?"

"Nope. Y'all go on and enjoy the flick."

"Sure you don't need a ride?"

I shake my head. "Thanks though."

"Anytime."

Parker and Roger don't need my help. Traffic has slowed down significantly and they're already starting to sweep away the bits of popcorn Reda hasn't gobbled up. I decide not to read anymore *Oth-*

ello. Instead, I climb up to the projection booth and sit beside Purlie. Wordlessly, he rolls a cigarette and offers it to me. I hold it the way I've seen all the starlets do. He strikes a match and the end of the cigarette glows like a small cherry. Smoke burns my tongue and the base of my throat, and I hack up a loogie I didn't even know existed. Purlie laughs.

"Ugh! That's awful!"

"Yeah, a bit, but nicotine is good for the creative process," Purlie takes the cigarette from me and pops it into his mouth. He looks so cool and rugged when he does it. It wouldn't surprise me one bit if he ends up riding a motorcycle westward toward some fantastic swashbuckling adventure. I'm spurred by a thought and a question escapes me before I've even processed the words.

"Hey, Purlie?"

"Hey, Delah."

"You ever read about weird stuff in school?"

"Weird stuff like how?"

I huff and press my chin against the lower rung of the crow's nest. Purlie is an intellectual. Anything I say will just sound stupid. "I dunno. Weird stuff."

"There's a ton of weird stuff, Delah. Gods turning into animals to seduce women... cannibals... I read a book about a man who was put on trial because he didn't cry at his mother's funeral."

My jaw locks and I have to work my dry tongue around before I can speak. "There've been stories about animal-men for a long time?"

"Since always. Think about it. In the Garden of Eden, a snake talks to Eve. A snake can't talk unless it's also a man. Of course, it could be that it was a normal man and was just called a snake... like calling someone who cheats you a rat. They aren't really, but they have a thieving, small-minded personality. You see?"

Purlie's hooked on this subject. I can tell by the way he has the same sort of fervor his father gets behind the pulpit. I bet this rough passion of Purlie's elevated him in all his classes, like he belongs in a group lecture where he can bounce off all his ideas and form new ones in quick succession. It makes me curious about why he dropped out, and also a little bit sad.

It embarrasses me that my thoughts can't move as fast as his. My lips tighten, holding back my admission of ignorance. If I say I have no idea what he's talking about, I'm worried Purlie will see me as a child. I don't want an answer for a child. I want the truth so that I can find some iota of closure in Kitty's senseless death. Swallowing my pride, I say, "No. I don't see."

"Point is," Purlie scratches his chin with a thumb. He doesn't sound impatient. "All stories come from something that was true. Writers like to expand on things, turn events colorful to fit into the box of what they are trying to say. Take *The Wolfman*, Lon Cheney Jr. Nineteen-forty-one. Sure, he turns into a werewolf when the moon is full but isn't that just an allegory for human nature? It's basically a rehash of Dr. Jekyll and Mr. Hyde."

"Do you think it's real though?"

Purlie peeks at me through the corners of his eye and flicks the butt of his cigarette into the gravel below. "Parts of it. Like I said, a story starts somewhere. Why?"

I tuck my chin into my shoulder, so he doesn't notice my blush in the glow of the projector. "I was just curious. That's all."

Ten minutes to the end of credits, Purlie gets up and begins moving around the booth again, preparing the cans, making sure the shelves are organized and away from anything that might be flammable. I climb back down the stairs and return to the box office, make sure everything is in its place, and grab my purse. Whether they know it or not, Purlie and Sandra-Lee have given me a lot to think about.

Dad arrives on time. His brown patrol car slides up to the employee entrance and Mrs. Dunne walks over to meet him.

She takes one of his hands in both of hers and the puffy blue veins swell as her grip tightens. "Daniel. You eating?"

"Yes. Of Course. Thank you for the pot roast. Best we ever had, wasn't it?"

"Yep," I say. "Thanks, Mrs. Dunne. For everything. I'll see you Saturday?"

"Say an hour before twilight?"

"Okay. Thanks again."

I climb into the car and hope the conversation between Mrs. Dunne and Dad doesn't last long. I want him to be on the road before we get stuck behind the line of cars leaving Starry Night Theater. A burst of hot wind pushes through the night and sends flecks of dirt to dance in spirals against the headlights of the patrol car.

Dad finally gets in and adjusts his mirrors before shifting gears. "How was work?"

"Fine. Sandra-Lee and Slick came. They offered to give me a ride home."

"Nice of them. I'm glad you have friends who care about you."

I reach forward to turn on the radio, but Dad hasn't finished speaking. "Delah, I'm so proud of you. You've been so strong through all this."

"Okay."

"I mean it."

"Thanks. Dad, how fast do stitches heal?"

He rubs his scruffy jaw with the bowl of his hand, forefinger and thumb, caught off guard by my swerve in conversation. "I don't rightly know. I think it depends. I had eight in my forehead that were taken out after two months. That was ages ago. When I was only a boy. Why?"

"I dunno," I shrug, and he doesn't push. Dad never asks questions he knows he'll get an answer to if he just waits. I try sometimes to ignore this trick of his entirely, but his silences always compel me to talk. "I saw Hardy yesterday. He looks a lot better. I just thought it would last longer or look worse. Or something."

"Maybe it's just new medicine? Things like this progress so quickly in the world and the body is a funny thing. It heals at the pace it wants to."

"I guess."

We drive up the dirt road leading to our house. Main Street, behind us, is nothing more than a string of lights, a glowworm in the dark. We pass Sheriff Muller's squat little cabin mostly hidden behind a grove of post oaks, the Anderson's well-lit home, and then our rocky acreage. There are no lights shining, no welcome or hope.

Before Kitty's death, I hadn't thought much of the world outside of home. I only dreamed of making it through high school, becoming a reasonable wife to a dutiful husband, and keeping up with Dad's ponies when he became too old. Kitty wanted to see France. She wanted to eat ice cream in an Italian plaza. She wanted her own manifest destiny in the shape of a Californian University. I thought of the last movie we saw together. Another Elvis flick where he and Tuesday Weld talk of their unhappy wild.

I wanna get out of here. I'm young. I want a good time out of life.
Then do it, Hun. Paint your toenails red and run away.

Could I do something like that? I can't imagine leaving Dad, but Maryneal is getting crushed by this unbearable sadness. Sandra-Lee is right, everyone hurts.

I say goodnight at the top of the stairs and Dad blows me a kiss. After I crawl into bed, I hear him shuffling from the kitchen to the living room, and I fall asleep to the low hum of the radio program he's turned on.

In the early hours, on my way to the bathroom at the end of the hall on the second floor, I see the light is still on in the living room. The radio hums, but no announcer speaks, no music creeps from the speakers. Dad's fingers steeple together, his unfocused eyes trail across the dusty rug. This is not my father I'm seeing, but Daniel Nix. This is a man who had children too young and lost one too soon. A man who holds himself together when he can. A man who acts as my father when he must. This person has the same unfamiliar face that appeared at Kitty's grave.

His expression shifts as the ripple of my shadow crosses him and I press myself against the wall, away from view. I feel like I've just stolen a secret and my heart thuds loudly against my ribs. I wait for him to call out to me, but he doesn't. So I sneak back up the steps to the attic room.

Further up the hill, another light flickers on and shines through the dark. It's the Diggs' house. At this distance, Hardy's window is no more than a yellow postage stamp, and I wonder what secrets keep him awake.

Chapter Nine

Dad wakes me up on Sunday morning right as the Andersons' rooster starts its daily holler. He's dressed in a dark brown suit, freshly shaved, and smells like Aqua Velva and moth balls. He gives my foot another wiggle after several minutes of non-movement.

"We're going to church."

It's not a request. Although he never pressured us to attend Sunday service, it was always understood we would go. As Nolan County's Deputy, attending service is just as much part of his job as it is a spiritual necessity. Dad waits for me to plant my feet on the ground before leaving me to get dressed. He keeps his face to the bedroom door. Since the night I found him sleeping in Kitty's bed, he hasn't looked to that side of the room.

I'm not sure what I'm supposed to wear. We didn't go last week because neither of us felt like talking much. It was the only time I've skipped a service and the relief was fantastic. What a thing it was to uncurl from my blankets at the hour I wanted, without the dreaded weight of duty flooding my lungs. Kitty's death has changed me drastically. I used to enjoy church and meeting my friends at Diggs' Pharmacy afterward for a soda or ice cream. Nothing about those things have changed. Only me, and I don't know how to get back to the person I was. I guess that's why Dad is so adamant about waking me up. If we return to routine, maybe we return to ourselves.

I own four dresses but two of them are too small for me now thanks to another growth spurt: a frilly pastel yellow that Kitty was going to stitch to her size, the plaid brown one that is long and thick for a harsh winter, and the green dress I wore all last summer with its capped sleeves and A-frame cut. It's my favorite but the skirt is too short now, so I'll have to give it up. These were all going to be Kitty's because she wanted to alter them into the dresses of her fashion magazines. Then there is the black dress Dad bought me for the funeral. It is the only one Kitty's never touched or examined or hoped to lay her hands on to give it an extra flare. It still hangs over the mirror of my wardrobe.

Am I meant to wear this one because my grief is so fresh? Or am I allowed the brown dress again because I must return to normalcy?

I take the brown dress out in defiance of the black. Thankfully, the summer heat hasn't properly set. I can manage to sit in this dress for a few hours. I braid my tight curls, although the edges fly away, haloing my face. It's the best I can do for a situation I'm not ready to deal with. I have less of an option when it comes to my shoes. Since my feet are the size of a boy's, and I'm not allowed to wear sneakers to church, my one pair of dress shoes have the same square cut pattern as Dad's. I've stopped being embarrassed about this for some time now. None of my classmates care about my shoes but I wish they weren't so boxy because of how it clashes with the soft draping of my dress.

Dad waits on the porch. He twiddles his mustard-yellow tie between his fingers and stares out at the patchy, uncut grass between the house and stable. "You look nice."

"So do you. I changed my mind. I like you without the beard."

He chuckles and steps aside so that I lead the way to the gate. Dad tries not to drive on Sundays, unless he has to go in for an evening shift.

It doesn't bother me. My boxy, leather shoes are comfortable, and the walk is pleasant most of the time.

We are among the first to arrive. Preacher John waits by the chapel's open door. His right hand extends to Dad's while the left clasps him on the shoulder. Near the front pews, Purlie stands beside his mother, Lucille. He gives me a short nod but returns to listening to elderly Mrs. Bankston about the proper way to prune a rose bush.

Sandra-Lee and Barbie arrive. The only time Sandra-Lee doesn't bat up her hair is on Sundays. Like me, she's gone for a simple braid. Hers lays much more smoothly against her scalp. She has on a new, blue tartan dress designed by her mother so that the lace collar will match her bobby socks.

Barbie comes to church, but her parents don't. It is one of the many scandals the old ones can gossip about for ages. Mr. and Mrs. Stine are artists and lived in Canada, then Maine, and then New York City before moving here to get away from toxic city pollution. They don't mind Barbie attending something as conventional as church but it's not what they believe. No one is sure what they believe. I asked Mr. Stine once and all he said was, "That Jesus was one righteous dude. I can't say the same about the rest of it."

Church is the only place Barbie wears a bra or a skirt. Like me, she prefers slacks, but she looks very elegant in her flowing white dress and her hair clipped back with a simple green jewel.

When Slick comes in with Mr. and Mrs. James, Sandra-Lee's shoulders become straighter and the shine in her eyes intensifies. The Jameses talk to the Goodwins, oblivious to the heated way Slick and Sandra-Lee stare at each other as they stay a respectful distance apart. Slick is naked without his Stetson. He has a good head of thick, sandalwood hair. He's combed it down with pomade. Although he cleans up well, Slick has officially grown out of his suit. His brown jacket is tight around his shoulders and biceps which restricts his movements and shows too much of his white button shirt.

Soon, the Diggs and Lawrences are in the chapel. The Andersons stroll in, displaying their fine clothes from another trip into Abilene. They are followed by Mr. Latimer and his frail wife, Petunia. The chatter swells. Folk come by to give me and Dad hugs of welcome and looks of concern.

"How ya holdin' up?"

"Do you need any help around the place?"

"How's ol' Tessie? She'll be dropping any day now?"

"Daniel, are you eating enough?"

"Delah, you look just beautiful!"

"Yeah, the most beautiful ogre." Sandra-Lee ribs me with her elbow in the spot I'm the most ticklish. I have to hold back a fit of giggles.

Hardy breaks away from his parents and joins us girls by the back of the church. It is remarkable how well he's recovered in such a short amount of time. Not long ago, the skin of his face and neck was crusted with scabs and swollen tight and black from all the bruising. Now the coloring is pale green and not so widespread, as though he's only come back from a wrestling match. The stitches down the side of his neck seem purely decoration.

"Good to see you," he says awkwardly.

"Yeah. It's been ages," I respond, and he smirks.

"Listen I—" Hardy cuts himself off because Preacher John has closed the red doors of our little chapel, and everyone begins moving to their family pews. The only noise now is the creaking benches and the old ones leaning into their handkerchiefs to stifle coughs. Preacher John begins with a prayer once we're seated, then directs us to open the hymnals. Petunia Latimer, Mrs. Dunne, and the Anderson twins lead us through "Amazing Grace", and "Hold onto God's Unchanging

Hand". After that, Mr. Roper, my History teacher, stands up to make a few announcements in the same speedy, no-nonsense tone he uses in the classroom.

For a little over an hour, Preacher John speaks in the book of Luke. He explains to us that the Kingdom of Heaven is shut off to those who falsely claim Christ as their savior. He says it's imperative we act in faith for ourselves, not for the sake of others. He says God knows what's in our hearts, so even if we do charity work or come to church three times a week, it won't matter if it's done because we want to be glorified by the community. He tells us that the following days should be spent in self-examination, to study our hearts and discover the truth of who we are versus who God wants us to be.

I hear half of the sermon, but it doesn't stick because I'm thinking about Madam Lulu. She, a pagan dabbling in witchcraft, also told me to keep my faith. It confuses me that she would tell me to pray to Jesus when Preacher John always says that people like her work to lead us away from the Lord. I want to ask Preacher John about this but doing so would reveal I've strayed from the path, that I also dabbled in witchcraft in my association with Madam Lulu.

What if Hardy is cursed? I look up from my bible over to the Diggs. They're at the front, just behind Purlie and his mother. What kind of curse would bless Hardy with a speedy recovery? Sandra-Lee said she saw what attacked us, that it ran on all fours. Kitty and I thought it was a coyote, but we saw the tattooed, forked-tongued man kill the bearded barker.

Is that what Madam Lulu means? Hardy is becoming some kind of animal?

Animals have better hearing. So, out of sheer curiosity, I breathe his name. So quiet Dad doesn't even look up from his note taking.

Hardy turns, pew creaking with the sudden gesture. He looks directly at me and my heart thuds against the base of my throat. His eyebrows lift and he mouths, "What?"

"Did you hear me?" I whisper back, keeping my hand over my mouth so he can't read my lips.

Hardy's eyes expand and his nostrils flare in a muted response. He turns back to face the front, shoulders stiff.

"What did you say?" Dad whispers beside me.

"Nothing."

We're guided into a closing song and prayer. Mr. Roper stands again to make more announcements, this time about the community and not just the church. In an afterthought, he adds that this month's social is being put together by Maryneal's junior year, so any volunteers are appreciated. By the time he is finished, Preacher John has opened the red doors again. He stands off to the side, at the bottom of the steps, to shake our hands as we leave and to listen to the old folks' commentary about his sermon.

I like that we sit at the back of the church, it means we're one of the first ones out. I stretch my legs and walk around the little rose garden while Dad and Preacher John talk of nothing in particular. Mr. Anderson slides up beside them and steals his own handshake. Mrs. Anderson, Martha, and Wilma stand prim and dutiful beside him.

He says, "Preacher, you be mindful of them rabbits of yours. Did you hear about Alfi Latimer's chickens?"

"I hadn't."

"They got raided last night! Some kinda ky-ote. Tore clean through the wire."

"I wondered why they arrived so late this morning." Preacher John shakes his head mournfully. "It's a darn shame."

"Well, wonder at it no more! There's about only two left. Don't think they'll lay though. Not after a scare like that. Rooster's gone and all."

"Oh, dear. We must do something for them," says Preacher John and he glances over the heads of his congregation to Mr. Latimer and Petunia who speak to the Lawrences, their closest neighbors.

I know it isn't my place to interrupt when men are talking but that hasn't ever stopped me before. Besides, I think it's funny Mr. Anderson gets so annoyed by this. I step over from the garden and tell them, "Barbie's parents have two new roosters. They're young still, but I know Mr. Stine only wants to keep one. I can ask if he's willing to donate the other."

Dad smiles and squeezes my shoulder. Wilma winks at me but Martha puts her attention to the shine of her white leather, pointed-toe flats.

"That's a fine idea, Delah," says Preacher John. "You tell them, from me, I'll pay for whatever they're asking."

"It's an Easter Egg chick. Is that the kind Mr. Latimer raises?"

"Never mind that now," says Mr. Anderson and he waves my question away with a swipe of his meaty hand. "What are you and Sheriff Muller going to do about the problem, Daniel?"

One of Dad's eyebrows shoot up into his peppered hairline and he almost laughs. "I suppose I've got to put a warrant out on it. Really, Charles, what do you expect me to do? This is the nature of beasts."

Mr. Anderson pops his lips together, flummoxed. He turns to Preacher John who only shrugs in agreement with Dad. Defeated and not knowing exactly how he lost in the conversation, he turns to the Jameses who have just exited the church. Slick towers awkwardly, in his too small suit, behind his parents. Dad and I start to leave but we hear my name. We're both surprised to see Hardy jogging to catch up.

"Heya, Delah. Mr. Nix. Is it alright if I walk her home?"

"Uhm." Dad stares at me and I can't think of a response other than lifting my shoulders and frowning in equal confusion. "Okay... yeah. Since it's on the way."

"Thanks. Delah?"

I hesitate and then begin to walk again. Dad looks like he intends to walk with us but bends down to check the laces on his shoe and suddenly he's a good distance behind. Hardy doesn't speak at first. He waits until we're well away from the rest of the community who flood out of the church garden and drown Dad into nothing more than another smudged face in the crowd. Since I don't know why Hardy wants to walk with me, I wait for him to speak.

Finally, he asks, "How'd you know my hearing got better?"

"What do you mean?"

"During the service, you whispered my name."

"I dunno. I just had the idea to is all."

He stops and squints at me. His freckled cheeks become flushed with an excitement he's hesitant to share. "Can I tell you something?"

"Sure."

"You can't breathe a word of it. Promise."

"Yes. I promise."

"Not to nobody!"

"I told you I promise!"

Hardy grabs my arms and forces me to look at his dilated pupils. "Swear it. Promise me again."

I cringe back from the heat of his breath. "Hardy."

"I'm serious," he whispers, his fingers digging deeper into the tender parts at my elbows.

"I promise."

Hardy lets go and steps away. "That's three times you promised me."

"What is it?" I don't want to walk with him alone anymore. The energy between us has turned frighteningly electric because he's been holding this secret for too long. My curiosity is the only thing that keeps me at his side.

He shifts his weight and glances over his shoulder to make sure no one else has caught up to us. "I think that ky-ote did something. When I was bit."

My heart shrivels into a tiny hard thing and clunks around my ribs before falling into my stomach. The sun is warm on my neck and in the part of my hair. Unseen mockingbirds whistle to each other and bees flutter between the White Dutch Clover that has unfurled along the hillside.

"Dad said it was a man."

"I know what I saw."

"But Sandra-Lee says she saw an animal, too."

Hardy's muscles unclench and his eyes grow wide with relief. "See! You *must* believe her! So believe me!"

I shake my head. "I don't know what to believe. I've lost my sister, Hardy. That's enough for me to deal with right now."

I press the backs of my hands to my cheeks. Tears are coming and I don't want to cry again. I don't want to make this about me or Kitty. This was so important to Hardy, and I've taken that from him, snuffed it out in my own grief.

He looks away from me and scrubs his face with his hands, shocked by my betrayal.

"I'm sorry," I say, even though I'm not really. I don't want this burden of his, but it seems that Kitty's death has tangled us together. He must feel like there's no one else he can share his secret with. I'm yoked to him now, for better or worse. "I didn't mean it like that. When did you start thinking something was wrong?"

"My hearing," he begins slow, unsure now of how I'll handle anything else he tells me. "My... I'm so hungry now. All the time! But I throw up everything... but... but watch this!"

The fervor is back in his expression and his muscles along his shoulders and jaw tenses again. With a sudden jolt, Hardy sprints up the hill. The air around me depresses the way it does when a rifle is fired. He's back before I can exhale. A flower bud is clutched between his forefinger and thumb. It's an iris from my front yard, which is still two miles away. I take it from him, the grooves of my fingertips trace the veins of the folded petals.

"How?"

One of the reasons Hardy joined the wrestling team was because he's one of the slowest runners at school. In gym, Hardy never broke out of a twelve-minute mile. He pushes hair from his damp brow and a wild grin stretches across his scarred face.

"That's what I'm saying! *How?* How can I do this unless that ky-ote did something to me?"

I don't say anything because Madam Lulu's warnings ring between my ears. Hardy doesn't mind my silence.

"I keep getting stronger!" he says. "Every day, there's something I can do better than I've ever done. Yesterday, I picked up Slick! We were just messin' around and I hip-checked him like nobody's business. I've *never* been able to load him on my back before!"

I clutch the iris close to my chest, at a loss for words because I can't process everything he's telling me. "It seems so incredible. Why don't you want to tell anyone? Not even your parents?"

Hardy deflates a little and I worry I've said the wrong thing. "Who would believe me? Who would think it was because I was bitten by that damn thing? They'd think I got the devil in me… or worse."

"The Traveler woman," I say. It's my turn to share a secret. "She warned me something like this would happen. Hours before Kitty was killed. When she found out you were bitten, she gave… she told me to use oil and pray to protect myself from you."

Hardy doesn't miss the hesitation but doesn't ask what I was about to say. I nearly told him about the silver bullet I've kept hanging on my bedside lamp since recovering it from our stable. Only, I can't bear to tell him that Madam Lulu wants me to kill him. I look at Hardy now and I see only the wonderful boy I've lived next door to my entire life. He doesn't pick fights in school. He makes good grades in all of his classes, and he helps out at his mother's pharmacy. He takes groceries up to old Jeb Burnel and even cleans out the gutters for him.

"You haven't got the devil in you," I say. "But, I think you're right. I think it's something."

We continue the walk to my house. With his newfound speed, I must be annoyingly slow in comparison. He slips his hand into mine and my breath catches, startled by the connection. I look at him and he smiles up at me. I never dreamed he would like me more than a friend and I'm not sure this hand holding is more than that. But it feels different. It has the same nice feeling that rolls around the lower half of my stomach whenever I see Barbie's long, brown hair catch in the wind.

He walks me all the way to the bottom step of our wraparound porch and waits until I'm safely inside. I don't go immediately to the attic but instead linger in the hallway. I let the heat of his hand tickle out of my skin and sink into the iris which has already started to wilt. By the time I make it upstairs and glance out the window, Hardy is at the steps of his house. He pauses and turns to look back, as though he can feel me watching, and grins.

Chapter Ten

Sheriff Muller is in our kitchen. His conversation with Dad echoes through the house and reaches the attic. I can't hear what is being said, only the timbre of his deep, charcoal voice. He visits sometimes, part of his job description as Sheriff for the entire County, but never this early. Curious as to what they're talking about, I slip out of bed and adjust my nightgown before sneaking downstairs. I listen in the shadows between the landing and the kitchen.

"Henson's in a right state, I'll tell you that much," grumbles Sheriff Muller. Although he's not very fat, he breathes heavily between words and often sounds like he's suffering a head cold.

"Wonder what's bringin' it so close to town," says Dad.

"Didn't take any of the hens like at the Latimer's but three died of shock just the same. Top her off, Dan?"

There is a clink of metal against ceramic and a slow, gentle glug of liquid hitting the base of a mug. Sheriff Muller slurps loudly and sighs.

Dad says, "What do you reckon? We could round up a posse and track it down. Might be infected."

"Might be."

Since they're talking about nothing the whole town wouldn't know about, I decide to head into the kitchen. Sheriff Muller's thick hands, gnarled with the early stages of arthritis, curve around a green, ceramic mug I made in art class. He presses the warm, uneven rim to his mustachioed mouth. Dad sees me standing in the archway, but Sheriff Muller starts again before Dad can mention I've come into the room.

"Dan, I know it's a pain to bring it up, but we still don't know who that man is. No one's come to claim the body. Sure you never seen him before?"

"Sure I'm sure," Dad answers quietly. "Delah, you?"

Sheriff Muller twists in his chair to look up at me. The skin of his neck folds into red clay. "Sweetheart, you ever see that man before?"

"He was a carnie." I fold my arms across my chest, embarrassed I hadn't thought about putting on a bra. There is a man, who is not family, in our house. "Barbie and me were walking around the tents and he sold us tickets to a strongman show."

Sheriff Muller scratches his mustache with the back of his thumb. "Carnival done moved across the way to Nig–"

"Really, Sheriff?" Dad cut in, exasperated, but Sheriff Muller slides right on through the conversation, without caring who or how he might offend with his language."–town. I might swing by with a photo of his face. See who knew him, but you know how those types are. They got no loyalty to the law."

He takes a final gulp of hot coffee, pushes himself onto his feet, then cups his hand over the grooves of his hat. Sheriff Muller fans himself with it, not because it's a hot morning, but because he's considering us. Trying to guess at our thoughts and, perhaps, thinking of a comforting word because he's realized the wound he so freely picked at has only just started to scab.

"County coroner called in this morning," he says, fixing his hat to cover his thinning hair. "That bald woman... the scam artist who came round bothering you. She's gone. I need you to confirm the I.D. Dan.

Think you can manage it?" I swallow the dry wedge that's appeared in my throat and turn to Dad. His frown lines crease and he nods. "How'd it happen?"

"I don't care." Sheriff Muller's sigh is equal parts exasperated and desperate. His expression shifts, becomes less hardened and he fiddles with his tie. "Self-inflicted by the looks of it. Drag lines on her arms."

"Poor woman," Dad says, so gently I almost don't hear it over the windchimes outside the kitchen window. A swelling of guilt pushes the dryness in my throat toward a sharp, wet prickling that fills up my navel cavity. Is it my fault she's dead? She blamed herself for Kitty's murder and I ignored the help she offered. I wrote it off as insanity, as quackery. The way it was said, *drag marks,* like it was more than self-harm. What if the truth of it is as sinister as she warned me and Barbie about? What if she didn't leave this life on her own but was trying to fight for it and the drag marks are from the same sort of creature that killed my sister?

The beast who ruined Kitty is dead, shot in front of my very eyes, but I can't believe that it would be anyone else. Not Hardy. *Please, God. Not Hardy.*

"How's your summer?" he finally asks me, drawing my attention away from this spiral of downward thinking.

"It's fine." I hug myself more fiercely, trapping my secrets behind my ribs. "Thanks for asking."

"You got a good head, Delah. Be a senior in the fall, won't you? Maybe think about Texas Woman's? Or Baylor?"

"I'll walk you out, Joe," says Dad. He guides Sheriff Muller from our small kitchen with an open gesture of his hands. They lean on Sheriff Muller's patrol car, which is nearly identical to Dad's, and talk a while longer. I use the excuse of rinsing out the homemade mug to watch them and wish I had Hardy's hearing. Could it be the unknown man they're speaking of or the coyote attacks on the chicken farms?

Dad returns to the kitchen, grim and ashen-faced. He forces a smile, but the way he eases into his chair at the kitchen table is too slow, too heavy. He speaks to his hands, head bowed with the weight of everything he's not telling me. "I told Joe about that woman who came on our property. He thinks she might've been involved. Guilt made her confess to you."

"But she said it wasn't a man that killed Kitty," I remind Dad. He looks at me then back to his fingers and a small, unconvinced sigh escapes him.

"Sometimes the brain tricks us into what we *want* to believe. It could be she doesn't believe any man capable of doing something... something so awful as murdering a young girl. Travelers see the world differently. Their culture is strange, and it could be she believes there is something worse than a man."

"She said Hardy was cursed, too, and—" I cut myself short. I've nearly exposed Hardy after I swore three times I wouldn't.

Dad's thin eyebrows pinch together. "And what?"

"And nothing. I think that's all she said. She was rambling."

Dad nods then slams his fists against the table. The laid-out plates and cutlery rattle. "I just want to know the bastard's name!"

The burst of anger vanishes as quickly as it came. He stares out the kitchen window. His whole-body tremors as his head falls lower and lower until it's in the space between his arms. The noise that comes out of him is a wordless, wet screech like cattle being branded with a fresh, hot iron. I don't know what to do, so I just sit there, stare at the marks on the table, and wait for him to stop.

Dad scoots back in his chair and stands. He walks over to me and presses my hair down with the flat of his hand.

"I'm sorry, honey. Why don't you get dressed for the day? I'll make us some breakfast."

I wander slowly back upstairs, rolling my fingers along the banister. The sound of bacon hitting the pan rises with me. I picture Dad cracking open the eggs, frying them in the bacon grease, and using the edge of his thumbnail to pick out the bits of shell he's accidentally dropped into the pan. It's amazing how quiet it is with just the two of us in a house that is determined to keep us silent and lost. Ten days. She's been dead ten days.

I can't stand the crushing grief anymore. So much of it is building inside of me I might go crazy. For the first time since the carnival, I go over to our Dansette and open it. I pick a random record from our collection and slide on Joey Dee & the Starliters and turn the dial all the way up. "Peppermint Twist" fills the bedroom and the music gets good to me. I jump and twist, let it overwhelm me, and delight in the sting of my hair as it whips around my face. I pump my fists in the air, run in place, let the words of the song rush out of me in frantic shouts until I've got no voice left. The song ends before I've finished dancing, and I stand there with an awkward huff.

Whatever possessed me has passed. The hem of my nightgown clings to my thighs and morning light pollinates the room, turning it gold. Three minutes of carelessness. I've never felt so free.

After breakfast, I ride my bike through the neighborhood. It's too early to visit Sandra-Lee or Barbie. Both of them prefer to sleep in during the summer and I don't know how they manage to do it. Even if I didn't have to muck the barn every morning, there's still the Andersons' rooster. I sometimes wonder if the sun would rise without the damn thing.

I ride past the square, wave to Mrs. Diggs in her shop and Preacher John as he strolls happily on the sidewalk opposite, toward Buzzy's

Dinner for his morning cup of coffee. Mr. and Mrs. Hooper drive by in their truck. He beeps his horn and rolls down his window as they come up alongside me. Little baby Gertrude makes bubbling noises. Mrs. Hooper appears nearly put together if not for the stain of spittle running down the shoulder of her maroon blouse.

"Mornin', Delah. Off to cause trouble?"

"Not too much."

Mr. Hooper isn't as thin as he used to be before Mrs. Hooper became pregnant and he's grown a thick beard to distract from the extra padding around his middle. "I'd love you to join our Ag Team in the fall," he says. "Now that Parker's graduated, we've got an opening."

"What's the animal?"

"Goat," he says. "Funny little thing, too. Very social."

"Maybe. I'll ask Dad."

"Oh! Someone made a poopie!" Mrs. Hooper says, sing-song, to Gertrude, and I decide in that moment I never want children.

She used to have her own identity before the baby came along and now she gets excited over changing diapers. Mr. Hooper shrugs and puts the truck into drive. He honks again and turns up the street toward Lone Apple Bank. I pedal around the rest of the square then double back and retrace the path we took to the carnival. I park my bicycle behind Starry Night's concession stand and turn to face the field.

It is disappointing and unremarkable. I breathe in the tang of grease hanging around from last night and the weird vinegar odor that comes off of movie theater garbage. Summer mornings in Maryneal are a beautiful, uncomplicated quiet. Another inhale and I've steadied myself. I have to do this. I have to see the place she died.

The soft, yellow-green grass is washed clean of any trace of my sister, but I know the exact spot she fell. It pulls me down to the earth like an anchor until my head spins and I am forced to sit.

There are traces of the carnival in the neighboring lot. Flag markers, divots where tent posts were hammered into the dirt, and the trails of where heavy equipment was wheeled away. I pull my knees to my chin and sit for a long time. Not even the grasshoppers are bothered by me. They spring from blades of grass, following horse flies while my hair soaks in the sun.

It isn't fair. I could have saved her if I had only done what Madam Lulu told me to. I should've done a lot of things differently and it's my fault Kitty is dead.

"Delah?"

I snap to attention and twist around to see Hardy standing a few paces away from me. He moves closer without making a sound. "You okay?"

"Yeah. I'm just thinking."

"Can I sit?"

I nod. He sits and plucks a thick blade of grass. He lines it up between the knuckles of his thumb and blows into it. The sound is like a sick duck, and he keeps making the sound until I shove him. He giggles then stretches out and hooks his arm underneath his head. "That cloud looks like Miss Hawthorne when she bends over."

I look in the direction he's pointing but there aren't any clouds. I punch him in the arm, and he laughs again.

"You're so gross!"

"You looked!"

"I just wanted to see if you were making up stories."

"You know what they say, 'curiosity killed the cat'." He chuckles and then sits up quickly. "Oh, Jesus! Delah... I didn't mean it like that."

"I know what you meant." I pluck a bit of grass out of his sandy hair. In the bright, cloudless morning, there's *almost* a red sheen to it. "Sheriff Muller was over at my house this morning," I say. "He said the Henson farm was attacked by a ky-ote last night. I was wondering... it wasn't you, was it?"

Hardy offers a dry stare. "What makes you say that?"

"Well... there hasn't been any kind of critter bothering farm animals in a while. Then you say that bite did something to you and all of a sudden chickens are getting slaughtered."

"I woke up warm and cozy in my bed. Like always." He pushes his hand over his scalp, attention focused on the abandoned lot in front of us. "You're letting your imagination run wild."

"Says the guy who's suddenly got superhuman speed."

"It's got nothing to do with me. Coincidence," Hardy mumbles and he picks at the bed of his nail with his teeth.

"Okay... but what if it is you?"

"Well it ain't."

"Someone's going to shoot the thing if it comes near town again."

"I said it ain't me!" Hardy growls and his fist slams down onto his knee.

"Okay," I say again, a little scared and more than a little pissed off. The realm of possibilities has expanded far beyond my understanding since everything happened. I don't think anything would surprise me now.

"Purlie knows a lot about things... maybe he knows what's happening to you."

Hardy looks at me with a strange wildness I've never seen in him before. "You're talking to Purlie?"

"No. I told you I wouldn't talk to anyone. I just think it might be a good idea."

"Okay, fine, whatever, but you *talk* to Purlie."

"Sure. We work together. He lives here. Everyone talks to everyone."

"I don't like Purlie," Hardy says, like his opinion is the final say on the matter.

"Why?"

"I think you should keep away from him. He looks at you funny."

"Maybe I like him looking at me funny," I say, and the words come out petulant.

"No, you don't."

"So? It's not really up to you!"

I push myself off the ground, dust my hands free of the little pebbles, grass, and dirt. "It's fine if you don't want help from him, but you can't go blindly into this. Talk to me when you grow-up."

Truth is, I'm scared to turn my back on Hardy, but I don't want to hang around when he's acting this way. I know the only way to see my way through this bad situation is by talking to someone who has worldly experience. Since Purlie is out of the question, Madam Lulu is the only other option. I have to know if there's a way to save Hardy from this curse without using the bullet she gave me.

Hardy watches me march toward my bicycle, but he doesn't call out or try to stop me or even offer any suggestion. He just tracks my movements and allows me to leave. I know, in those few minutes it takes for me to get my bicycle and ride west, he could have run me down. There is something animal in him. I can see the change, feel it under my skin, like a rabbit knowing it's being stalked.

It takes me an hour to bike to Bitter Creek. Only a few old Indians live out here. They moved in when down here it was because of the Indian Relocation Act and a lot of them worked at the cement plant but with that closing down, all the jobs promised to them dried up. Most of the families turned tail on Bitter Creek and moved out to Sweetwater or to further, more profitable communities. Soon it will be another forgotten place, unable to be found on a map.

I pedal down the tarmac, past the ruined cotton fields, the scant farmhouses, and the remains of a gas station. Beyond Bitter Creek is Wastella. Only the poorest or nonwhite families live on the fringes of this town and the carnival is set up there, like Sheriff Muller said it would be. I never thought much about where the carnival traveled after it left Maryneal. I guess they don't care much whether it's black or white, as long as they get paid. The carnies are setting up for the day, opening tents and hanging prizes in order of size and color. Some of the rides are spinning and whirling through practice runs. I slow my peddling and search for Madam Lulu's wagon.

No one is bothered by me as I move slowly up and down the rows, searching for a sign that might point me in the right direction. Beside a row of target games, I catch a glimpse of the tattooed man with the forked tongue.

"Hey!" I holler with a wave my hands and quicken my pace to catch up to him before he disappears into one of the burlesque tents. "S'cuse me! Sir!"

He pauses and blinks at the idea of anyone calling him sir.

"I just want to know where that fortune teller is. Madam Lulu's her name."

His small, dark eyes scan over me, and he reaches to scratch his bald head. The back of his wide hand and knuckles are tattooed with a garland of thorny roses. His expression softens. "You're the girl whose sister was killed."

I nod and wait.

"I didn't recognize you. It was so dark... Everyone's real sorry to hear it. That man wasn't one of ours."

"Okay. Thank you. Do you know where that woman is?"

He presses the flat of his hand over his bald head again. The back of his neck is peeling with sunburn. "Can't say. She didn't come with us. But if it's fortunes you need, those Injuns living in Bitter Creek will sell you something. 'Bout all their good for."

"Thanks anyway," I say.

Chapter Eleven

The trip back to Maryneal is much longer with cloudy disappointment hanging over. I become uneasy at how dangerously close I ride alongside the highway. I pump my legs faster as I approach one of the steep hills. As cars zip by, I get dragged back in the slipstream. I want to give up. I want to just lay down, stretch my arms and legs open to the sun, and wait for the buzzards to come.

Hardy waits on my porch swing and gently pushes himself with the toe of his shoe as he watches the lane. Sweat forms around the hooks of my overalls and down my spine but I do my best to not look exhausted. I ignore him and push my bike through the gate and lean it against our cedar tree.

He says, "I'm sorry about earlier today."

"You didn't need to be so mean. I was just trying to help."

"I know. I'm just scared, you know?" He follows me inside and helps himself to a pitcher of water that sweats idly on the kitchen table.

I don't need to turn the lights on during the day because my house has so many windows. Sunshine spreads through in oranges and golds, tanning the rooms. Dust angels swirl with the disruption Hardy and I make as we move from foyer to stairs. I'm not sure why he's following me and my heart sticks in my throat, but I don't mind it, so I don't ask. A pocket of my thoughts is black with the idea he is hunting me, but I push the idea away.

"Well? Are you going to talk to me or do I get the silent treatment the whole time?"

"I biked all the way to Wastella and back to try and help you. I don't have the lungs to fight with you right now."

Hardy hovers awkwardly in the threshold of the bedroom door. His clear blue eyes pan over to Kitty's neatly made bed and the corners of his mouth fold in. He enters slowly, barely picking up his feet. Hypnotized, Hardy's fingers stretch out to the pale lace that frames the pillow where my sister used to sleep.

"Bobby Davis is real cut up about the whole thing," Hardy says quietly as he withdraws his hand. "Said he wanted to ask her to the Church Social."

"Well, I'm *sorry* for Bobby's loss!" I spit.

Hardy glances at me over his shoulder and shrugs. He walks around the bedroom, touching things with his index and middle fingers. He pauses over the collage on my wall then strolls over to the Dansette and The Fleetwoods album out of its sleeve. Flipping it in his hands, Hardy glances at me over his shoulder for approval, then places it carefully into the player. The sound of the needle connecting to the vinyl expands in the silence. I'm suddenly aware of the fact it isn't just Hardy in the room now, but a boy. This has never happened before. I've seen enough films to know what I'm supposed to do but it doesn't seem right. Dad won't like this and I'm not sure I want to be alone with him.

He shifts as he listens to the music and his face pinches together. "Remember *The Curse of the Werewolf*? Mrs. Dunne played it at her Halloween Midnight Madness."

"I remember it." I sink onto my bed and hug my pillow as I watch him continue to examine the layout of the room.

"Well... the cursed man turns into a werewolf at the full moon, right?"

"Sure."

"It's only two weeks until the next full moon."

I pluck at a thread on the corner of my pillow. "Do you reckon that's what this is?"

Hardy crosses the room and sits down beside me. The bed groans and his entire body heats up my left side.

Is this what Sandra-Lee feels like when Slick gets this close to her? I've felt this kind of fear before, but it usually comes with the buttery warmth of watching Barbie. My face turns red with the shame of wanting to be closer to Barbie than to Hardy or Manny or any other boy.

I don't understand why Hardy looks at me the way he is right now, or why he doesn't like Purlie looking at me in the same way. It feels like his eyes are pushing into mine and he reaches forward, memorizing the lines of my face with the pads of his fingers.

"Do you think that's real?" I ask, unable to move.

"You saw how fast I can run! How good I can hear! How strong I'm becoming! I mean..." Hardy is breathless with an excitement that launches him away from me. My muscles unwind with relief.

He paces the length of the room as though caged. "Delah, you saw! You must understand. Don't you?"

I shake my head and then nod. "What will you do?"

"I don't know. What if it is like that traveler said? What if it's like in the movies and I lose control?"

I turn to check that the silver bullet necklace hasn't fallen off my bedside lamp. Hardy doesn't notice. I think of taking it down and hiding it in my pocket, but I'm worried the movement will bring it to his attention more, so I leave it.

"Maybe there's a way to keep control of yourself?" I offer. "If this is really happening, then we have to make sure you'll be safe, and you don't hurt anyone else!"

"But you said the woman is gone. Who else would know?"

"Purlie."

A rumble of displeasure comes from him, and he turns to look at me. "You like him?"

"He reads a lot. He might know what to do."

"I don't want him in my business! Besides, you didn't answer my question."

"I haven't thought about it. What does it matter?"

Hardy flicks the flat of his hand in the air, annoyed by the direction our conversation has gone.

"What about the Indians?"

"What about them?" he bites out.

"Didn't Manny's mom get one when his sister was sick with pneumonia? Maybe they know something about whatever it is that's happening to you."

"Yeah? Maybe!"

"It's not that far," I say. My legs ache from riding my bicycle farther than I'd ever thought possible. But if I've done it once, then I can do it again.

Hardy returns to the spot beside me and my pulse picks up again. His eyes float down to my mouth, and I suck in my lower lip, self-conscious of how chapped it is.

"We should go. They might know what to do."

His breath is hot, and his nose is close to mine. Cotton puffs of pale hair grow around his mouth. He's so close to me I can see the looping veins of his irises. A thousand miles away, the front door bangs open. Sandra-Lee and Barbie call out for me as they charge up the stairs.

"Hey! Delah!"

"Remember you promised not to tell," Hardy whispers, and he escapes through the open window. My hair hasn't even settled when the others barge in.

"Delah!" cries Barbie, exasperated. "Where have you been all day?"

Has this whole thing been an overly vivid dream? I close my slack jaw and tear my gaze from the window. "I... I got up early and just rode my bike for a while."

Was Hardy trying to kiss me? Part of me wants to share that with my two best friends but the other part of me wants to keep it a tightly bundled secret. Barbie and Sandra-Lee perch themselves on my bed.

Sandra-Lee says, "You sure you're okay? You're really pale."

"I'm fine."

"Fine enough to help us with the color scheme for the dance?" asks Barbie. She stretches out on my bed and brandishes a folder filled with notes and swatches of paint. "Wilma is holding a staff meeting at her house, but we wanted to see if you could come before we went over."

"Yeah. That sounds like fun. Let me just turn this off." I crossover to the record player and take the needle off my album.

I want, want you to know,

I love you, I love you so.

Please hold, hold me so tight.

All through, all through the night...

I will never be able to listen to this song without thinking about Hardy and how my insides disappeared when his mouth was so close to mine.

Chapter Twelve

Martha and Wilma have the biggest house in Maryneal. It's a two story with four bedrooms and two bathrooms. Several years ago, Mr. Anderson built a bomb shelter in the back and stockpiled it with canned goods, blankets, and reading material. Martha and Wilma share a bedroom because one of the extra rooms is for visiting family only. The other is home for an unsettling collection of porcelain dolls. Most of them are only two feet tall, displayed on pedestals, or in their original packaging. Most of the dolls are girls, dressed in gauzy evening gowns, tutus, and themed holiday jumpers. There are a few boys, red lipped and pale skinned, nearly identical in lacy clothing with only the shorter hair giving away their sex. Two dolls are three feet in height and have actual human hair and dead, glass eyes that roll around in their heads when moved.

I only know about the doll room because I had to go in there to get extra paper and, in all honesty, I nearly ran from the house screaming. It certainly explains why the Anderson Twins look like porcelain figurines and are far more delicate and prim than any other woman in Maryneal.

The afternoon turns gray and cloudy but there is no promise of rain, only humidity. It slinks into the house like an unwanted guest, clinging to our skin and hair. Sandra-Lee presses her face against the oscillating fan set up in the room. Wilma stretches out in her white, wicker chair and passes a paper fan lazily in front of her face. Martha and Barbie stand by the open window, smoking Virginia Slims stolen from Mrs. Anderson's vanity drawer. We've been looking over the lay-outs and plans of the Church Social for nearly two hours and haven't gotten past arguing over the color scheme. Martha shakes her head to Barbie's plea of pastel green and pink. Her bubblegum curls, set high on top of her head at the start of the day, are in need of a hairspray touch up.

"It's too similar to how Preacher John had Petunia decorate the church for Easter."

"What about an Underwater theme?" Wilma suggests. "Oooh, it could be so classy! Blue and silver. Bubbles everywhere!"

"No!" Martha wails. "That is *not* classy. It's tacky."

"Well, what do *you* want?" I snap. "Since this is clearly your grand party! The whole town gathered just to see you in a new expensive dress. Oh-la-la!"

I've been quiet most of the time. My only job is to decorate the posters we'll put up around the square and in the shops, but I can't do that if a theme isn't chosen. Martha stares at me in blank horror because I had the audacity to interrupt. Wilma shakes with silent laughter.

"Something... something *cool*," she says at last.

"Like a jazz club?" asks Sandra-Lee. "We all dress like beatniks and flappers?"

"Maybe," says Martha with a pretty twist of her nose.

"We couldn't," says Barbie. "Remember when Miss Hawthorne read us a bit of *On the Road* and Mrs. Bertrand got sore with her? It was too counter-culture."

"What about an ancient Greek theme?" says Martha. "White and gold."

"The snacks can be served on grape leaves!" Wilma bounces with excitement.

"We can make a paper mâché chariot for the pictures!" adds Barbie.

"I can see if Dad'll let us use Navajo Blue or Bonnie Wee Dancer. He'll probably say yes."

I envision myself in a toga, one sun-brown shoulder exposed. My hair is tamed and plated. I look elegant riding side saddle on Navajo Blue. I picture Barbie and Sandra-Lee in similar outfits, reclining, open mouthed as Hardy, Slick, and Manny feed us dates. Wilma flutters around as a cherub Cupid. Martha has become disfigured, her head replaced with a mule's.

"That's actually not a horrible idea," Martha says to me. "Can you braid ribbons in their manes?"

"Sure. It's easy." Guilt tugs at the base of my throat because Martha is trying to be nice, and she's opened her home to us. I shouldn't have snapped at her earlier but how can I explain my attitude away unless I admit that Hardy's curse is on my mind.

"You know what would be fun?" asks Wilma. "We can have Cupid's arrows deliver date requests!"

"How would that work?" asks Sandra-Lee.

"Well..." Wilma taps her pencil against her pointed chin. "The boys write down their name and the name of the girl they want to ask out and... someone brings it to the girl, and she tells the Cupid yes or no."

"Maybe," says Martha. "But it's a *Church* Social, not the prom. I don't think Preacher John would like it much if we turn this into a dating game."

Barbie snuffs out her cigarette and flicks it into the yard below. She gives an excited wiggle and sits beside me. "This will be the best social yet! Not anything like the ones planned by Petunia Latimer and her old fuddy-duddy bridge club."

I take a sheet of paper, a ruler, and pencil out of my book bag to make a mock-up of what the posters will look like. "What did the ancient Greeks call their parties?"

"Symposiums," says Sandra-Lee. She pulls out a pocket mirror and fixes her pale, blonde bangs so they cover up the spattering of acne that appeared overnight.

"Ugh!" says Wilma. "That sounds like a boring lecture!"

"It wasn't," says Sandra-Lee. "Drinking and dancing and music."

"We'll call it something else," says Martha.

"Olympia?" I suggest. "Ambrosia?"

"I am not having a social that's named after a salad."

"Call it a Toga Party then," I say. "Purlie told me that's what they do in college whenever there's a get together."

"It isn't a college party!" Martha half-screeches before she remembers she is supposed to be an angel of delicate hospitality. "We are organizing the monthly Church Social."

"Well, you aren't coming up with any ideas! Besides, this is Barbie's team. She makes the final say." I close my folder and get to my feet with a huff of annoyance. "Honestly, Wilma, I don't know how you put up with such an insufferable brat!"

I'm out the front door and at my bicycle before Sandra-Lee and Barbie can catch up. Barbie starts in on her own list of complaints about Martha and Sandra-Lee makes approving noises.

With plenty of the day left to do nothing in particular, we decide to ride out to the school and watch the wrestling team do a little off-season work. Coach Bertrand doesn't like anyone on the varsity team slacking on their fitness so the track and field remains open even when the rest of the school is closed for break.

We abandon our bicycles next to the bleachers. By the looks of things, their practice is nearly over, and Coach is making the team do laps around the ceder track to end the day.

Barbie groans as we plod up the first few steps of the empty bleachers. "My boobs are sweaty."

"You should wear a bra, then," says Sandra-Lee with a little smirk.

"Don't oppress me!" Barbie wails in mock horror and she leans back, resting her forearms on the hot metal bench behind her. "Seriously. Tomorrow, let's go swimming."

Manny and Hardy pass us and wave. Slick isn't far behind, and he blows Sandra-Lee a kiss as he passes. She squeals and Coach Bertrand's whistle snaps a warning.

"I think I'm going to marry that boy," Sandra-Lee sighs. Her blush rests pretty on her face.

"Isn't it too early for that?" I ask.

"I suppose. I could give him a test drive first..." She glances at us from the corner of her eye. Barbie and I stop. My jaw unhinges.

"You don't mean?" says Barbie, but she can't finish the question.

Sandra-Lee grins and her blush deepens. "I don't know yet. I'm just thinking about it."

"You're supposed to be married first," I say.

"Says who?"

"Preacher John... and Jesus," says Barbie lightly. "No one important. Go for it, girl!"

The boys pass us again. Barbie frowns and says, "I wonder what they look like naked."

"I guess like those paintings or that Statue of David," says Sandra-Lee.

"Seems kinda small compared to the rest of him," I say, thoughtfully, and Barbie cups her hand over her face giggling wildly.

"That's because you're forced to see Ambition's every morning when you go and feed the ponies," she says. Sandra-Lee doesn't laugh. All the color has drained from her face.

"Oh. Oh my gosh… you don't think it'll be like that size, do you?"

"Only one way to find out!" I say and Barbie makes wet kissing noises until Sandra-Lee is begging us to stop.

Hardy passes us and we turn to see how far back Manny and Slick are. Slick is red-faced and puffing. Manny looks livid and his knees are pumping high as he angles himself to gain speed.

"Wow!" says Barbie, surprised as they pass us a third time. "That's a different outcome than what I expected."

"If their speed is any indication," I add to Sandra-Lee, "you and Slick will be at it all night."

She lets out a little gasp and Barbie shrieks with laughter, but my focus is on Hardy. He's directly opposite us, having rounded the first bend.

"Slow down," I hiss through my teeth so that the others can't hear me. His blotchy, red face turns, and I give him a pointed look I hope he can see from across the pitch. As subtly as he can, he back pedals. Manny is now neck and neck to him and begins to take the lead. Even at the pace Hardy was going it wasn't at his new potential.

I see the strain in his neck, the way his calves bulge with the desire to push into the air like a rocket. Our ponies do this when the weather is glorious and bold. Their flanks ripple with anticipation, and once we let them out of the paddock, they let loose with a frenzy.

Manny finishes ahead of everyone on the team, which is the standard way of things at our school. The muscles around Hardy's nose and mouth are outlined in a blistering rage but there's not much he can do right now. Coach blows his whistle a final time and the wrestling team marches back to the gymnasium.

"I want you boys showered before you leave here!" he shouts. "I'm sick of y'all making my locker rooms smell like ass!"

We watch the team trudge off the field, hunched shoulders glistening with sweat and baked red by the heat of the afternoon. We follow, taking our bikes up the hill to the gymnasium entrance and wait for Hardy, Manny, and Slick to come out of the locker rooms. Coach watches us warily from the shadow of his baseball cap. No one except the team is allowed to go into the school between semesters and for some reason he's under the impression we're here to break in. He looks awful, eyes puffy and bloodshot. The veins around his nose and cheeks are a lattice of thin purple lines.

"Delah," Coach addresses me suddenly.

"Please don't," I say quickly. I don't need to hear any more condolences.

He grunts and tugs at the curve of his baseball cap. No one says anything. We don't want to talk around Coach because he's an adult and he doesn't want to hear us anyway. Coach hates it when we talk during gym and right now he might blow a gasket. The thin slash of his mouth twists into a quiver and his attention is fixed on the locker rooms inside the cool gymnasium. He puts the whistle to his mouth and blows sharply. It makes Barbie jump and that puts me and Sandra-Lee into a fit of nervous giggles.

The wrestling team marches out. Coach counts the heads of everyone before vanishing into the dark interior to make sure nobody has straggled behind or left something on the benches.

"So, Hardy owes me movie tickets because I beat him. Anything good showing this week?" asks Manny. He puffs out his chest smugly.

Hardy looks ready to rip Manny's throat out with his bare hands. I've never seen him so angry and a chill rolls down my spine.

"*State Fair*," I say, avoiding Hardy's gaze. I could probably score him free tickets, since it's my fault he lost the race. "And a new John Wayne. *The Man Who Shot...* someone. I don't remember."

"Heck, I saw that one already," says Slick. "Dad and me, we up to Sweetwater to get some materials for our fence. Popped in at the Cineplex... but I wouldn't mind seeing it again," he adds and looks down at Sandra-Lee. "If you want."

"Say, we can do double dates!" Manny says brightly and he nudges me in the elbow with a loose fist. A deep rumble of warning comes from Hardy. I ignore this but Slick lifts an eyebrow, his eyes flickering from me to Hardy as though he's trying to solve a problem in our advanced algebra class.

"I have to work," I tell Manny politely.

"Maybe Wilma will go with you," Slick suggests.

"Sure. Maybe. She's a bit of alright." Manny nods, trying to convince himself this is a fine idea.

I tuck my head and pretend to have trouble with getting my bike free of where I parked it. Whenever I imagined what my wedding would be like, I never considered Manny or Hardy as options. The groom never has a face.

If I go with Manny, we'll end up in the flatbed of Slick's truck. Manny will probably paw awkwardly at my blouse. Easy enough to imagine but I don't get the same sort of thrill that Sandra-Lee talks about when Slick holds her close. I remember Kitty telling me how Manny thought I was interesting and suggesting he's nice enough, gently pushing me toward the idea of hitching my yoke to his.

As we push our bikes out of the school yard, Barbie says, "So, we finally figured out what the theme of our Social is going to be. We could really use y'alls help with the decorating."

"Nope," says Manny. "That's girl work."

"But we need a chariot built!" says Barbie. "How are we supposed to do that?"

"We'll pitch in," says Slick.

"Dude! So whipped!" Manny moans.

"At least I'm dating someone other than Rosy Palm and her five friends."

Sandra-Lee slaps Slick's arm. He shrugs because Barbie and I are laughing. Manny's sunburned cheeks deepen in color.

"So, what do you say?" Barbie asks him. "Bonus points if you help Slick and I'll put in a good word for you with Wilma."

I lag back from the group because Hardy gives me a pointed look and I know it must be over his mysterious circumstances. He's had time to calm down and return to his normal, genial self.

"We need to talk about stuff. When can we go to the—"

Barbie wheels around, sees that we're far behind, and coasts back down to us. She hops off her blue bicycle and gives us both a wide grin. "Hey! I wanted to talk with you about getting your mom's store involved in the dance? Walk me home?"

"Can't," says Hardy. "I have to be at the store and count inventory."

Barbie flicks back her long hair and flashes a dazzling white smile. "I'll walk you to the store, then! You can help me convince her. See ya, Delah!" she says as we approach the cross street.

"Wait! Did you want to spend the night tonight?"

"Oh! A slumber party!" she says and shouts up to Sandra-Lee. "Sleepover at Delah's!"

Slick wolf whistles and Sandra-Lee slaps his arm again then leans in to hug his massive arm. "Okay!"

I swing onto my bike and wave goodbye and Hardy does his best to hide his disappointment. I catch up to Slick and Sandra-Lee, then we part ways, and I take the high road that leads to my house. Slick follows Sandra-Lee in the opposite direction.

I'm glad for my spur of the moment invitation for the girls to come over and I know Dad won't mind. Quite suddenly I'm aware of my loneliness. The click of my bicycle's chain has replaced the warm sound of chatter, the conversation Kitty and I might be having were she still alive. For the first time I think of Kitty's friends and how they must be hurting with the same loneliness. I've been selfish to think Dad and I are the only ones who miss her company.

I gain a burst of speed and pedal up the hill to my house, determined to call each of Kitty's friends and invite them over as well. In minutes, my bicycle is abandoned by our cedar tree. I'm up the steps, through the door, and in the living room staring at our rotary phone. I don't reach for it. I don't even try. My resolve vanishes.

Dad isn't back home from work either. It's one of his long nights. That means it's my turn to make dinner. Kitty and I used to alternate nights, but I don't have anyone to share chores with anymore. This forgetfulness has happened a lot lately. I keep wanting to come home to share the off-color jokes Purlie, Parker, and Roger tell at work. In the mornings, I want to share my dreams with her and ask her opinions on my clothes. Much of the time I want nothing in particular. I just want her to be there. This is the hardest thing of all. Not having Kitty is like having my ring finger removed. I am utterly incomplete.

Having chores does help keep me from drowning in thoughts like these, so I decide to make hamburgers for dinner. I've just finished chopping the onion and mixing it into the ground beef when Dad's patrol car eases up the driveway. Through the kitchen window, I see him shut off the engine, then let his hands slide from the steering wheel and into his lap. His wide, hazel eyes stare off into the middle distance as though he is captivated by Bonnie Wee Dancer and Navajo Blue.

Tessie Western Spark and Ambition have sequestered themselves to a muddy dip in the pasture. A few weeks ago, Tessie's udder distended. She's become more irritable and restless. The foal could drop any day.

I have to force myself to quit watching Dad. He has become that secret self again when he thinks nobody is around.

After draining the pan of fat into the tin can we keep by the stove, I clean my hands free of the onion smell with lemon. Pulp oozes between my fingers and burns the paper cuts around my knuckles. It's bad enough I've lost Kitty, but now I'm losing Dad, too.

He takes his time coming inside. His boots scuff against the porch steps. The screen door creaking open. In the hallway, he slips out of his shoes and removes his gun belt.

"Smells good," he mutters, coming into the kitchen as he loosens his brown tie.

"Thanks." I use a spatula to shift the raw patties onto a frying pan which has been warming on the gas stove. Dad nods and helps himself to a glass of water. Then he sets the table for two.

"Barbie and Sandra-Lee are coming over to spend the night."

"Excellent!" He smiles at me but in a distant, polite sort of way. His thoughts are with somebody else.

"How was work?"

"Oh, same old song and dance. Dwayne Henson's bull got out and made a mess of things running up and down the country road. It turned up in the Lawrences' vegetable garden. Trampled Laura's prize-winning turnips. I went over to help settle compensation between her and Dwayne."

Meat sizzles on the stove, bubbles with brown grease, and the kitchen fills with the heavy aroma. I push open the window above the sink so some of the heat escapes before the room turns unbearably hot.

"First the hens and now this? He's not having much luck these days. Did his coop get fixed any?"

Dad drags his hand over his jaw. "Hell, Henson and Latimer are both having a time of it, what with the ky-ote. You know Petunia's cough came back."

"No. I didn't know. Will she be alright?"

Dad's head shifts softly from side to side, unsure of Petunia's outcome. "Can't say. Her mother barely survived the dust pneumonia while she was pregnant with Petunia and the doctor reckons that's accountable for her frailness. Latimer said they might try to trade with the Indian for a bit of medicine, but he doesn't want to leave Petunia by herself. She isn't much for traveling any distance at the moment."

"I could go," I say and try to not sound too hopeful. It's just the excuse I need to get out to Bitter Creek without Dad questioning the motives. I could go again without telling him, of course, but I'm already keeping so many secrets from him.

Again, Dad looks uncertain. "I was planning of doing it myself. Me and Muller are thinking the folks out there might know Kitty's murderer."

I feel the swell of ocean between us deepen. We used to not have secrets. I used to need Dad's opinion on everything, and I want to tell him now that I *need* to visit Bitter Creek. Only I can't do that without telling him the one thing I promised Hardy I wouldn't. Dad senses something is chewing me from the inside out and clears his throat. He drags his thumb over a spot on the table's soft wooden surface. "It might be good if you come. It might give you closure."

"I don't want closure! Finding the name of some bastard madman isn't going to bring Kitty back! What's the point?"

He looks up, shocked. It feels good to yell at him and not get punished for it. I want to shout some more but Dad's dark hazel eyes are swimming, and it crushes me worse than never getting to see my sister again. I'm not supposed to see this face. He's let the mask slip. "Why are you so determined to keep her dead?"

I turn back to the stove and press the spatula to the meat and watch as it pops and slides around the base of the skillet. I finish making the hamburgers in silence and transfer the patties onto a large, mustard yellow plate which has a paper towel on it to catch the excess grease.

"I'm not hungry."

"Okay," Dad says, utterly defeated.

"I sliced the tomatoes and lettuce already. They're in the ice box."

"Thank you." I'm at the foot of the stairs when I hear his chair scrape against the floorboards and Dad rounds the corner. "Delah?"

"What?"

"I love you so much. Okay?"

"I know that. I love you, too."

He gives a succinct nod and returns to his lonely place at the kitchen table. I make it to the top of the stairs before the house creaks and settles around me, urging me to turn around. A low, steady sigh escapes my tightly squeezed lungs.

I return to the kitchen. Dad glances up from the hamburger fixings.

"I guess I am kinda hungry."

"I'll fix your plate."

We eat with our elbows on the table, haloed in the lamp hanging over us as the night grows.

Chapter Thirteen

B arbie and Sandra-Lee arrive just as the sun starts to set. They lean their bicycles against mine and hurry up the porch, not bothering to knock. Dad greets them each with a side hug and allows us to disappear up to the attic. He has a set evening routine of his own: crossword puzzles while he listens to *Moon River*, the most boring radio program ever to exist. It's just some old man reading poetry over dreamy organ music.

We don't have a television, not many people do in Maryneal, but Dad has several radio programs he listens to religiously. *Gunsmoke* and *The Romance of Helen Trent* were our favorites before they went off air a few years ago. Now there's *Ranger Bill* and *Yours Truly, Johnny Dollar*, which are good enough programs. I'll join him when he turns the dial to the soaps, but *Moon River* gives me a headache and I always fall asleep.

Barbie spreads out the magazines she bought from Diggs' Pharmacy and Sandra-Lee unrolls her sleeping bag. They avoid the other end of the room where Kitty's bed remains a white lace tombstone.

"So," says Sandra-Lee, wrapping her hair in tissue paper before covering it all in a baby blue hairnet.

"What?" asks Barbie and her sly grin disappears under the fabric of her shirt.

I avert my eyes. This isn't the first time we've undressed in front of each other. In the locker room after gym class, we're always baring skin. But I let my gaze linger too long and I feel guilty. She doesn't have the same tan lines as Sandra-Lee and I do. The skin around her nipples is as bronzed as the rest of her and I think she must spend her mornings sunbathing without her clothes. Does she have a secret place to do that without even her parents knowing?

Sandra-Lee had already changed into her pajamas, but she'd done it while in the bathroom. I feel like I ought to do the same. Do they explore me with covert looks, too? Or is it just my own curiosity silently probing at the differences in our bodies? There is a hidden truth in me I'm not willing to face but I know it's there because I wish I could keep looking at Barbie. I'm enchanted by her willingness to be so free and unashamed of her nudity.

"So," Sandra-Lee says again. "Did you ask Hardy to the Church Social?"

"No!" Barbie answers in a light squeal. "Delah and I are going stag. Isn't that right?"

"Best decision we ever made," I say, flicking my magazine closed. I stretch out and pop my toes.

"But you want to ask Hardy, don't you?" Sandra-Lee probes with a knowing smile.

"What have you heard?" asks Barbie, suddenly breathless.

"Nothing... I'm just noticing."

I've barely shimmied into my own cotton nightgown, when several plinks against my window grab our attention. At first I think it's a bug attracted to the light from my bedside lamp, but two more pebbles are flung against the glass in quick succession. The three of us rush to the other side of the room and draw back the curtains. We make out two shadows standing outside the stretch of light coming from the living room where Dad is hopefully on the couch asleep.

Barbie pushes open the window and we stick our heads out in unison.

"What?" I whisper.

"Can we come up?" asks Hardy.

"Shhh!" says Sandra-Lee. She and Barbie look at me. It's my decision, after all.

"Why?" I whisper. There's no answer because we've just heard creaking from downstairs. Barbie and Sandra-Lee turn to stare at the bedroom door and they don't see how Hardy's eyes are the silver pearl of things that can see at night. My skin rolls and my bones chill.

"Well?" Slick's sonorous voice drifts up to us, rough in its attempt to stay quiet. "Can we?"

He dips back into the shadows again because there is movement from the house. The living room light clicks off and, after a few minutes, Dad climbs the stairs and drifts to his own bedroom.

"Oh... okay. Fine."

We step away from the window. Sandra-Lee's smile is so wide it looks like it might split the skin around her ears. Barbie mimes clapping and spins on the spot.

Slick's bulky figure slinks surprisingly catlike up the exposed trellis that lines the side of the house. He becomes less graceful as he stumbles through the window. We pause in case his entrance was heard, but Dad doesn't investigate. Hardy climbs up next. He doesn't make a sound as his feet hit the floor. Neither of them are wearing shoes.

"Where's the third stooge?" Sandra-Lee asks, voice low.

"Didn't want to face the wrath of mama bear if he was caught sneaking out," says Slick. He hops onto my bed and stretches out. The springs of my mattress groan loudly in protest. He takes up most of the bed but that doesn't stop Sandra-Lee from wiggling into the crook of his arm.

"So does this mean you're going to help us with decorating ideas for the Social?" asks Barbie.

"Uh, nope!" says Hardy. "You're having a slumber party. We invited ourselves over."

"What's a party without a few smart fellas?" adds Slick.

"Yeah. I was wondering when the smart ones were going to show up," I say, and he smirks.

"It's rude to not bring a snack to a party," says Sandra-Lee.

"Hon, I'm all the snack you need," Slick answers. He flexes his arm and that pushes Sandra-Lee closer to him. She stifles a giggle as he covers her mouth with a swift kiss.

"Wow," mutters Hardy. "Y'all need to find a different room."

Slick shields himself and Sandra-Lee with his Stetson, then continues to kiss her with dramatic smacking noises.

"But where will you sleep?" asks Barbie. All eyes flicker to Kitty's bed.

"The floor," Hardy says evenly.

"I guess that's okay," I mumble. "There's extra blankets downstairs."

I leave them to sneak through the house to retrieve spare blankets and pillows from the linen closet. Dad is reading in his bed, and he rolls toward his lamp, exposing the ridges of his spine and loose cotton underwear. I move as quickly and silently as I can, avoiding the aged spots that make the floor talk loudly.

When I return, Hardy hasn't moved from beside the window. I fluff up the spare pillow and lay it on the side of the room that's the furthest from the window. Then I unfold the blanket and shake out some of the dust before putting it on the floor, too. It smells slightly of mothballs.

"Thanks," he says.

He looks around the room again. Barbie drops to her knees and pulls out the Monopoly boardgame from underneath my bed. Slick and Sandra-Lee sit down on the floor with us and the game goes on for hours, each of us having to keep silent to avoid getting caught. At first I'm not aware of my envy at Barbie's ease with Hardy, but bile builds each time I see her skin brush against his or when she leans, braless and willowy, across from him to collect her piece and move it around the board. Hardy doesn't move away from the subtle advances, and I hate him for it.

It's nearly two in the morning when Sandra-Lee yawns wide and makes her way over to her sleeping bag. Slick drags over his pillow and blanket, then stretches out beside her. On the other side of me, Barbie and Hardy make up their beds. I turn off my bedside lamp. Hardy strips down to his boxers and folds his clothes neatly before placing them above his pillow. No one speaks. Instead, we listen to the sound of each other and take in the novelty of sleeping next to boys we aren't married to. Slowly, Barbie and Sandra-Lee's breathing becomes unpatterned. Slick snores gently into the crook of his arm.

I'm still awake. Hardy shifts his head and opens his eyes. They shine in the fracked moonlight. I pull my thick blanket up to my chin, my pulse thumping with a wild excitement in my ears. The angle of his head changes. Can he hear my heart? Can he taste the way my fear floats into the air?

When I was a child, I was scared of the monsters hiding in the shadows of the room. Dad used to come in and chase away those dark unknowns. The monsters weren't real then, but what am I supposed to do now that there *is* one, not sleeping, beside me?

Chapter Fourteen

I 've always been a light sleeper, so when I hear Dad groan and fart as he rises out of bed the following morning, I reach down and nudge Hardy awake. His skin radiates heat of a terrible fever. He snaps up so quickly I swallow a scream of surprise and draw my hand protectively into my breastbone. Hardy stares up with me, unfocused and cotton mouthed.

"What is it?"

"Time to go."

I roll over and wake the others but Hardy's rough hand tugs at my wrist. He steals a glance at Barbie, sleeping as though she's pricked her finger on a spinning wheel.

"Check them," he mouths to me, then makes a shushing gesture. There is a dark crust underneath his fingernail.

I lift and twist my head enough to see Sandra-Lee and Slick haven't stirred from the commotion I've made. Sandra-Lee fits perfectly into the bowl of Slick's body. They look so pure in their embrace, so happy. I turn back to Hardy and nod.

He shifts cautiously into an upright position and moves closer. "I had a strange dream. I was running through the fields. Sometimes just barefoot, other times I was using my hands to make me faster. I woke up with a raw taste in my throat."

"Raw like what?"

"I don't know. I think I bit my tongue in my sleep... I didn't go anywhere did I?"

"I don't think so."

Behind him, Barbie groans and pushes a knuckle into the soft pockets of her eyes. "Too early for talking," she mumbles and then rolls onto her other side and falls back to sleep.

Hardy pushes himself up to his feet. The muscles around his ribs and spine ripple like the sketching of a sea monster in the corner of a treasure map. There is an unseen depth of how big the creature really is just beneath the surface.

He pulls on his shirt and pants, then straightens up with an agitated sigh. "It was so real. This is the second time I've been to Manny's and—"

I cut him off and say, with more certainty than I feel, "You stayed here the whole night. Y'all should go now before Dad catches you."

Hardy nods and tiptoes over to Slick and kicks his leg.

Slick wakes with a loud, startled grunt. "Already?" he mumbles. He rolls onto his back and stretches, bare feet sticking out the bottom of his blanket. Sandra-Lee wakes in time to peck a kiss on his cheek. The boys leave through the window and jog lazily to Hardy's Queen Anne style house at the end of our dirt road.

I gather up my hair and pull it into a tight bun. My eyes are open, and sleep has dragged itself from my body but I'm not here, or anywhere in particular. I've been caught up by the frail moments of the morning when Hardy and I shared a binding secret and how it pressed around the others as they slept.

"Ugh," says Sandra-Lee around a yawn as she unwraps tissue from her batted hair. "I can't believe I let him see my hair like this."

I pull on a paisley blouse and a clean pair of dungarees then pause to reconsider my standard wardrobe choice. I slip out of the denim and into a skirt that matches my top. My waist and the sudden growth of my breasts are more visible this way. It's not the tough plain fabric that hangs like a box from my broad shoulders like the ones I wear to church. If I wasn't so worn out, I'd look like one of Mrs. Anderson's porcelain dolls. Sandra-Lee fixes the dents in her hair and dresses in the bathroom. She's chosen to wear a pale-yellow sundress that makes the red of her lipstick pop and shows off the surprisingly athletic curve of her thighs. It takes a lot of coaxing to wake Barbie, but we manage to do so, eventually. Once up, she dresses in a halter and blue slacks then pulls her long hair into pigtails and decides not to fuss with any make-up. In muted, sleepy tones, we make plans on stopping at Diggs' Pharmacy for bottles of coke before making our way out to Sweetwater.

Dad is downstairs, dressed in his maroon striped bathrobe, and setting the coffee pot to boil. There is fresh squeezed orange juice on the table and pancakes browning in the griddle.

"Y'all look nice," he says to us. For the first time since Kitty's death, there is a shine behind his small eyes.

"Thank you," says Sandra-Lee, passing a hand over the back of her skirt before she sits.

"Heck, yes!" Barbie claps her hands and slings herself into a vacant seat. "Bacon!"

Her parents don't eat any type of pork. One of the reasons Barbie rarely invites us over to her house for sleepovers is because she doesn't want to subject us to rice cakes and flavorless oatmeal. But there is a lot of bacon... more than any of us could eat. Dad stacks pancakes the size of sand dollars onto a plate that is already full of fluffy, golden disks.

"What's with all the extra?" I ask.

"I guess I just got carried away," he answers, scooping out the last of the batter onto the griddle where it sizzles and pops in bacon fat.

Sandra-Lee, Barbie, and I tense at the sudden knock on the door. Dad pats his hands clean against a kitchen towel. "Mind the stove. I'll see who it is."

We wait, and my thoughts go fuzzy with an unnamed dread. The soles of Dad's house slippers scrape along the entryway and come to a stop.

"Boys? What a surprise!" He doesn't sound surprised at all, but he doesn't sound angry either. Barbie and Sandra-Lee exchange looks. Do they also think Hardy and Slick's appearance is too bold a move?

"Hiya, Mr. Nix." Slick's low mumble carries an unbothered authority. It's as if he knows the whole world is his for the taking. "We were wondering if the girls wanted to take a trip down to Lake Sweetwater."

Dad leads them into the kitchen. "Well how about that. They were planning on a trip today... Have y'all had your breakfast?"

My cheeks and nose are splotched red. This isn't the first time I've wondered if Dad has the superhuman ability to read minds, but I'm curious as to how much he actually knows. Did he just expect that the boys would show up? Does he know they slept in my room last night? How could he when I didn't hear him creak up the stairs to check on me during the night? Maybe I'm not as light a sleeper as I thought.

Slick and Hardy follow Dad into the kitchen. I don't know why I was surprised to see Manny with them. They are dressed in high waist and belted swimming trunks, which expose the palest parts of their legs that haven't had a chance to bake in the sun. Their unbuttoned shirts hang from shoulders, ready to be cast aside in the frenzied dash to the lake's cool shallows. As always, whenever I see Slick without his Stetson, I'm amazed by the amount of hair he has on his head. Hardy's chest is covered in thick scars. Five parallel marks stretch from his collar bone. Only Manny seems underdeveloped, the hairs around his nipples like curling eyelashes.

Our kitchen quickly fills with chatter as everyone loads down their plates and digs in. Dad learned how to cook working at Buzzy's Diner. It was ages ago, before he left for the police academy. I don't do much talking. Instead, I listen to Dad swapping stories, asking if anyone wants refills on juice and telling jokes as he slowly comes out of this cocoon he's built around himself the last few weeks. His familiar, cherubic grin is hitched back into place. In this bright moment, he is the person I've always known and loved.

Between Slick and Hardy, no food is left behind. Hardy even uses the stiff corners of toast to soak up trails of ketchup and grease off his plate. We offer to wash and dry the dishes, but Dad shoos us.

"Y'all go swim. There's plenty of time for chores when you've grown-up."

We pile into Slick's apple green Chevy, stopping first at Sandra-Lee's and Barbie's house to collect their swimsuits and towels. Sandra-Lee's father is hesitant to let her go. He's just coming off another night shift at the cement plant and doesn't like the idea of her in another town without anyone he knows chaperoning. It takes Slick about ten minutes to change Mr. Goodwin's mind. While he's working his magic, Mrs. Goodwin slaps together a picnic basket full of ham sandwiches, pickles, and dried plums. I'm glad they aren't as perceptive as Dad. Had the Goodwins known Slick cradled Sandra-Lee in his arms the entire night, Mr. Goodwin would have taken down the

rifle from where it hung above the fireplace and shot him in the foot...
or worse.

While we wait for Sandra-Lee and Slick to come back out of the
house, Manny drums his fingers along with the music playing on
the radio. I'm stretched out in the flatbed with Barbie and Hardy.
The blistery morning light heats the metal and turns us into sausages
rolling in a frying pan.

Once we're back on the road, Slick kicks up the speed, turning out
of Maryneal and onto Highway 70. There's nothing on either side
of us but stretches of desert shrub, splashing green throughout the
rocky red earth. A few longhorns plod their way lazily behind barbed
wire fences. Eighteen wheelers thunder by, hurrying to the next big
city. Manny laughs loudly at a joke we can't hear because of the wind
whistling around the back of the truck. It's no good trying to talk.
Conversation gets lost in the slipstream. Instead, Barbie shifts her feet
and begins to tickle Hardy's hairy ankle with the nail of her small toe.
Red-faced and sore at this quiet exchange, I turn away.

There are places at the lake where we can change without prying
eyes and the boys wait for us by the truck. I change into my red,
cherry print bubble swimsuit, ordered from the Sears catalog that
comes every Christmas, and hurry back to them. Slick pulled into a
spot beside a few other kids from Sweetwater High, and while they're
busy syncing up radio stations, I manage to get a private word in with
Hardy.

"So, do you remember anything else from your dream?" I ask him.

"Why?" He keeps his voice low.

"I was thinking the dreams might help us somehow. Maybe the
Indians can translate it?"

An involuntary shudder pulls at his lopsided face as he turns his thoughts inward. "I ran to Manny's. That raw taste I woke up with? I remembered it's because I killed his cat with my teeth."

"But you didn't go anywhere."

"How can you be sure?" His question comes out in a half-whine.

"You'd never do that to poor ol' Tufty!" I assure him. Manny's cat, a stubborn old thing that was at least one-third bobcat, was the wrestling team's unofficial mascot. "It was just a dream, see? We'll go to Bitter Creek and have someone break it down for us."

Barbie and Sandra-Lee ramble in our direction, towels slung over their arms. Sandra-Lee tucks her hair into a floral swim cap. It matches her blue knitted swimsuit with a cute sweetheart neckline. Barbie is the only girl I know who has a fashionable bikini. It's strapless and a radiant orange that makes her easy to spot on a crowded beach. I can't wait to see the looks of shock and irritation on Martha's weasel little face when she realizes she's not the only one in vogue this summer.

Hardy, Slick, and Manny allow their eyes to drift to Barbie's exposed ribs. The extra bit of revealed skin is acknowledged and then taken with the tide as Slick turns back to messing with his radio and Manny challenges us to race him to the water.

It's the perfect day for a swim. A few clouds come in from the east and give us an occasional curtain of shade. Almost everyone from school is at the lake and there are hardly any adults. A few kids from Wastella show up and bring with them a portable player and some great albums, including Chuck Berry's *New Juke Box Hits* and James Brown's *Good, Good Twistin'*.

It's late in the afternoon, and I'm sun-bathing on the stretch of the dock beside Barbie when a shadow falls over us. I open my eyes, and I can't see who it is at first. The sun is behind a broad build.

"Heya, Delah. Barbie."

"Hey, Purlie," yawns Barbie. "You're blocking my light."

He shifts to balance on his calves and then drops his bottom to the dock. He wears speedo style swim trunks, and I'm reminded of Elvis in *Blue Hawaii*. Only, Purlie is thickly muscled and there is an arrow of dusty bronze hair that starts at his belly button and disappears into the hemline of his suit. "Delah... I was wondering. Would it be okay if you..."

I sit up, caught off guard by Purlie's uncertainty. My hair falls loose around my bare, sun brown shoulders and I start messing with it rather than look at him. "What's up, Purlie?"

"I was wondering if you wanted to go to the Social with me?" He clears his throat and adds quickly, "I haven't been to one since I've come back, and it'd be nice to go with someone I get along with."

"Oh. Gosh! I... I'm going with Barbie," I say lamely and glance over at her for help.

She doesn't say anything but eyes him with a curious quirk of her brow.

"Well, save a dance for me?" He tries to shrug off my dismissal but can't altogether hide the disappointment in his voice.

"She's not going with me," Barbie says. She sits up and flicks back a bead of sweat from her high forehead.

"Yes, we are." The words are practically a sneer. As much as I like Purlie, and as stoically handsome as he is, I can't imagine dating him anymore than I can imagine myself necking Manny. "We already agreed."

"*Delah*," she says pointedly. "That was before a cute boy decided to ask you."

Purlie clears his throat again and pulls a hand rolled cigarette from the front pocket of his shirt. He lights it and takes a deep inhale. The tobacco smells like old raisins. "Only if you're interested. It's okay if you're not."

"I'll ask Hardy," says Barbie, grinning wide. "So, we're squared up. It's perfect!"

I don't want to be in this situation, never thought that I'd have to be. It wouldn't be hard for me to tell Purlie no but then I remember Manny trying to wriggle me into a double date. If I had to go to the Social with a boy, I'd rather it be someone I could talk to without fuss. I give Purlie the warmest grin that I can. "Sure. We can go. No problem."

My chest caves in with a bitter hurt.

"Okay," he says with a nod and smoke comes out of his nostrils like ribbons. "This is good. I'll pick you up around seven."

He pushes himself off the dock and leaves a little too quickly, perhaps wanting to ensure I can't change my mind. He joins Manny and Hardy who are attempting to build a bonfire.

Barbie rakes her fingers through her hair and wiggles her eyebrows. "What a catch! I had no idea he was interested in you."

I don't try to hide the feelings of betrayal that pull down the corners of my mouth. I let her see all the wounded, unexpressed yearning, then drop myself into the water and swim underneath the dock. It's cool here and the wet wood is an almost clean smell after Purlie's cigarette smoke. I let the gentle waves push around me and lap against the moss-covered pillars, the cold water a balm to my burned skin.

A little splash from behind lets me know that Barbie has jumped in, but I don't turn to her. I make her swim to me.

"Purlie is good for you," she says, treading the water. She's not sure what she's supposed to apologize for. "He's smart. He's nice. He's what men are expected to be, and he doesn't think women should be inferior to him."

"How do you know?" I let myself drift a little distance from her.

Barbie chews her lower lip, thinking. "Because he's gone to college. He sees how things work. Don't you like him?"

"Sure, I like him."

"Then why don't you go with him?"

I don't say anything at first. Overhead, girls and boys are running up and down the dock, launching themselves into the water and far away from us. Barbie swims closer so that we won't be overheard by the wrong people. She's thinking what I'm thinking. One of those girls could be Wilma or Martha. They might overhear and the gossip would find its way back to Purlie.

"Because I'm not fond of him." I hesitate, not trusting myself to speak anymore. Barbie is as close to me as Hardy was when he first found his way into the attic room. The only difference is I don't feel like I'm expected to lean into Barbie. I *want* to. She waits for me to speak again, wide eyed and clueless. I don't know what I'm supposed to do with this thought of kissing her the way I ought to kiss a boy, so I let myself sink a little until water gets into my mouth. The words bubble out of me.

"I'm fond of you."

Barbie doesn't blink. She doesn't say anything, but the color deepens in her cheeks. Then she repeats herself, her soft voice tilted into a gentle warning. "Purlie is good for you."

She doesn't remove her eyes from mine, but she starts to swim away, and I reach out, clutching her narrow wrist. My nose and eyes sting with shame. "Please don't tell."

Barbie rolls her wrist downward, until her fingers thread into mine and she squeezes. "I won't tell. I'll keep it to the end of our days."

She slowly floats backward to the edge of the shade beneath the dock, bronze hair trailing in the water's surface like water moccasins or the leaves of oak trees that fall into the tide in winter. I know I've ruined our friendship. No matter what happens from now on, Barbie and I cannot be the same. It's clear in the tiny way the skin above her nose knits together she is thinking of this, too.

Our attention is pulled upward by another thundering group of kids sprinting to the edge of the dock to jump into the cold, green lake.

"C'mon," says Barbie. "Let's go see what the others are doing."

Sandra-Lee and Slick recline on large bath towels, lips locked and oblivious to their surroundings. Martha and Wilma have wedged themselves between Manny and Hardy. Both are wearing adorable, pastel romper swimsuits. Wilma tilts the wide brim of her sunhat away from her face as Barbie and I approach. She waves and pushes Hardy over to make room for us. Martha files her nails, ignoring me. I have to bite down on my thumb to keep from laughing at her swim cap that looks remarkably like a pineapple.

There are a few charred sticks and candy wrappers inside of the pit the boys created but no fire. It's much too hot for one anyway, although I'm sure they'll try and start another one up again when the sun begins to set behind the tree line.

"Oh it's just awful!" Wilma continues in the vein of conversation Barbie and I walked in on. "Lauren Willoby and Roger Landis are off again. Now she won't have anyone to go to the dance with. She just got her dress fitted, too! She went all the way to Dallas to get it."

Barbie sits in the open space Wilma created and nudges Manny. "Hey, you should ask her! Just don't put mascara on your mouth again."

"He simply *can't* ask Lauren!" Martha moans without looking up from her nail file.

"Why not?" asks Hardy.

"It's an awful match. Most everyone who goes to the Social ends up together. That's what happened with my parents. And yours!"

"Mine met at one of Herbert Huncke's parties," Barbie says.

"Nobody cares," Martha sighs.

"I care," I say. "Who's Herbert Huncke?"

"Some poet."

"Point is!" Martha interjects again. "If you're from Maryneal, you wind up getting married to the man you go to the church socials with! And having a name like Lauren Lawrence is just asking for trouble."

Manny touches the sparse mustache hairs around the corners of his upper lip. He ignores Martha. "We had fun. She's good people but…" He inhales deeply and puts a pocket of air into his cheek. "I was thinking of asking you, Delah."

"Oh!" says Wilma with a mingle of giddy delight and shared embarrassment. "That is so sweet. Isn't it sweet?"

"Hmm," says Martha.

Before I can tell Manny I can't go with him, Wilma bursts out, "But she's going with Purlie."

To the right of me, Sandra-Lee detaches from Slick with a wet pop. Across from the fire pit, Hardy turns to flint, his jaw tight. I begin to bundle up my hair into a thick braid and avoid everyone.

"How can you *possibly* know that?" ask Barbie. "It just happened!'

Wilma shrugs and for a wild moment I think she must know of what happened beneath the docks. "I asked if he was going with anyone when we got here. He told me he asked you."

The tension in my lungs is punctured and I'm overwhelmed with relief.

"Say, girls," says Sandra-Lee as Slick begins to press himself into the swoop of her neck. "Let's get new dresses next week!"

"Honey, I don't care what you wear," says Slick.

"Good thing I'm not getting the dress for you then, isn't it?" teases Sandra-Lee.

I don't think Hardman's in Sweetwater carry your size Delah," says Martha. She tucks her nail file away and gives her little straw purse a prim snap.

"Yes they do!" Sandra-Lee says. "We were there just last spring and lots of dresses were long enough for her! Weren't they?"

I shrug. There were dresses that fit but none that were particularly charming or in the colors I liked best. It amazes me how Martha thinks I'm self-conscious about being six feet tall. I've always been the tallest and broadest of the girls in our class. Why should it bother me when I haven't known how to be any other way?

"Martha, I'm starting to think you're running out of material. Why not pick on my hair? Or are you jealous that you have to spend two hours curling yours and I just wake up glorious like this?"

I flick my messy braid as I stand, and it smacks her in the face. The others laugh, even Wilma, who tries so hard to stay on her sister's unbearable side.

"Preach!" Manny shouts and he holds out the flat of his hand. "And slide me some skin!"

We slap hands. Martha jumps up from her place in the sand and gathers her swimsuit cover in one arm, the other reaches down to tug Wilma away. "Well! I think it's real bold of you gallivanting around with an *older* boy! Especially when you should be mourning. You're some kind of girl, Delah, acting like Kitty doesn't even matter to you. Why's that? Because she was prettier and now you don't have anyone to compete with!"

"Oh my *God*, Martha!" whispers Wilma. She snatches her hand away. "I can't believe—"

My skin has gone numb. A frantic drumming in my ears deafens me and possesses my body. The lines around Martha blur as I pick up a charred log and swing it against her leg. She shrieks as the wood splinters and falls from my hands. With another war cry, she lunges at me. We claw at each other, bellowing wordlessly. Spittle flies. Hair is torn.

Slick drags me off of Martha, but I keep kicking out at her. Hardy and Wilma flank her. Wilma desperately attempts to cover an exposed nipple. I nearly break free from Slick, my fists balled and ready to turn her smug face purple. Slick tightens his grip and lifts me over his shoulder.

"Time to go!" he shouts.

Manny and Barbie collect our blankets and picnic basket. Hardy trails after us, glancing over his shoulder to make sure Martha isn't going to attack us when our backs are turned.

We don't talk as Slick speeds down the highway. Barbie wraps her arms around me, and I cry until my lungs give out and snot has crusted around my nose. The highway seems to stretch, keeping me further away from my bed. My lip is puffy and swollen from where Martha decked me, and I can taste the tang of my own blood each time I press my tongue to it.

Finally, Slick slows in front of my house. Barbie offers me another reassuring hug and Sandra-Lee gets out of the truck to do the same. "She's a complete bitch!"

From inside the cab, Manny nods. "You got every right to be happy, Delah! You of all people got the right."

"Thanks, Manny."

"You decked her real good," adds Slick. "I'll show you a few tricks for next time."

I manage to quirk a smile. "Thanks, but I don't want a next time."

I wave them off and slink inside, bitter and defeated. My skin is so burned that when I peel off my swimsuit there are pale lines etching around my shoulders and panty line. The house is empty. I am empty, and my confession to Barbie becomes a distant hiccup, a memory belonging to somebody else. It doesn't matter what Manny or Sandra-Lee say. Martha is right about me. I'm a horrible person.

Chapter Fifteen

B reakfast with just me and Dad is unusually quiet. He isn't fully awake and leans into the chicory heat rising out of his coffee mug. He hasn't asked me about my busted lip but I'm sure by the time he sees Martha he'll have made a connection. Maybe I'll get lucky, and he won't run into the Andersons on his patrol. It could be he already knows and has resigned himself to the situation.

"How's Tessie this morning?" he asks, scrubbing his unshaven face with one hand.

"Grumpy." I dip the edge of my toast into runny egg yolk, playing with my food instead of eating it. "Could be any day."

"Good. I'll check on her before—"

He cuts himself off and lifts his neck to peer out the kitchen's window. Mr. Hooper's Ford lurches to a stop outside of our gate and he springs from the driver's side, nearly forgetting to shift the gears into park. His tufty brown hair is plastered to a splotchy, sweaty brow. Dad pushes himself from his chair and is out the front door in seconds to meet Mr. Hooper in the yard. He talks with his hands, gesturing in sharp rhythm to the space behind him. Dad nods and his stance becomes increasingly stiff. His right hand slips into the hook of his hip where his gun would be if he were wearing his belt.

"I tell you it's a damn massacre, Daniel!"

"Could be the ky–"

"It ain't no damn animal! It's carnage!"

"Alright, I'll meet you up at the barn. Let me just get some pants on."

"I'll wait."

"No. You go on. Make sure no one else wanders in to tamper with anything."

"Right."

They split. Mr. Hooper back into his Ford and Dad bounding up the stairs to change in his uniform. I stay at the kitchen table and stare at my egg spread and congeal. I'm numb with a terrible thought that sinks below my stomach. Dad is back downstairs and out the front door.

"I'll see you at dinner," he shouts over his shoulder as the screen door slams.

With that, I'm thundering up to the attic to change. I don't worry about a bra or a different shirt because I'm not sure how much time I have. I jump into overalls and bundle my hair on top of my head, then tug on my socks as I hop back down to the first floor and out the door where my bicycle leans against the cedar tree. I'm only a little bothered by the fact the breakfast dishes are left on the table, but I convince myself they can stay there until I've done my bit of snooping.

The gut-wrenching thought grows black and expands inside of me. I need to see what Mr. Hooper is talking about for myself. Either to confirm my suspicions or soothe them away. Mr. Hooper doesn't own enough property to have a barn, and as the Ag teacher, he's always checking on the animals at school, even during break. I know that's where they are heading, and I want to get there in time to hear what is being said and before Dad swings his patrol car around and sees me pedaling in that direction.

I'm halfway down our dirt road when Barbie and Sandra-Lee come around the bend.

"Where are you going in such a hurry?" asks Barbie.

"Ag barn!" I shout, zooming past them. "Something's up!"

Sandra-Lee and Barbie whip their bicycles around and follow me without question. We become a streamline of pink, blue, and yellow wheels tickering through Main Street, around the corners of houses, and up to the school. Coach's shrill whistle breaks apart the cloudless sky. The wrestling team is out on the track again, feet pounding against the cedar and chalk, each trying not to be the slowest one. The Ag building is on the far side of the track. Dad's patrol car is parked right in front of the barn doors.

We stow our bicycles beneath the bleachers and slink around to the side of the building. The warm smell of manure and fresh alfalfa spreads across the stalls and out the windows. There's usually some manner of neighing and grunting coming out of the barn. Not today. Today there is a tense silence, and I realize there aren't any birds in the area that usually hang around to pick off grain or mites. There's not even grackles hiding underneath Mr. Hooper's Ford. My skin goes numb with the utter wrongness hanging in the air.

"What is it?" Sandra-Lee asks in a hoarse whisper, and I know she must feel the charge in the air.

The closer we get to the barn. The familiar, earthy scent is gone. In its place is a metallic, acrid stench. Voices rise and pitch in uneven shocks. Not just Mr. Hooper and Dad, but also Principal Bertrand. Hers is the only voice that remains neutral and forced into calm.

"No one thing could've done this."

"It's gotta be an animal. I can't think of what else..." Dad mumbles.

"The Indians?" asks Mr. Hooper.

"Get your head outta your ass, Brad!" Dad snaps.

"Some of them do strange things."

"Bah! You're watching too many movies. Forget about the Indians."

"I say it was an animal," agrees Principal Bertrand. "We best call Sheriff Muller in any case. Could be a pack of wild dogs."

"I've never seen a ky-ote, rabid or otherwise, do this," insists Mr. Hooper. "We would hear them in the twilight by this point. If it ain't the Indians, it's some kind of satanic ritual."

"Brad," Dad warns again. "We can't go jumpin'—"

"That's right! We can't and that includes conclusion on a wild pack, Daniel! Lookit. You know as well as I do, ky-otes go after one or two maybe. They stick to small game. They don't hop around taking *everything*!"

I press myself to the side of the building that is furthest away from the barn door and watch Principal Bertrand and Mr. Hooper march back up the hill to the offices. After a moment of hesitation, Dad follows. I exchange nervous looks with Barbie and Sandra-Lee. "I'm going in."

"Don't," says Barbie and she reaches out to hold me back, but I've already stood. I move quickly inside the barn at a crouch, just in case Dad turns to look down at the barn from the school.

At first, I don't see what's wrong. The hay-covered path cutting down the center of the stables looks how it always does. The brushes are in place by the wash station, the bridles, blankets, and hoof picks are in order. The brooms are stacked neatly by the barn door. Sandra-Lee and Barbie sneak in close behind me. We breathe through our mouths in short staccatos because the stench threatens to knock us off our feet. Overwhelming anxiety peels back the layers of my skin as we make our way over to the first stall. My teeth chatter and my insides turn into a thin soup. I'm afraid that whatever creature has done this still lurks in the barn and will hear me breathing. This fear glues my feet to the earth and my knees can't bend into motion.

"Jesus God," mutters Barbie and she stumbles back beside me.

Sandra-Lee says nothing. She covers her eyes with the pads of her fingers and gags.

This propels me forward again and I peer inside the stall. Noonie, our prized pig, is gutted. There's nothing left of her except a wide stain of blood. The front half of her, skin and bone, and snout twisted in glassy horror is shoved against the stable door. The back half of her is missing. I push past to the next stall to the other pigs. Arnold and Lil' Bit are shredded bits of flesh and hoof. Further down, the goats have been reduced to intestine and splatters of fur. There is no evidence of Reggie the Ram.

Nothing survived. There are only pieces. Shards of bone. Bloodied tufts of fur. The shit that has leaked out of every single one of these poor creatures as they listened to the slaughter around them.

I launch myself out of the barn and make it all the way back to the underside of the bleachers before vomit bursts out of me.

Barbie keeps muttering, "Oh my God."

Tears stain her cheeks. Sandra-Lee trembles and slides down into the cool grass. She stares unblinking into the middle distance.

Chapter Sixteen

Preacher John paces in front of the church's red doors, nodding solemnly as people filter in for the impromptu town meeting. Even the cement plant has closed down for a few hours. The plant's foreman, Mr. Slidle, and his wife Meryl sit next to Mr. and Mrs. Anderson. It's rare to see the Slidles, mostly because they live in Roscoe and attend the Methodist church. Their presence is a mark of importance to the situation at hand.

Women wave paper fans in front of their faces. Men mutter to each other, hats in their hands. The air is stagnant with sweat. Purlie moves around the perimeter of the church, pushing open the windows. Pews groan with the weight of families taking their seats. Sheriff Muller and Dad stand at the front with Mr. Bishop, the mayor of Nolan County. All three of them are stone pillars of silence. Mr. Bishop's underarms have discolored his white button-up with sweat, and he dabs a cloth against his receding hairline.

Once everyone is accounted for, Preacher John steps in but leaves the doors open in a desperate attempt to push the heat out of the room. He sits at the front between his wife, Lucille, and Purlie. I sit in the back with Barbie, Sandra-Lee, and Martha and Wilma. Unlike Sunday mornings, we aren't in our family pews. Instead, the adults mingle up toward the front. The younger kids aren't allowed to sit in on town meetings, but it wouldn't surprise me if they were bunched up around one of the open windows.

Mr. Bishop clears his throat and moves to the pulpit. He is an incredibly thin man, almost skeletal, and he moves like his joints are made of rusted gears.

"I think we should open up the meeting with prayer. Would you, Preacher?"

Preacher John moves slowly to the front. His hands spread over the surface of the pulpit as though the right words would sink into his flesh from the wood. He bows his head and there is a gentle wave of creaking as everyone assembled bows their heads, too.

"Lord... God our Father. Look over us in this hour of uncertainty. For our struggle is not against flesh and blood, but against the rulers and the powers of this present darkness that have fallen on our community. Amen."

The singular voice of many respond. "Amen."

Mr. Bishop nods and slides back behind the pulpit after Preacher John returns to his seat. He clears his throat again. "I've had a discussion with Deputy Nix and Sheriff Muller about the goings on..."

"It ain't a damn animal!" Mr. Hooper jumps from his seat. Mrs. Hooper shifts baby Gertrude into one arm and puts a hand on Mr. Hooper's elbow but he shakes her off.

"Well, it ain't the Indians!" Dad shouts back. "I'm sick of this talk, Bradley Hooper!"

"We *all* know how you feel about them! Sympathizing... partnering up—"

Purlie stands now, too. "Don't you be slinging mud, Brad! Not when you went down to Bitter Creek yourself to get the missus medicine when you thought Gertrude mightn't survive."

"We've all gone to Bitter Creek to get remedies now and again," says Mrs. Diggs, but she remains seated. "They're good people. Kind people. It's like Preacher John says, what we're dealing with is a darkness that's got nothing to do with a different culture than our own."

"You think it's some kinda booger-man running around the dark then?" asks old Jeb Burnel. He hacks out a laugh that turns into a wet cough.

"It may not be the Indians," says Mr. Anderson coolly, "but I'm with Brad on this one. No animal could be doing this. We've had nothing but slaughter in this town since Kitty was murdered. Beg your pardon, Deputy, but I have suspicions that it's all related to her."

Dad says nothing but some of the color drains from his face and he gives one nod of consideration to what Mr. Anderson suggests. Barbie slips her fingers into mine and gives my hand a brief, reassuring squeeze.

"Now hang on," says Mayor Bishop. He lifts abnormally flat palms to calm the room. "Take your seats everyone and let us discuss this civil-like."

"You go on and tell us, Mayor!" grumbles Jeb Burnel. "Ain't no one else in the entire county having such trouble! You go on and speak truth!"

Mayor Bishop frowns. "It's true. There seems to be a concentrated interest in Maryneal, but Sheriff Muller and I are working—"

"You keepin' from us, Mayor?" asks Mr. Latimer suddenly. "I hear tell that the body of that madman who done Kitty Nix wrong has gone missin'. You tell us here and now!"

Mrs. Lawrence shrieks, "It's the Devil's work!"

She faints into Mr. Lawrence's arms and Manny leaps out of his seat to run to her aid. They take her out of the church for some fresh air as chaos erupts.

Purlie and Mr. Hooper shout into the frail inch of space between their noses. Other men attempt to calm them by shouting their own grievances. Petunia Latimer fans herself more vigorously and joins in the fray. Mr. Latimer starts in on Mrs. Diggs and Mr. Diggs pushes into him, telling him off for speaking to his wife. Mr. Anderson slaps a fist into an open hand demanding to be heard. No one is making sense of anything.

Mayor Bishop has lost control of the room.

From where he stands, Dad speaks to his feet. He squares his shoulders and repeats himself. This time the single word comes out of him like a foghorn. "ENOUGH!"

It takes everyone a few minutes to realize he's said anything, but it starts to quiet down. Dad looks at Mayor Bishop, who stands nonplussed at the pulpit.

"I am sending out additional law enforcement to patrol Maryneal until we find the culprit who is violating the livestock. Sheriff Muller is leading an inquiry into neighboring towns. If you see something, say something to one of these men here." He gestures to Dad and Sheriff Muller. "I ask that we all remain calm."

"What about the body?" asks Mr. Anderson. "Has it gone missing?"

"We are investigating those claims as well," Sheriff Muller says, and his tone is such that no one attempts to pry for more information.

"Patrolling ain't enough," snaps Jeb Burnel. "Specially if there *is* some kinda booger-man."

This gets a small response of nervous laughter. From behind me, Hardy taps my shoulder, and whispers in my ear. "Let's cut."

I nod but I'm not sure how to go about leaving without everyone else seeing us and becoming disrupted by our sudden departure. I stand up slowly and fan myself, as though I'm overcome with the heat.

I have to push my way past Barbie and Sandra-Lee, straddling their legs as I make my way past the isle.

"You okay?" Barbie whispers.

"I just need air," I whisper back. Dad sees me leaving, too, and gives a terse nod. I imagine he wishes he could escape the town meeting with me. Hardy remains seated next to Slick and the vacant space where Manny was moments before his mother went into hysterics.

It's much cooler outside, despite the lack of a breeze. Dusk settles with the first stars appearing like little pinpricks of silver against the cloudless evening. The Lawrences are in the church's garden. Manny's sister, Maria, looks up and gives me the briefest of waves. It's a signal that everything is fine and there's no need for me to come over and get in their business. I think about what Manny said, weeks ago, about one of the Indians making a remedy for Maria's pneumonia. That night at the carnival seems like a different universe. Everything was roses and pure simplicity.

I begin my walk toward Main Street and the square. My thoughts travel back to Kitty's savaged body and how similar it looked to the gore I witnessed this afternoon in the Ag building. Worry settles into me like the sting of sorrow that once again filled my nose and eyes. I don't hear Hardy approach from behind me but I'm learning to expect his silent appearances.

"Hey," he says to get my attention.

"What's up?"

We walk a little ways. Past his parents' drug store, Buzzy's Diner, and Lone Apple Bank. Everything has closed so that no one would miss the town meeting.

"I think Purlie's all wrong for you."

"Jesus. We're talking about this?" I press my thumbs into the tear ducts of my eyes and sniff.

"Well... yeah?" He assesses me in the growing dark. He keeps pace with me as we take the road back up to our houses.

"Did you do it?"

"Do what?"

"Did you kill all the animals?"

"I don't know."

His honesty catches me off guard and I stop so I can face him. The muscles in his shoulders and neck are tense. He keeps walking toward the fields that separate our dirt road from the town square. A small penny whistle voice in the back of my skull tells me not to follow.

I ignore it.

"I went to bed early yesterday. And then that stupid rooster woke me up like always."

"That's all?" I ask.

Hardy shakes his head and strands of hair fall over his forehead. "No. My hands were sticky with... I dunno... goo. There were dark chunks of it in my nails and teeth. But I don't remember doing anything."

"But how? How did no one see you?"

"I don't know!" He huffs and crosses his arms, hugging himself. "I don't mean to scare you, but Delah..." Hardy pauses, unsure of what to say or where to put his hands. There's nothing around us but the hard sky and green earth. He waits for me to walk in front of him. I hesitate, not wanting to turn my back to him and I wonder if, like all animals, he can smell fear. I can't calculate how close I'd make it to my house before Hardy runs me down, but the odds aren't good.

"Delah."

"What?"

"I woke up, and for the first time in days, and I don't feel sick or starved! I feel more *human* than I've ever felt! Does that make sense?"

I shake my head, and Hardy turns on the spot, searching for something he can use to his advantage.

"Watch this."

He marches over to a fence post, buried deep into the Andersons' property line, and pulls it up with one hand. The barbwire bounces and tightens. Three feet of weed and root fall from the bottom of the wooden post. He puts it back into the hole and runs further up the dirt road to red sandstone boulders that stick up from the ocean of grass. He uses both hands this time but picks up a sandstone like it's only a melon. With a satisfied grunt, Hardy shot-puts it and it lands several yards into the Andersons' field. The inside of my mouth turns to cotton.

Hardy is giddy with adrenaline, and he latches onto my arms and shakes me a little. "Don't you understand? I don't want to stop getting stronger and faster! I–I don't know how to describe it. This isn't like *anything* I've ever felt before!"

"But look at what happened to that man! Look what it made him do!" I cry out, throwing my arms up to push him off of me. "That Traveler woman warned me that you're cursed! It might feel amazing now but what's going to happen when you aren't satisfied with picking off livestock? What then?"

Hardy chews his lip and the cute freckle there disappears behind white teeth that are too sharp for a human mouth. "That bastard wasn't in control. I can be."

"You don't know that."

He reaches out for me, but I think how easily he might throw me and I shrivel into myself and out his touch. His hand swings limply to his side. He looks knocked down and I'm sorry I've hurt his feelings. He has no one else to talk to about this and I remind myself he's just handling his fear in a different way than I am.

His eyebrows knit together. "I can do this. I know I can get control of this."

"Okay, but we have to go talk to that medicine woman in Bitter Creek. She must have something that can help."

Hardy crosses his arms over his chest again and I turn to look back at the town square far behind us. Truck lights flicker on, and the community is starting to thread out of the church. I can't hear anything from this distance, but I don't think anyone feels satisfied by the outcome of the meeting. I certainly don't. Even if I had no clue about Hardy's condition, I wouldn't have found bringing in more law enforcement a final solution to the problem. Honestly, what does Mayor Bishop think will happen? Some police officer is going to come upon a coyote in the act and apprehend the thing?

Hardy walks me all the way to my porch steps and waits for me to get inside before he sprints to his house. The lights of his bedroom are on by the time I've made it to mine and I roll my eyes, almost amused by him showing off. Then I remind myself that Hardy can do all these amazing things because he tried to save my sister. Kitty's wonderfully cheerful face swims to the forefront of my mind and it aches all the way to the bone. I hope Hardy can control this thing inside him. He's already done so much damage to the livelihood of the farmers in our community. I can't imagine what he might do when he wakes up to find human blood staining his hands. Would he act so carefree then?

Chapter Seventeen

We meet early the next morning at the end of our lane. Hardy has a Schwinn like me, but his is built with a narrow, triangular frame. I take the lead since I know where to go. It's the same route I took a few days before when I searched for Madam Lulu. A few times Hardy speeds ahead of me but forces himself to slow down. He must be annoyed by this but is kind enough to not complain.

We turn off the highway and pedal through back roads, unfinished and riddled with potholes. Even though the day has just begun, it's dreadfully hot and crushing with humidity. Sweat trickles down my neck and nose. I want to be back to Maryneal before the weather turns unbearable, but at the same time, I don't want to rush this. I'll take my skin frying in the afternoon sun if it means Hardy will have a cure from this medicine woman.

Bitter Creek is a ghost town. The scars of a once prosperous settlement are visible, sticking out of the tumbleweeds and the brown grass. Buildings made of strong timber or brick, the roofs caved in, windows without glass. We pass by a dilapidated sod house, the frame of a rusted Model A Ford, and a windmill that has been choked into stillness by overgrown creepers. Only a handful of people, most all of them Indian, buried their knuckles into the earth like old tree roots and refused to leave.

We finally stop in front of a green shotgun house. Several wind chimes, made of seashell, wood, and found glass hang from the low porch. Ivy crawls up the sides, pulling slats of wood away from the support beams and the foundation. The front yard has given up any attempt to thrive but there is moss in the shallow basin of a concrete bird bath. I sweep back several tight curls that have run away from the bun at the top of my head.

Hardy swings off his bicycle and marches up to the front door. A thick spread of sweat covers his back and jewels the toughened, new scars stretching from ear to shoulder. I follow him up the haphazard, flagstone path.

"Should we knock?" I ask, coming up behind him.

He doesn't move and I understand why. For weeks, we've been going on a fantastic assumption: he was bitten by a madman and now he can perform superhuman feats. It has been our secret, pulling us together in ways that are indescribable and deeper than a binding ritual. Once we talk to this woman, our foundation will crack. We are allowing someone else into this universe of ours. We are selling our secret and at what cost?

I reach over him and knock because I'm unable to live in this cloud of unknowing. Hardy sucks air in through his teeth. Nothing happens and the knots in my shoulders begin to release.

"Who are you?"

We scamper off the porch and I tumble into a woman. Her upper body lurches backward, arms flailing to keep balance. Her large, woven basket falls to the ground like a stone. Bottles and jars clank together. A tartan cloth drops and is trampled underfoot. Hardy bends quickly to help her up while I stand there like an idiot, mumbling apologies.

"It's fine! I tell you, it's fine!" She swats Hardy away from a small vial of what looks like water and tucks it deep into her basket. "Who are you?"

"We just... I'm Hardy Diggs," he says, pointing to himself. He slaps me in the arm with the back of his hand. "This is Delah Nix. We came for help."

The hard lines of her brow and mouth become smooth. "The girl whose sister was killed? I talked to your father. It is a terrible loss."

"Thank you." I'm not sure what else to say.

"We're looking for that medicine woman," says Hardy.

"That's me. What do you want?"

Hardy and I exchange looks. She doesn't look like an Indian. Her skin is brown from laboring outdoors but there is a flush of sunburn pink to her cheeks. Her eyes are blue, and her hair is not as flat-black as I've come to expect from the few I've seen pass into Maryneal to buy goods. She does not have a wide face or stout body. In fact, she'd be remarkably plain if she weren't so bony and angular.

"You're the one that helped Maria Lawrence?" asked Hardy, taking in her horse-like face with some apprehension.

"I don't know. Maybe. Lawrence? She the one that had the pneumonia." The woman shrugs and opens the door to her house. She throws her question over one shoulder and it sounds more like a statement. "You were expecting a shriveled old witch covered in warts?"

Our eyes flicker to each other again, like searching for an exit door or the corner of a security blanket tucked away in some far corner of a strange room. A bubble of insanity swells up my throat and I stick my knuckles against my teeth to keep from laughing. This whole thing is a joke! We'd set ourselves up and discovered nothing but a spinster living in happy isolation.

The screen door claps shut as she disappears into the cool interior of her house. Then she flickers briefly back into view.

"Are we going to talk about your sickness? Or do you just plan on standing there, decorating my yard?"

"How did you know?" asks Hardy, teeth clenched, and I'm reminded of a rabid dog.

The woman lifts one shoulder and pushes the screen door open with the toe of her flat, leather shoe. "Why else are you here?"

I go into the house and Hardy follows closely, peeking over my shoulder at all the curiosities that hang from the walls and ceiling. It is musty and thick with sage inside the green shotgun house. Many of the rooms we pass through are without furniture but carpeted in thick brown shag. She leads us to a room that must have been a bedroom, but instead of a bed there is only an awful suede couch covered in throw blankets and two stiff chairs. Beside the bare window is a garden rack she must use to clean the carpet.

"Sit wherever and we'll talk about this. Tea?"

"No thank you," I say, and Hardy shakes his head.

"Okay then. If you need to use the toilet, there is an outhouse out back."

She takes her basket to the kitchen and sets it on a tall workbench. Herbs and dried flowers hang from the ceiling. There are candles and books stacked along in untidy rows and a pot of something in the sink. Hardy sits and shifts to remove a large, pink and yellow crochet pillow from underneath him. I sit next to him and tuck one knee under my chin and stare up at the corners of peeling wallpaper.

The woman comes back in from the kitchen and moves around the room, drawing back curtains and opening windows, humming softly to herself. It sounds like a prayer but in a language I don't understand.

When she finishes, she eases into one of the armchairs and folds her hands on top of her denim skirt.

"I told your father I don't know the man that killed your sister."

"Was that a lie?" Hardy asks, his eyes hard as flint.

She shakes her head and breathes a slow calm back into the room. "No. He's not from our community. He's a traveler. A man without family. But we know what he is."

We wait as she studies the anticipation turning into sweat across our already damp foreheads. Her thin lips twitch. "There are many names for this type of man. All you need to concern yourself with is that he was a witch. Someone who goes on all fours with a dark purpose. He was expired in the correct way."

"Do you know what happened to his body? They're saying it's gone missing."

The woman shrugs. "I would hazard to guess that the people who knew him did something with it to ensure that his evil would not rise up again."

"Those are the other Travelers?" I ask. "From the carnival? They said they didn't know him."

She shrugs.

"Like what kind of thing did they do?" asks Hardy, leaning into the empty space.

"Perhaps they will bury him standing. I'm not sure."

"But I need to know why he did what he did!" My fist slams against my calf as a final punctuation.

Again, the woman scans me with a thoughtful grace, and I hate her for it. "I'm sorry if it seems unfair to you, but it isn't wise to talk about—"

"He ripped Kitty apart! He bit Hardy! He—"

The woman hisses. "Bit you?"

"And scratched." Hardy leans forward and pulls back the collar of his white undershirt so that she can see the scars more clearly. "It wasn't bad as I thought. Healed really quick."

She scoots forward and touches the raised skin with rounded fingernails. The thin lines of her mouth deepen.

"We want to know how we can prevent Hardy from doing anything awful like that man," I explain.

"Do you have blood lust? The desire to eat only raw flesh? The inability to eat other foods? Strange dreams?"

Hardy nods and her hand snaps back and curls against her bony sternum. Hardy shifts, uncomfortably. "Tell me there's a way to keep this in control."

The woman's blue eyes shine and her thick eyebrows peak, wrinkling the tight skin above her nose. "Your blood is poison. It's in God's hands now."

Her words slam into me like I'm made out of drywall and all that escapes my lungs is a cloud of dust.

"Isn't there anything that can slow it down?" Hardy's voice cracks and I'm briefly swept away to a thousand summers ago when we were children searching for earthworms underneath the bricks and stones of Mrs. Diggs's front garden.

Hardy's blood is poison? That means he's already dead and I will myself to face this terrible idea so I might see the solution inside the tragedy.

The medicine woman turns an unblinking focus onto me. "You have silver?"

"Yes."

"True silver?"

"I think so." I think of the bullet necklace that Madam Lulu gave me, and the medicine woman seems to pluck the image out of memory. She bobs her head thoughtfully.

"Keep that on you at all times." She stands lightly onto her small feet. With a flick of her wrist we are beckoned into the kitchen. "Keep quiet while I'm working. I need to think about this."

"What are you going to do?" asks Hardy.

She arches a thick eyebrow. "I asked for silence."

"Sorry."

We watch as she shifts from cupboard to cupboard, sometimes taking out a slender bottle or thick jar to examine the labels, other times, shrugging and closing the rough doors with a disgruntled sigh. After half an hour, she's collected a number of twigs, herbs, and liquids. With slow, deliberate measures, she begins to mix ingredients into a wooden molcajete. When she is finished, she puts the paste into a tiny glass vial with a cork stopper.

"I can't promise anything, but this may slow down the blood. Put a bit of it on your tongue before you go to bed each night. It will taste bitter, but it is made with traditional wards."

Hardy takes the vial and gingerly tucks it into his front pocket. The woman shoos him with another flick of her bony wrist. "Now, go outside. I need to talk with Delah alone."

She doesn't speak as he walks through the house, feet shuffling against the shag. The screen door creaks and slams on its hinges. I whisper without turning to face her. "He's got really good hearing now. It might do you no good, him standing outside."

"You know what you must do if it comes to it?" she asks me, ignoring my statement. I want to tell her I have no idea what she's talking about, but I can't lie with those depressingly large blue eyes boring into me. I nod once, slowly. My pulse wrenches to a stop.

"If it is clear that the medicine is not working, do what needs to be done. And don't come back here."

She guides me to the door with the flat of her hand. Hardy straightens as he sees me and hops onto his Schwinn. The woman folds her arms tightly around herself. She watches us leave and I think of Dad and how he liked to watch me and Kitty leave for school each morning. There's so many things I still want to ask, like what's in the paste she gave Hardy, and why no one ever wants to see me a second time.

All of Hardy's energy has left him and now I'm the one who has to stop to wait for him to catch up. At first I think it's because he's exhausted. The temperature has crept upward and the stretch of highway is covered in wavering mirages of water. Scrub brush and post oaks scatter around the tall grasses and I can't think of why anything bad should come to this place of silent peace. What had we done to deserve this fate?

"What's going to happen to me?" he asks, pedaling up to me. His white shirt sticks to every curve of muscle around his torso. He's gone pale with dread.

"What do you mean? I thought you liked becoming fast and strong."

"I do! But that Indian... she made it seem like I was going to die from it."

"You won't."

Hardy clicks his tongue and rolls his eyes at me. "Yeah but she asked you if you know what to do if it comes down to it."

"I won't let anything come down to it," I say, determined to make that statement true.

We veer off the highway and onto the small roads that crisscross into town. We stop to catch our breath, underneath the shade of the towering cement plant, and watch buzzards circle low in the horizon.

"So, what are you supposed to do if it comes to it?" Hardy asks. I'm not sure if I should say at first but Hardy has trusted me with so much already. The least I can do is tell him the truth. I start with my palm reading and work my way up to the morning in the stables when Madam Lulu presented me with the silver bullet. I even tell him that Sandra-Lee didn't think it was a man that killed Kitty either.

"But you didn't tell Sandra Lee about me?" Hardy asks. The wildness in him has expanded.

"No. You asked me not to. Besides, she told me that before you showed me... what all you could do."

"I'll walk you home if you want."

The sun burns our necks, and I wish for clouds to roll in from the western mountains. The strong odor of Hardy's aftershave mingles with wild honeysuckle. The spokes of my bicycle tick-tick in the fear that has muted us. This thing we are dealing with is growing too big. It's like drowning.

We pass by Main Street, taking the back roads through the hills to avoid being seen by Hardy's mother, in case she's standing outside the pharmacy chatting with Buzzy like she so often does.

"How's the ponies?" Hardy asks once we're close to my house.

"Fine. Tessie's going to drop her foal any day."

"Can I see?"

"Okay."

We lean our bicycles underneath the cedar tree and walk to the barn. Ambition and Navajo Blue idle in the fields. Their long tails swish away flies from landing on their flanks. Bonnie Wee Dancer canters up to me and pushes her piebald muzzle into my hand. I spread my fingers over her wet nostrils and up to the tuft of stiff hair between her ears. She nickers nervously, inhaling Hardy's prominent scent. He's a stranger and God knows what else. The fact that I'm with him means that she can trust him, and she remains calm, but when Hardy reaches out to her, she canters back, shaking her head. She may accept him here but everything about him is a danger. The other ponies look on curiously but slowly migrate to the furthest point of the paddock. Hardy's frown deepens.

Tessie is in her stable, laying as comfortably as she can in a pile of hay. Her tail flicks with annoyance and her velvet muzzle wiggles around the dusty ground for something to chew on, too tired to stand and eat from her bucket. She grunts at Hardy and me as we stick our heads over the stall's half door to look at her.

"How do you know it's only a few days?" he asks.

"Because she's bagged up weeks ago and she's not doing much walking now."

"She's pretty."

"Yeah. Her foals usually sell at good prices. If it's a boy, we might keep it. Ambition's getting too old to stud."

Sunlight leaks in through the roof's uneven slats and pollinates the barn. Swallows have taken over the rafters and their blue, forked tails cast the briefest of shadows as they dart in and out with twigs and strings for their nests. Last year, when Kitty and I attempted to grow a vegetable garden, the swallows and grackles took the hair we collected from the barber's and threaded through the tomatoes and cabbages. They used it to build their nests and in the morning light we could catch glints of fine silver and long curls stuck in between the twigs. With the hair gone from our garden, the rabbits and voles came in the night, unafraid, to eat everything.

"Last night you asked me who I thought was right for you."

"Yeah?" I'm unsure of where this sudden change in conversation has come from but I don't like the direction it's heading.

Hardy reaches up and tucks a lock of my curls back behind my ear. His mouth is very close to mine and my gaze focuses on the freckle of his lower lip. Everything else becomes a blur as the freckle disappears into me. My whole body stiffens and my joints lock. He breathes into my mouth. I feel his teeth against my tongue and then his own tongue pushes past mine. It swirls around the soft, wrinkled skin of my palate. His hands slide down my back. An abrupt cold prickles my skin as one of his hands slips into the gap between my shirt and overalls.

I jerk away from his invasion but Hardy's mouth presses more forcefully into mine. His hand makes a second attempt, fingers tight against me. Everything inside me screams and shatters apart but I can't manage to force sound out of my throat. I'm disgusted by the wetness of his breath against me. He moves his mouth from mine. A thread of saliva is determined to keep us together as he shifts his head downward to kiss my neck.

Finally the wind is knocked back into me and I gasp, "Don't!"

Hardy pushes his mouth back against mine. My gaze flutters up to the swallows, darting freely in and out of the stables. His hands are hard and stone against my spine, holding me in place. I manage to roll my mouth away.

"Stop! Stop!" I wish my voice didn't crack. "Hardy..."

A wild, hot sting scraps across my back in his determination to get at my bra. I scream as my skin is split open and slap my hands around his ears. He stumbles backward, shocked. The pain in my back spreads quickly. A sticky wetness rolls down and collects in the elastic lining of my panties. A brilliant hate lights me on fire, and I swing my fist into his face. The impact of my knuckles against his nose comes in a welcome crunch. Blood dribbles over his mouth.

"You piece of shit!" I hiss, shaking the pain and his blood free of my hand. "I said stop!"

Hardy's eyes are glazed and crooked. His fingers brush against his broken nose. "Did I hurt you?"

"Yes!" The skin around my spine burns tight, like the time I fell out of our cedar tree and slammed flat against the earth. It's hard to breathe and my legs are dissolving. The oatmeal I ate this morning churns up from my stomach to the base of my tongue. I need to lay down, but I think any movement might make the nausea worse.

"I told you to stop!"

"I thought it was a good stop!"

"There's no such thing!"

He reaches for me, and I swing my fist, but he dodges a second impact. "Get away from me! Don't you *ever* touch me again!"

Tessie whinnies nervously from her straw bed. Hardy wipes at the blood spurting out his nostrils. "I guess I should just leave then."

"Yeah? No shit."

He shuffles to the barn doors like a dog that's been caught pissing on the carpet and looks over his shoulder at me. "Can I check on you tomorrow?"

"I don't know. I can't even think right now."

"I'm sorry. I... I thought you might like kissing."

I pick up the nearest thing to me, a hoof pick, and chuck it at his head. His arms swing up for cover as he sprints from the barn.

It took everything I had left in me to stand straight and not collapse in front of him. The pain burns with spreading white pinpricks that rush out from the points of contact where Hardy's nails dug in. I know he's cut me deep and I'm not sure how bad it is until I can make it safely to my bathroom. But I'm not leaving the barn until enough time has passed for him to get off the property.

Tessie snorts loudly again and sticks her head over the stable door. I give her a reassuring pat on the nose before staggering back to the house. Each breath comes in short bursts of agony. Each step is a small victory. The staircase becomes Mount Everest, and my feet have become useless by the time I make it to the bathroom on the second floor. I sink onto the toilet and sit there for a long time. Ages. Nearly vomiting but not quite able to.

When I feel like I can start moving again, I unhook the brass buttons of my overalls with trembling fingers. The removal of my shirt is a slow torture. The burn of infection spreads out from my spine, and I have to rest again once it is off of me. The back of the shirt is torn in four long, vertical scratches and blood has soaked through the veins of the fabric. My bra is even harder to unhook, and I cry freely in ugly gasps. When I'm naked from the waist up, I lean forward and hold onto the towel rack for support. I turn my back to the mirror and use another handheld one to see the damage.

The cuts start between my shoulder blades and end at the midpoint of my back. Blood oozes slowly out of the two center lines and all four are flaming and purple at the edges. Bending slowly at the knees, I take the brown bottle of rubbing alcohol from underneath the bathroom sink and brace myself for the bubbling sting. It takes an exhausting amount of effort for me to cut large squares of gauze and cover them in Monkey Blood, because I can't spread the medicine on my own. Then I have to figure out a way to tape it to my back. In the end I lay what I can against my skin and then press myself against the wall to secure the tape.

My face and neck are ashen and blue. I'm worried I've lost too much blood, but I don't feel sick anymore. Only numb. It's hours before Dad is supposed to come home, and I wish he was here. I wish I didn't have such a terrible secret that I had to keep from him. I clean up and shamble to the attic bedroom. My bedroom. I need to stop thinking of it as a place to share.

I wince as I ease onto the mattress. I haven't stopped crying, but all the liquid has left me. All that remains are dry, aching sobs. I can't find support and it hurts to keep shifting around. Finally, I get in an okay position on my side, my back straight, but my arms and legs curled forward around a lumpy pillow.

I can see the barn from one of the windows and Hardy's house further up the hill. I should have drawn the curtains before collapsing into bed, but I don't have the energy to get back up again. So, I squeeze my eyes shut and hope to dream away the bad thing that happened. Sleep rolls over me in stages and at some point I think I hear Barbie and Sandra-Lee knocking at the door, calling out to me. Walking around the sides of the house.

When I wake up again, it's dark, and I'm sweating through my thin nightgown and the bed sheets. There is a level of blackness that surrounds the attic, and I know it's past midnight. I hear Dad breathing heavy in his own sleep and I'm sorry that I didn't get to welcome him home.

At first, I'm not sure what has caused me to wake up. The pain between my shoulders has decreased some, and despite my sweating, the room is not too hot. Then I hear it. The long, icy howl of a coyote. Several heartbeats later, others answer, their calls as brittle as the starlight and just as overwhelming.

Chapter Eighteen

"Focus, Delah!" says Martha, snapping her fingers. We've gathered under the gazebo in the square to finish preparing for the Church Social. It seemed like a good idea at the time, but storm clouds have rolled in, and we're bogged down by the humidity in the air. Martha gets cranky when it's humid because it ruins the set of her bubble curls and makes little clusters of pimples appear on her pointed chin. "You really dropped the ball on us yesterday and I need those posters done now. Thank you."

"Sorry. I told you I was sick." It's not really a lie. I could hardly move after Hardy attacked me, but I wasn't in the mood to try to explain to everyone what happened. I felt like this violation was just part of the secret world he and I were weaving together, and I was helpless to it.

"Give her a break," Barbie snaps. She stretches, folding her arms underneath her hair to lift it from her neck. I hand her a spare hair ribbon and she takes it with a relieved smile. "She's having a hard enough time without your dragon breath ruining her day."

I've never been more grateful for my friends. Martha must believe me though because I'm still pale and slow moving. I've decided there's no other explanation to Hardy other than the poison in his blood is taking over. He's not entirely in control of himself right now, that much is clear, and I should have been better prepared. Lately, his moods have ticked back and forth with the speed of a metronome. I understand this. Hardy is no longer the sweet boy I've lived next door to my entire life. He is a live wire. In spite of what I know, I cannot forgive him.

Wilma attempts to lighten the mood but there is no fixing the sourness between me and Martha. "Daddy's going to take us to Abilene to buy new dresses. He says he'll take whoever wants to go."

Sandra-Lee wiggles excitedly in her seat. "I'll ask my parents tonight. When were you going to go?"

"Tomorrow! Oh, it'll be such fun!" says Wilma, clapping her hands together. "We can all get the latest trends! I'm thinking satin gloves that come all the way up the elbow."

She draws her finely painted nail up the length of her arm and I visualize her as a perfectly quaffed debutante.

"Isn't it a little much for a church social?" I ask.

"You're kidding," sighs Martha. "It's not a church social. It's *the* Church Social."

"That explains it," sniggers Barbie, and that gets me laughing, but it comes out of me in a dried-up huff.

"You'll never guess who asked me to the dance!" continues Wilma, refusing to let the rift between us and her sister ruin a perfectly good conversation.

"Who?" asks Sandra-Lee with polite interest.

"Parker Armstrong!"

"No! He didn't!"

"He sure did! Just yesterday after the town meeting, didn't he Martha?"

Martha gives a superior little head wiggle.

"That's good," I say as I finish outlining a poster in glitter. It's not really turning out the way I want it to, and I blame the weather, but the truth is my heart isn't in decorating anymore. "I like Parker. He's a real cut-up at work."

"Oh! I forgot y'all worked together!" Wilma leans forward and grabs my hand. Golden flecks spray out of my hand and land on the gazebo floor. "What kind of woman do you think he likes? I want to dress just right for him."

"I think you're the type he likes, otherwise he would've asked Martha."

"You can uninvite yourself from coming to Abilene with us, Delah!" Martha squeaks.

"She didn't mean it like that, dummy!" says Sandra-Lee. "She meant y'all look the same but act different. That's all."

"That's right," I say. I'm glad Parker picked Wilma over Martha. Wilma may be a gossip, but she's got a golden heart. Martha snagged a date already and it amazes me that flat-faced Albert Crue would sign himself up for punishment. Then again, Albert's mother is about as mean as acid spit so maybe he thinks all women ought to be that way.

"What about you?" asks Wilma, again trying to make the peace.

"Slick, obviously," says Sandra-Lee.

"I'm working on it," says Barbie with a small laugh. "I haven't mustered the courage to ask Hardy."

"Delah, you can tell him," suggests Wilma. "You're about as thick as thieves with him as you are with us."

"Yeah. I can do that, no problem," I say.

I try to sound even-toned. Some sadness leaks its way in and Barbie blushes, thinking of the moment we shared under the dock at Lake Sweetwater. But the truth is, I don't want to subject her to Hardy. Not when he's no longer himself. I keep thinking about the swallows and their forked tails darting in and out of the stables wishing I was like them and able to escape. Out of all the things that would haunt me and make my skin crawl, I didn't think it would be little birds.

"You'll be a great item," says Wilma. "I mean… the scars sort of add to his look."

"I hardly notice them," sighs Martha and her gaze flits over to Diggs' Pharmacy where Hardy helps his mother stock the shelves. Poor Albert Crue. He has no idea what he's getting into, hitching his yoke to the likes of Martha Anderson.

We pause in conversation to watch a brown and white patrol car ease down Main Street and take a slow turn around the square. Inside are two cops from Roscoe. One has a large mustache, and the other is drinking out of a paper cup so I can't really see what he looks like. The one with the mustache looks like he wishes he were anywhere but here. He slows as he passes us, and his partner looks through the passenger window. No mustache and a weak chin. He doesn't look happy to be patrolling around Maryneal either. They consider the five of us and drive on.

We finish making our posters around noon. Right about that time, Slick rolls up in his truck and Manny is in the cab with him.

"You girls want to get outta here?" asks Manny. "Do something fun for a change?"

"Absolutely!" says Sandra-Lee. She collects her purse and strides toward the truck. "Out Manny! That's my seat."

"I was keeping it warm, m'lady."

Barbie and I help gather the poster materials. "We'll put these up tomorrow once the glue dries," I say and look at Wilma, expecting her to stand and come with us. Her gaze slides nervously to Martha.

"It's not ladylike to sit in the bed of a truck," says Martha.

"We live in the middle of nowhere," I say with a resigned sigh. "No one cares how much of a Lady you are. Prince Charming doesn't even know you exist. So, for the love of God, don't ruin Wilma's life just because you're a bitch."

"At least—" begins Martha but Wilma cuts her off.

"It's not ladylike to be cruel either. Why don't you just hush." She stands and dusts off the seat of her skirt and then her hands. "I'll see y'all here tomorrow and we can decide the best places to put the posters, okay?"

"Bye, Wilma. Sorry."

"See you tomorrow Wilma," says Barbie and she hops into the bed of Slick's truck.

I'm not as quick to jump in because of my injured back and I brace myself for the number of potholes he's bound to speed over. Manny joins us in the back and bombards us with questions on the best way to invite Lauren Willoby to the Social.

"Just be yourself."

"Don't put mascara on your mouth again."

"Buy her flowers."

"Don't burp or fart."

"But you just told me to be myself!"

"Good! Make her laugh." I wince as a shock of fire radiates through me. Slick deliberately ran over a pothole just to hear Sandra-Lee's delighted squeal. "She likes a good joke."

We stop at Barbie's house first. Her mother, an eggshell of a woman hidden under the giant brim of a sunhat, is weeding in the garden. She tilts her head up and waves a dirty, gloved hand. "Say you'll stay? I've just made lemonade!"

Slick pokes his head around Sandra-Lee to address Mrs. Stine while Manny helps Barbie out of the truck bed. "That's mighty kind, Mrs. Stine, but I'm just the driver. Up to the girls."

"I'll have some," I say. It's been a while since I've had Mrs. Stine's sweet lemonade, and my back needs a break.

"Me too!" Sandra-Lee says, and she slides awkwardly out of the cab, adjusting her skirt.

Mrs. Stine's smile widens. All thirty-two perfect teeth flash. She peels off her gloves one finger at a time. "Right this way. Shoes at the door if you don't mind."

"Ma, the Anderson twins invited us to Abilene to pick out dresses tomorrow. Can I go?"

"I don't see why not. I'll ask your father to write out a check tonight."

Slick takes off his Stetson as he steps inside and holds it to his expansive chest. He steps out of his boots and Sandra-Lee props herself against his arm so she can slide out of her Mary Janes.

Mrs. Stine's kitchen is immaculately clean, and she takes her time crushing ice and placing it into small cups. Her lemonade, chilled and properly presented in blue carnival glass, is distributed evenly among us. I've never had lemonade that tastes as smooth and as sweet as hers. She makes a plate of cucumber sandwiches as well. It's only when she sits down that Slick notices she's not wearing a bra. He clears his throat and averts his eyes. Manny stares without shame. Barbie never wears a bra, unless she's at church, so I'm curious as to why the boys are acting this way.

"That's some wallpaper you got there," mumbles Slick. The borders of the kitchen are decorated with dancing pigs wearing laurels around their ears.

"I couldn't resist." She has a China doll laugh. "There was a similar one with hens, but I thought, well, we have enough of the real thing, don't we?"

Her comment reminds me of the coyote that raided the Latimers's chicken coup and the massacre in the Ag building.

And Kitty.

Mrs. Stine puts her hand between my shoulders. I jerk, unprepared by the sting. Heat rises to my face, and everyone looks at me as though I've shouted an unforgivable curse word.

"Is everything alright, Delah?"

"Yes," I manage at last. "I was just far and away."

"You look like something's troubling you," Mrs. Stine tries again.

"Not really. I was just thinking about all my chores," I say, giving her the politest smile I can. I never used to lie like this.

Mrs. Stine nods and raises an eyebrow to Barbie. "I know another young lady that has chores as well."

Barbie groans dramatically and places the back of her hand against her forehead. "There's just no rest for the weary."

Slick slips his hand out from under the table. He'd been holding Sandra-Lee's, not sure of whether or not Barbie's mother was as strict on public affection as his own mother. As he stands, the chair scrapes against the linoleum floor. "I'll take that as a hint we best be going."

"Thank you for the lemonade and sandwiches," says Sandra-Lee, following Slick to the door.

"Yeah! You're the best," echoes Manny and he steals another sandwich for the road.

"You're welcome! Anytime."

She hugs each of us. Even though it's painful, if I could, I'd sink into her arms. I needed that hug worse than I ever imagined.

Slick takes me home next. He puts the Chevy into park and stares out past the ponies' barn, all the way to Hardy's house on top of the hill. The veins in his forearms tighten and his knuckles turn white against the steering wheel. His eyes become hard slits of a snake's, and I want to ask what's going on in his mind.

"Don't forget to ask your Dad if you can go tomorrow!" Sandra-Lee says, sticking her head out the window. "What have you got going the rest of the night?"

"Work. Unless it gets rained out." All I want to do is curl underneath the hot showerhead and figure out a way to peel off the gauze without it ripping open the newly formed scabs. If I'm lucky it'll rain but there hasn't been much luck in Maryneal.

Manny hops out of the truck and helps me down. I shudder and swallow the urge to vomit when his thin fingers accidentally brush against my hips.

"Maybe we'll come by," he says brightly.

I'm glad he doesn't hold any hard feelings in my rejection of him. This town is too small to hold grudges against anyone.

"Sure. Yeah. You haven't seen the new films yet."

I stand by the gate and wave them off as Slick makes a three-pointed turn and heads back down to the square.

"Delah!" Dad calls from the stables sliding door. He skips in place and waves his hand, then cups it around his mouth and yells, "C'mon! Come quick!"

It takes me a second to realize what's happening. I launch myself off of the porch and sprint up to the stables. Grass clings to my shoes and sticks into my ankles. I nearly trip as my toes graze over the opening of a rabbit hole. It doesn't matter. I'd fall flat on my face and still keep going. Tessie is giving birth!

Dad's grin stretches him out into the man I remember before the sadness in him started to suck out the marrow of his bones. I slow down once inside the barn, not wanting to agitate Tessie or the other ponies who are trotting around the paddock.

Tessie's grunts and heavy whickering bounces off the walls of the birthing stall, which has been scrubbed clean and sprinkled with lime. New hay laid out for soft bedding and all the feeding tubes and buckets have been removed. She's on her side, shifting that heavy head of hers through a pile of hay. Her lips wiggle and move with the contractions. Her snout is wet with the grunting snot of each push. She is covered in lather and her liquid brown eyes dance wildly between me, Dad, and the barn swallows above.

The birth of a colt is an astonishing thing to witness. There is nothing and then, quite suddenly, new life slipping out of a pearly veined sack. All that blood and gruesome stretching and all that pain to create the purest, gentlest creature.

"I'm glad you're here," Dad says. "I was worried I'd have to do it alone and you'd miss out!"

He wraps her tail in nylon stockings so that the foal won't get dirty as it comes out. I ease down beside Tessie, resting my hand on her shuddering flesh, and begin to wash her udder, legs, and buttocks with warm, soapy water and a soft cloth. The other ponies occasionally poke their heads in and give curious snorts. Slow splatters of rain begin a calm rhythm on the roof. The contractions quicken and I step back from her, taking the water bucket and cloth with me. Dad steps back, too. She lays down again and stands again. The amber liquid of her water sack flows out of her vulva and down her quivering legs. We leave her alone in the birthing stall.

Five minutes pass. Ten. Fifteen. Tessie's grunting continues and we can see, from where we wait, she continues to stand and lay down between contractions.

"Go get the rope bridle," Dad says.

He removes the shirt of his uniform and hangs it over the railing of Navajo Blue's stall. Then he pulls on a pair of elbow length, green rubber gloves and begins covering them with lube. I get the bridle and return to the birthing stall. Tessie's decided to stand again. I tie her to one of the walls so she doesn't lay back down while Dad is inside of her. He wiggles his hands into Tessie's uterus, and she stamps a back leg, annoyed.

"Do I need to call the vet?" I ask between shushing sounds as I run my hand over Tessie's velvet nose.

"Naw. Foal's fine, just too big."

He takes the obstetrical chain and loops it around the forelegs of the foal, then pulls with Tessie's contractions. Tessie lets out a final sigh and blood splatters up Dad's arms and across his white undershirt. The foal shakes its head and breaks free from the sack. I slip off the bridle then help clear the mucus away from the foal's nose. Tessie rests while we work. Soon she'll start cleaning off the sack and after she tears off the umbilical cord, I'll have to disinfect the foal's navel stump with iodine and then collect the after birth.

Dad and I watch as the foal begins to root for Tessie's udder. Navajo Blue and Bonnie Wee Dancer come in from the rain and stick their heads out of their stalls. They nod slowly, welcoming the newest addition with tiny clicks and grunts. Ambition, too, shows some interest. The foal is a beautiful stud. Piebald cream and dusty roan.

"What do we call him?" Dad asks, following me out of the birthing stall as he peels off his rubber gloves.

"I don't know. We don't have to name him today, do we?"

He shakes his head and trudges over to the hose at the other end of the barn to wash himself clean. He takes off the soiled undershirt and pauses, holding it in his toughened hands, examining the pattern spreading across the fabric. His chin trembles, but with a deep inhale, hitches his smile back into place. "I have to get back to work. It's a miracle I came home for lunch or Tessie might have had a harder time of it. Will you let me know if anything is wrong with the after birth?"

"Sure," I say. "I don't think Mrs. Dunne will open the theater tonight if it stays rainy."

Dad takes his uniform shirt off Navajo Blue's door and flicks the strands of dust and hay clean of it. "Okay then. I'll see you at dinner."

We walk to the house together. Dad gets a new undershirt and puts it on before buttoning up his uniform. He runs a thumb over his brass deputy's badge and straightens his tie. I've only come inside to grab something to read and take it back to the stables. Sometimes it can take up to two hours before the after birth appears and I haven't read any *Othello* since I brought it to work with me the other night. I've got nothing better to do while I wait, so I might as well attempt to understand what I'm supposed to read for my senior year. Maybe Purlie can talk me through some of the complicated language.

I ought to call him anyway. I haven't seen him since the town meeting, and we didn't have a chance to talk then. We need to figure out where to meet before the Social and how we're going to dress. A flutter of anxiety pulses through my chest. What if he tries to kiss me? Will he stop if I ask him to?

I'm not far in *Othello* and keep rereading the same three pages, trying to make sense of Desdemona's relationship with Iago, when the after birth finally comes out of Tessie. I set aside my book and yank on a pair of green rubber gloves. It's heavy with liquids and slips in my grasp as I struggle to put it in a trash bag so it can dry out and be weighed properly. The foal and Tessie are doing fine. I leave them in peace, make sure the other ponies are filled with food and water, then wash my hands and take up my book and sprint back to the house. Icy rain slants in the wind, which is still warm. A flash of lightning tears through the solid mass of gray-black cloud. I count the seconds between it and the clap of thunder. The wind chime Kitty and I made clanks together.

I step out of my soaking shoes and socks and leave them on the porch. Part of me wants to sit outside and watch the storm as it passes by, but I've worked myself up enough courage to call Purlie, so I step inside with determination. My book, wet from the down poor, slips between my nervous fingers.

Our avocado green telephone sits on an end table in the living room. As much as I've pleaded with Dad to get my own, I don't think he'll ever go for it. It's not so bad but sometimes I wish I could have a private conversation, or at least have the phone set up in a different room so I don't have to compete with the radio whenever Dad turns on one of his serials.

I push my pinky into the dial and call Purlie. The plastic rotary whirls back into place, and each drawn out number causes me to hesitate and reconsider. If I start calling him up like this, he might take it as genuine interest. I like Purlie, he's clever and fun to be around. So why does going out with him feel like a type of prison?

He picks up on the fifth ring. "Gates residence. Purlie speaking."

His sounds so formal that for a second, I think I've dialed the wrong number, and I don't say anything.

"Hello?"

"It's Delah."

"Oh. Hey! How are you?" Purlie's voice crackles through the receiver and becomes much more relaxed.

"Fine. You?"

"Fine."

I don't know what to say next. If Kitty were alive, she'd know what to do. I can picture her, perched on the armrest of our sofa, one hand cupped over a silent giggle while the other motions for me to keep talking. It is such a rich image I can almost reach out and touch her. A sob snags the base of my tongue.

"I... uhm."

"I've been meaning to call you," says Purlie, saving me. "You were sick the other day and I didn't want to bother you."

"How did you know I was sick?" I ask, stupidly. There's not any sort of privacy in a town as small as Maryneal. Except, somehow, Hardy and I have managed to hide his secret. Haven't we?

"Well... I tried calling but your Dad picked up and said you went to bed early. You're better now?"

"Yeah. Thanks. It was just..."

"You don't have to explain yourself to me," he says kindly. "Sickness of the heart. You can't control when it's going to hit."

I wish it had been heartache from Kitty's death instead of the burning betrayal of Hardy violating me the way he had. Am I a bad person for letting what happened between us overwhelm my grief for Kitty? Was it, perhaps, my punishment for wanting her death to stop hurting?

"So what's up?"

My fingers twist around the phone's cord. "Nothing. I was just calling. I figured I was supposed to call. Tessie gave birth this afternoon."

"Mazel tov!"

"What?"

"It means congratulations. I had a roommate in college who said it all the time. I guess it just sort of rubbed off."

"Oh, okay. Well, thanks."

"Can I take you to dinner?"

"When?"

"Tonight. Why not? Do you have any other plans?"

"Well. No, but I told Dad I'd be here tonight."

"I'll come by then and ask him if I can take you away for a few hours. Is that... is that okay?"

"Uhm. Sure. That's fine. What if Mrs. Dunne opens up Starry Night?"

"She won't," he says lightly. "We just talked. Even if it stops raining, the area's flooded, and she doesn't want anyone's tires getting stuck."

Another clap of thunder distracts me, and I wonder if it's going to let up in time for a dinner date. Purlie's end crackles again. "Okay. I'll come by at six."

"How should I dress?" I blurt out and then blush furiously. I ought to know how to dress for a dinner date. Purlie chuckles with an inhale and I picture the fine paper of his hand rolled cigarette disintegrating.

"Dress however you want. I'll come by at six."

He hangs up his end but I'm still holding the receiver close to my mouth. I'm going on a date tonight and I'm not sure what I'm supposed to do or how I'm supposed to act. Martha's mocking tone swims luridly into my thoughts.

I think it's real bold of you gallivanting around with an older boy. Especially when you should be mourning.

I shake her ugly face away and march upstairs to shower and clean the wounds on my back. They're tender to the touch but not swollen with pus. The gauze keeps molding to my skin, though, whenever scabs start to form. I have to rip them off and reapply the stinging Monkey Blood and new squares of itchy bandages each time. I want to knock Hardy's teeth into tomorrow or at least break his nose again.

Dad returns home around five and the rain has eased. We tug on our wellingtons and trudge to the barn to check on the ponies and see if the after birth is dry enough to examine. I enjoy the smell of wet hay as much as manure. It's a strange comfort, welcoming, almost akin to walking into Mrs. Stine's house just as she's pulling a batch of cookies out of the oven.

Dad pulls on his green rubber gloves which are clean and hanging to dry next to where we keep the hoof picks. He pulls the after birth out of the trash bag, weighs it in his hands, and examines the color. After birth, dried out, looks like pants with one leg shorter than the other. There aren't any tears in the placenta that we can see and that's a good sign, despite Tessie's slightly difficult birth. If there were bits missing, it might mean that some is still clinging to Tessie's uterus and that can cause an infection. Dad bags the placenta back up and ties the end of the bag into a tight knot before throwing it into the trash bin we keep around back.

"Hey, Dad."

"Hey, what?"

"Purlie wants to take me out to dinner tonight."

He looks up at me and blinks. "Purlie? I see."

"Is that okay?"

He shrugs. "I just thought you and Hardy were... you know."

"We're just friends."

"Not you and Purlie though?"

We walk slowly back to the house. There's a break in the rain and the earth smells raw in its new dampness. "Purlie and I are friends, too. He's just taking me out to dinner."

We leave our wellingtons on the porch. Dad takes off his belt and hangs it on a hook by the front door, then loosens his tie. "Where's he taking you?"

"I didn't ask."

"When will you be home?"

"I'm not sure. After we eat, I guess?"

Dad scrubs his face with his hand and wanders slowly into the living room. He crosses his arms and looks around for nothing in particular. "I guess. Sure. I'll talk with him while you're getting ready."

I look down at my overalls, grass stained and damp around the ankles, and my shirt that I've been wearing all day. I thought I was ready, but I should make some sort of effort to show I appreciate Purlie wanting to take me anywhere. There isn't much time before he arrives, so I hurry up the stairs and undress. My bandages are still clean and I'm not too worried about them bleeding through. If I wanted, I could wear a light-colored blouse.

Kitty watches me from her vanity, delicate and translucent. Our final night replays again and I retrace the little dance steps we took around the attic. I delight in the memory. What would her keen, fashionable eye dress me in? It doesn't matter how many times I convince myself to push through and move on with my life. Every little thing becomes a treasure that I can't share with Kitty, a moment that I can't spread out or examine into the late hours of the night. I suppose I could talk to Barbie and Sandra-Lee about my date with Purlie. If I'd thought of it sooner, I'd've invited them over to help me prepare, but it would be hollow without Kitty's input.

I tug on a green blouse and a clean pair of khakis that hug my hips but aren't uncomfortably tight. The doorbell rings as I'm twisting my hair into a tight braid and my heart flutters in my chest as Dad's gentle tone drifts through the floorboards.

Chapter Nineteen

A dialogue between them begins but I can't quite make out exactly what they are saying. I don't want to go downstairs. I want to hide in the attic forever. If Purlie likes me enough, he can visit me here. I want to sleep for five hundred years. I want to run away. I don't want to force myself to be with him just because I want to touch and hold Barbie the way I'm supposed to with him. These are things I need my sister for. I need her help, her support.

I need her courage.

I hesitate by the bedroom door and then cross to Kitty's vanity. Three tubes of lipstick are lined neatly beneath the curved mirror, gathering dust. I pluck up the one closest to me and uncap it. It's pale pink, nearly the same color of my own lips. The arrow of color slides out of the tube, and I touch it to my lower lip, drawing up and down its natural curve. It's as though she's guiding my hand, armoring me with makeup. Amazingly, I don't feel guilty for using Kitty's lipstick. I feel protected and emboldened.

With a deep inhale I open the bedroom door and make my way to the living room. The stairs seem to become unending, but Dad and Purlie's conversation is getting louder. They're talking about the madman's missing body and the extra police officers patrolling the town.

"Here she is," Dad stands from his chair. Purlie, catecorner to him on the sofa, stands as well.

"You look nice," he says. He's slicked back his rusty hair with pomade and shaved the perpetual stubble off his jaw line.

"Yes, you do," Dad agrees and his wide hazel eyes swim. "Very spruced up."

"Okay," I say, and I look down at my feet.

"We're only going down to Buzzy's," says Purlie, giving me a reassuring grin.

Dad claps him on the shoulder and follows us to the yard. "Just have her home by nine."

"Of course, sir."

Purlie holds open the door of his flashy red impala wagon and waits for me to get situated before closing the door. The upholstery is fresh and white with tan stitching and a silver cross hangs from the rearview mirror. I keep my hands folded together and pressed between my knees. He's treating this with such formality I wonder how I should tell him to quit acting this way. I want to have dinner with the Purlie I work with, not Purlie Gates clean and pressed.

"This'll be fun," he assures me with a nervous smile as he slides in behind the wheel. His hair brushes the roof of the car. Purlie takes a pair of black, Brookline glasses out of his shirt pocket and fixes them up the bridge of his nose before switching the gears into drive.

"I didn't know you needed glasses."

"Just for driving. Sometimes when I'm setting up the projector. My depth perception is a little off, is all."

Purlie reaches forward and I think he's going to put his hand on my leg. My vision blurs. I shrink away, but his intention is to turn on the radio. He stares at me, fingers hovering over the dial, and frowns. "What just happened?"

"Sorry… I thought that… never mind."

He presses his index and middle finger to the radio and Elvis warbles through the speakers. Purlie keeps his eyes on the road, avoiding potholes, and pats his hand against the steering wheel to the beat of the music. I relax a little. Gene Chandler comes on next, and I catch myself singing along with Purlie.

He tries to hit the high notes, and I giggle at his cracking voice.

"Like you can do better?" he asks but he's grinning just the same.

We park on the square, and I get out of the car before he has time to come around and open the door for me. He rolls his eyes and leads the way to Buzzy's Diner. I'm hit with the smell of pancakes and bacon grease once he pushes the glass plated door open. Apparently, everyone else in town had the same idea as Purlie.

Men squeeze around the L-shape of the bar, slurping coffee and cutting into steak and egg dinners before heading on to the night shift at the cement plant. The Anderson twins are on a double date with Albert and Parker. Petunia Latimer chit-chats with Mrs. Dunne and pauses to cough into a pink handkerchief. Reda sticks her gray snout out from under Mrs. Dunne's legs and sniffs hopefully for a bit of sausage.

Barbie and Sandra-Lee are in the back corner booth with Slick and Hardy. Barbie stands and waves us over.

"Is it okay if we sit with them?" I ask Purlie. He tucks his glasses back into the pocket of his shirt and smiles. I like that he has dimples. I never paid much attention to them before, probably because he keeps them hidden under all that rust-colored stubble.

"Tus amigos son mis amigos."

"Is that like mazel tav?"

"Nope. Spanish. I know a handful of about every language there is. But I can't hold a conversation in anything but English."

"Then why learn the language?"

"To pick up chicks." Purlie wiggles his eyebrows until I snort, and we sit down with the others.

"You look cute!" says Barbie, wedged up against the window because Hardy scooted over to make room for me.

I pointedly take the seat next to Slick and Sandra-Lee. I don't want to look at him, but I'd rather do that than feel the heat of his thigh against mine. Nobody notices the uncomfortable, unspoken exchange between us.

Purlie takes the seat next to Hardy and reaches across him and Barbie to snag a menu. The booth is a tight fit. Purlie, Slick, and I are all six feet or over. Our knees knock together no matter which way we twist in our seats. Sandra-Lee and Barbie aren't bothered, but Hardy looks almost miserable. This fills me with a sick tingle of pleasure. I hope he stays that way all night.

Manny's sister works here part time and we're sitting at one of her tables. She swings by on her roller skates, tray filled with the sodas everyone ordered.

"Hey, Delah! Purlie!" she says brightly. "What's your poison?"

I order a coke, and Purlie asks for coffee with cream but no sugar. She turns effortlessly on the skates, then returns promptly and drops off our drinks and sets of silverware wrapped in napkins. "Let me just check on the Andersons and I'll be back to take your orders."

Maria scoots down the terrazzo floor, bobbing to the music coming out of the jukebox at the front of the diner.

"Where is Manny anyway?" asks Hardy, trying to sound relaxed.

"At the graveyard with Lauren Willoby," Sandra-Lee whispers.

"Classic," says Hardy.

I slide my paper straw into the frosted neck of my coke and watch Purlie measure out his cream. I think of Kitty stretched out beneath Manny and Lauren, disturbed from sleep by their slurping wet kisses. Purlie pours it in a thin trickle and his lips move slightly as he counts under his breath. He takes up his coffee spoon and stirs, counting again. I'm glad he was fine with sitting here. It makes going on a date with him easier, safer somehow, like he's become part of our circle.

"Dag, I'm starving!" moans Slick to the right of me. "Coach had us running all afternoon and nothin'—I mean nothin'—has touched the sides."

"Does he still start the practice at sunup?" asks Purlie with a smirk. "I don't miss those days."

"Say," says Slick, tilting back his Stetson. "Y'all went to college on wrestling? How can I get that same deal?"

"Talk to Coach," says Purlie with a shrug. "And don't blow out your knee in the middle of a tournament."

"Is that what happened to you?" asks Hardy.

"It's okay. I learned what I needed to learn. Some folk aren't made for college."

Sandra-Lee leans onto the lime Formica tabletop, cutting off the boys' conversation. "So, did you ask your Dad if you can come to Abilene tomorrow?"

I let out a little, exhausted moan. "I completely forgot."

"What?" asks Barbie. "Why? Make sure you ask him tonight!"

"Tessie gave birth," I answer with a smile. "We were distracted all afternoon."

"Oh! Yay! What's it look like?"

"It's red and white. A little boy. But we don't have a name yet."

"Gosh," sighs Sandra-Lee. "So sweet! That's wonderful."

"He's a real cutie," I say.

"That's great," says Hardy. "You told me you were hoping it was a boy."

"Yeah," I repeat, not hiding the tight anger that's swelled up because he thought he could speak to me. "Thanks."

Hardy is trying to apologize in a way that is safe among mixed company, but I'm not ready to forgive him. Maria returns with fresh drinks for everyone and tucks her round tray beneath one arm so both her hands are free to write down our orders. We all order burgers and onion rings. Slick asks for an extra patty and a side of bacon. Barbie and I order a vanilla shake to split.

"Y'all ever dip French Fries into a shake before?" asks Purlie.

"Disgusting!" gasps Sandra-Lee.

"Maria!" shouts Purlie. "Can we get another shake and an order of fries?"

"Okay!" she shouts back.

"I promise you, it's amazing," says Purlie.

"What put that in your head?" asks Hardy. "Who comes up with that?"

Purlie smirks. "College, amigo. It's full of experiences."

"Yeah but... how?"

"Short answer? Reefer."

Slick snorts into his coke and bubbles form around the melting ice cubes. Sandra-Lee gives an excited little gasp. "You? Smoking illegal substances? But your dad is a preacher!"

"Aw, heck, Sandra-Lee. It's only been under legal scrutiny for the past twenty-five years. A millennium ago, God said 'Let the land produce vegetation: seed bearing plants and trees'. That's all reefer is. Sometimes you just gotta delight in God's creations."

"You want to share a little of that delight?" asks Slick.

"You wouldn't!" Sandra-Lee gasps.

"I'll share with you," says Slick, then he adds with a wink, "Let's delight in creation."

"Well," she chews her lip.

Barbie laughs and lifts her hands in the air, in a take-it-or-leave-it gesture.

"I don't know how good an idea it is," I say, swirling my paper straw around my drink. "I mean... it made you crazy enough to eat French Fries with ice cream."

Purlie's grin is mischievous. To Slick he says, "I'll see what I can do. No promises."

Maria returns with half of our order. There's so much food she has to make two more trips. Slick piles bacon into his double patty burger and begins wolfing it down. Purlie picks up a fry and presents it to us, the professor putting on dramatics for his captivated students, and dips it down past the cream and into the vanilla shake. Then he pops it into his mouth and chews happily.

"It's not a trick?" I ask, taking a fry and mimicking him.

"Only one way to find out," he says. I put the littlest bit up to my teeth and bite down. An explosion of hot and cold, salty and sweet, hits my tongue.

"Okay! You win," I say, eating the rest. "My new favorite treat."

"Exactly!" says Purlie and he dips another into the shake. Barbie and Sandra-Lee try it, too. Slick swallows his mouthful and grabs a fistful of fries to dip. Then he tries it with an onion ring.

"Oh... nope. Don't go down that path. Definitely not the same," he moans, spitting the onion ring into a paper napkin.

We all laugh at his disgruntled expression. Hardy is the only one who doesn't try the weird combination. Instead, he gives Purlie a hard look, the pupils of his eyes glint dangerously in the ways I've seen when the beast in him starts to grow, and he stretches his arm around

Barbie's shoulders. I tense, flashes of pain and the inability to escape roll through me. It's only when Barbie leans into him that my muscles relax again.

Maria clears our plates and the boys order thick slices of chess pie. "One day," she warns them, "your metabolisms will shut down and you won't be able to eat nothing but salad."

"That'll be the day," says Purlie in his best John Wayne impression.

After pie and more coffee, Purlie lights a cigarette and leans back to look outside at the night sky. Sandra-Lee and Barbie are both trying to tie our milkshake's cherry stems into knots using only their teeth and tongues. Slick is almost in a food coma, the brim of his Stetson pulled down low.

"Looks like we'll have a full moon during the Church Social," Purlie says on an exhale of a cloud of smoke.

Hardy's eyes flicker to me. It was a full moon the night Kitty was murdered. In just a few days we'll know for certain if that paste the medicine woman made for him actually works.

Purlie taps cigarette ash into an empty coffee cup and checks his watch. "I'm supposed to get you home."

"Is it nine already?" I ask. "I was having a good time."

"I was, too," pouts Barbie. "We need to do this again."

"Absolutely," agrees Sandra-Lee.

I don't mind it so much this time when Purlie opens the passenger door to his impala wagon. If this is how every date will be with him, I would do it again. I certainly don't have any more trepidation about going to the Church Social with him. Maybe that's why he wanted to take me to dinner, so I can ease into the idea. Purlie puts on his glasses before starting the car.

"You had a good time?" he asks.

The radio comes on automatically, but the Top 40 is no longer playing. It's a news program with some monotone reporters reading off bulletins in a trans-Atlantic accent.

"I did."

"Cool."

We're silent for a little while because Purlie seems invested in the reports. At the commercial break, I twist in my seat to look at him. His hands stay at ten-and-two on the steering wheel as he swerves around a pothole, but his chin angles a little toward me and he smiles enough for a dimple to appear. "What?"

"Do you think it's really possible? Like the man said?" I ask, gesturing to the radio. "Putting people on the moon?"

"Doubt that the stars are fire, doubt that the sun doth move."

"You're quoting something."

"Yep."

"I'm not doubting... I just can't imagine it."

I roll down the window and stick my head out to better catch a glimpse of the waxing moon. It burns fluorescent against the smaller pinpricks of stars surrounding it. "Why do we obsess over the moon?" I ask, softly. "What power does it have over us?"

"It's the exploration of the unknown," says Purlie in studied seriousness. "Space is that which marries Science and God."

"How do you mean?"

"We're made of carbon. Stars are made of carbon. In the old religions, people associated the planets and stars with gods. God created us in His own image. If He is the stuff of stars, then so must we be."

"He must have been depressed the day he created Martha Anderson."

A surprised shout of laughter jumps from Purlie just as he pulls to a stop in front of my house. "The point is. One old story feeds into another until it propels us to look, not to the past, but to the future. We have a desire to travel to the furthest parts of the universe so that we might be closer to God as we choose to see Him. The space program is this generation's Tower of Babel."

"Do you think they'll find God?" I ask.

"No clue," Purlie says, and he turns off the car. It's ten minutes before my curfew. "And honestly? I don't really care. I like the discussion more than the actuality."

His hands slide off the steering wheel and I'm nervous again. I'm not ready for him to touch me. I've just started getting used to the idea of sharing my time with him.

"Can I ask you a serious question?"

"Okay," I say, pressing my knees against my hands to keep from sprinting off in the other direction.

Purlie studies me over the tops of his glasses and shuts off the radio. He doesn't try to touch me the way Hardy has. He doesn't even find an excuse to scoot closer to me. I'm grateful for it but at the same time it worries me. I don't know what he's thinking or planning.

"Are you a lesbian?"

"A... a what?"

"Do you have a sexual attraction toward women?"

Heat rushes to my face. I can't look at him anymore. I focus on my whitened knuckles and the dark hair on my arms as they rise.

"It's okay if you do," he says kindly.

"What makes you think that I do?"

"The way you looked at Barbie tonight."

"I don't like Hardy with her."

"And Hardy doesn't like you with me. Tough titties for him."

"I don't know," I admit, and I force myself to straighten up. Purlie is not making me feel ashamed of this. "About women. I don't know. I like Barbie."

"That's okay, too. I'll still take you to the Social, if you want, but I don't mind if you don't."

I exhale slowly and inhale again. "I... thank you. I'll still go with you."

Purlie holds out a hand. "It's a deal then."

We give each other a firm, gentleman's handshake.

"Truth be told, Delah," he says, releasing himself from my grip. "I wouldn't mind if you settled for me. I'd mind if you settled for Hardy... but... well, anyway. There's so much you could learn about yourself if you cut out of Maryneal. But if you don't want to do that, I'll be your fallback. That's all I'm saying."

"You mean if I decide to not go to college and to get married and push out babies, I should propose to you?"

"Technically, I should propose to you."

"Can I think on it?"

"Will you let me walk you to the door so your father doesn't think badly of me?"

"Yes. I guess that's fine."

He steps out and rounds the front of his car, the headlights stretching him long and lean across the acreage. Purlie has just offered me so much and I can't soak it all in. I can picture Barbie and Sandra-Lee screaming in delight. Dad's tears would be joyous for a change. Martha would be enraged. Here I have a brawny, well-built man who is educated. She has only Albert Crue. But is it what I want? If I asked Kitty, she might be shocked at the notion of me wanting to kiss Barbie or seeing if there were other girls in the world to kiss me back, but I think she'd want me to be happy, too.

Purlie opens the door and waits for me to climb out. I slip my hand into his and even in this half-darkness, I can see he's blushing. My gesture is not a yes, but it is a definitely, maybe.

"Thank you, Purlie. For everything."

"Sure, sure."

"Maybe we can go out again, once we're back from buying new dresses?"

"I'll take you up on that." He gives me a loose salute and walks back to his wagon, a new spring in his step.

Dad is waiting up for me, listening to *Yours Truly, Johnny Dollar* and working on a crossword puzzle at the back of the newspaper.

"Hi," I say, stunned at the lightness lifting me up on my toes. But I don't mind it. I wish I could feel like this always.

"Hi back. You had a good time then?"

"I did. We ended up sitting at a table with everyone."

"Will you see him again?"

"Would you mind it?"

"Not at all. Not if he returns you to me every night this happy."

"Can I go to Abilene tomorrow with Barbie and Sandra-Lee to get a new dress? Mr. Anderson is driving us."

He folds the paper and gives me a curious once over. "I think that'll be fine. Just get your chores done before then."

"Thanks, Dad. Goodnight."

"Night."

I check on my bandages again before changing into my cotton nightgown. I'm not tired, but I stretch out on my bed anyway, replaying the night out and capturing the best moments that made a golden halo around my heart. I imagine Kitty in her own coffin-bed, a smug grin spreading on her face. A thin line of lipstick smears her teeth.

Several hours later, an icy howl shocks me out of sleep. It's so much closer than before. My skin prickles and the howl comes again. Ambition lets out a wild shriek. I hear Dad curse. He thunders out of his bedroom and down the stairs. The screen door bangs open at the same time he lets loose a warning shot in the dark.

I leap from bed and chase after Dad. He pulls the trigger of his shotgun again. Underneath the staggering whinnies from our ponies, I hear a painful yelp.

"Shit," Dad growls. "I only clipped the damn thing!"

He scoops down to pick up the hot shotgun shells that have landed in the mud by his feet. It's almost comical, the two of us standing there, Dad only in his underwear and wellingtons, shotgun in hand, me in my nightgown and eclipsing him in height by an inch.

We march up to the barn and check on everyone. None of the ponies are injured, just rattled and nervous. We double check the stalls and make sure all the doors are bolted shut and that the dirt hasn't been dug up by anything attempting to sneak in.

"Go on to the house," Dad yawns. He slings the gun over his shoulder. "I'll spend the night in here. Just in case."

"There's a spare blanket in the closet," I remind him, and he nods. We both check on Tessie and the foal a second time. Fear hasn't had time to settle in the newborn yet, but Tessie's nostrils flare.

"Go on, Delah. Big day tomorrow... dresses and such," Dad says, yawning again.

I slide the stable door shut but don't immediately walk back to the house. Instead I watch for any movement in Hardy's bedroom, but I don't see anything, even though the moon is so bright it can light the path up to his front door. The shadows are too broad and deep but I'm certain it was him skulking around our property. Dread pierces the balloon of joy that filled my lungs only hours ago. The medicine woman's paste isn't working. Hardy is getting worse.

Chapter Twenty

By next morning, I'm dressed and out the door before the Anderson's rooster crows. Dad sits up and the tough wool blanket slides loosely off his shoulders. He's thinner than he was before Kitty died and there's more gray in his sideburns, too. I've brought him his bathrobe and a cup of coffee.

"Thanks," he says, stifling a yawn. "Don't worry about feeding them. I'll do it before work."

"Okay. Did you sleep any?"

"Some. That ky-ote didn't come 'round again."

"Maybe we should get a dog," I suggest.

"Heck, I'll just name this new foal poodle and be done with it."

He gives me a wry smile and I laugh a little bit.

"Do you need money? For shopping today?"

"I was going to use some of my paycheck."

"Save it. I'm only sorry Anderson is taking you and not me."

I shrug and pluck some dirt off a bridle. I wish he was going with me, too. I wish Martha would get sick and have to stay home. "Thanks, Dad."

"Okay. I'll leave you some cash on the table before I head out."

I hug him and hike up to Hardy's house. It's squat and yellow, trimmed in brown, and wildflowers overtake the front yard. There's a porch swing I often see Mr. Diggs sitting on while he drinks his morning coffee and sketches on a drawing pad. I miss his art classes.

A few Blue Jays flit through the field between our houses, chirping at each other, but they don't go near the bird feeder Mr. Diggs made out of discarded bottles. The tall grasses brush against my pants leg, disturbing the grasshoppers and gnats that settle there. The sun hasn't risen over the crest of the horizon and the cement plant that eclipses the town stands as a looming flat-faced figure, nothing more than a cardboard cutout. I'm not worried I'll be disturbing the household. Mrs. Diggs is usually at her pharmacy by this time and Hardy is awake, scarfing down breakfast before team practice.

I pull open the screen door and knock. Nothing. There is no scuffling of feet or sizzle of a frying pan dropping into the wet basin of the sink. I move around the edge of the house and lean over the rose bushes to tap on Hardy's bedroom window. The curtains are drawn but a sliver of light shines through the cracks. I tap again.

He moves toward the window with a creaking slowness. His eyes snap from a half-sleep to a wide-eyed intensity when he parts the thin white curtains. He steps away but I put my hands on my hips and stare him down.

In a harsh whisper, I say, "Hardy Diggs, you open this window right now! I need to talk to you!"

His shoulders sag and he presses the palms of his hands against the glass. There are fresh cuts against the toughened skin, and his nails have dirt trapped underneath them. The window slides up a fraction, enough for us to speak to each other but not for me to climb in. "What?"

"Was that you last night skulking around the barn?"

"I don't know what you're talking about," he mumbles. The bags under his eyes are deep and threading from the corners of his tear ducts. "I wasn't doing anything."

"Well, are you at least taking the stuff that medicine woman made for you?"

Hardy avoids the question. He avoids looking at me. Instead, he asks, "You want to kill me, Delah?"

"No."

"Yes, you do."

"I don't." I snake my hand through the window and clutch onto his wrist. He flinches at my touch, as though I'm made out of flame. "I want you to be cured."

"I've got to get ready for practice." Hardy shakes loose and a long, aching breath beats around his rib cage. I've never seen anyone so defeated, not even when Dad flung himself over Kitty's closed casket.

He starts to close the window before my hand is out and it snaps with a finality. Through the widened gap in the curtains, I see Hardy's naked back. Along the base of it, near the hip, is a bloody arrow where he was nicked by buckshot. I swallow the swollen brick of my tongue.

"Hardy!" I hiss. "Hardy! Take that paste! Or so help me God! Don't... don't become this thing!"

He's back at the window in the space of a second and his fist slams against the glass, cracking it. I stumble backward, determined to not break eye contact with him. If I turn and run, will he chase me? Will he throw me into the grass and ruin me? My teeth grind together to keep my heart from exploding out of my mouth. Hardy's expression turns from an animal rage to that of a frightened child. He yanks the curtains shut and his silhouette disappears into the deeper parts of the house. I realize now he had kept the window down to keep himself from getting out. A cold shudder spreads across my neck and down the cuts of my spine.

Chapter Twenty-One

The Andersons's rooster crows, bringing me back into my body. How long have I sat here, dumbstruck? I pick myself off the ground and hurry back down the hill to my house. Dad has gone to work, his coffee mug is upturned in the sink next to a dish that held toast and jam. I climb the stairs to my room, passing the bathroom where steam is still collected from his morning shower. He might have just left, and I didn't hear the wheels of his patrol car slide out of the drive.

All I want is to be held by him, cradled into a false sense of security as he soothes the shaking fear out of me. I'm not sure of what will happen next, but the Hardy I've known my whole life is gone. It's somebody else wearing a familiar skin.

The silver bullet, on its thin leather rope, has not moved from where I've kept it all this time. It's a talisman collecting dust. I've been so convinced there was another alternative to what I have to do, but now I know this little bit of silver is the only thing that will work.

Morning creeps by in a slow progression and daily chores, like mucking the stables, doesn't seem to eat away the hours. If Kitty were alive, we'd spend our morning sunbathing and riding down to the square to get an ice cream at Diggs Pharmacy. We'd talk about my date with Purlie and debate on how pretty his rust-colored hair is. Her absence is marked by silence and when I put *Clap Hands, Here Comes Charlie!* onto our Dansette, it only feels like I'm slapping a band-aid onto a gaping wound.

I stretch out on Kitty's bed and stare at the vaulted ceiling. This, like putting on her lipstick, seems a necessary violation. I haven't touched anything of hers since she died and I don't think Dad has either, not since he slept in her bed that one night. The blue and purple quilt absorbs the dampness of my hands as I spread them. The grooves of my fingers absorb the smooth texture of each square, the slightly strained corners where the stitching has started to come undone. A bit of lace from her heart-shaped pillow tickles the back of my neck. I never understood how Kitty was able to sleep with this pillow, but she was almost like lace herself.

I wish someone would explain death to me. Preacher John says it's God's way of taking us home and we can't question His reasons. I think that's unfair. Don't I have a right to question the murder of a thirteen-year-old girl? Don't I deserve an answer? And what about Dad? Isn't he owed an explanation? Sometimes, I catch myself not thinking about her and I don't know if that's okay. Does that mean I'm starting to cope with her absence or that I never loved her as much as I thought I did? Who am I supposed to be now that I am without my partner in life?

Far down below, another universe away, the doorbell rings. I've turned up the volume so loud again, I barely hear the bell over Ella Fitzgerald's up-tempo rhythm. I slide off of Kitty's bed and stand before the Dansette, wondering if I can just skip out of the dress shopping. After all, Martha doesn't want me there and she'll probably try and hurt my feelings again for wanting to go to the Social. But what am I supposed to do? Stretch out underneath the sod and rot alongside my sister's remains?

Sandra-Lee and Barbie wait for me on the steps of the porch. Sandra-Lee has a darling white and yellow polka-dot scarf twirled around the high curve of her hair, giving it even more volume than I thought possible. She's in a matching white blouse and yellow skirt, soft tennis shoes and bobby socks, like she's dressed for the first day of school rather than a trip to Abilene. Barbie's long brown hair is in a fishbone braid. She's wearing blue slacks and a crew neck cardigan. Her freshly painted toenails are exposed in her sandals. I'm surprised to see her in a brassiere, which has shaped her small breasts into dangerous bullets.

"I'm under-dressed," I say, helplessly, holding out my arms. My overalls are stained at the knees, and I haven't checked, but I suspect that there are bits of hay in my hair.

"Not for us," says Sandra-Lee, lightly getting to her feet. "But probably for Martha and you know her parents are worse. Let's see what armor is tucked away in your wardrobe."

"What's the point?" I sigh as Sandra-Lee leads the way up to the attic room and Barbie takes the rear, like I plan on somehow escaping through the back.

"To look pretty for Purlie tomorrow night."

"To look pretty for yourself," adds Barbie and I'm reminded of Kitty again.

Sandra-Lee opens my wardrobe and examines the dresses that are now several inches too short for me. The wire hangers slide against the wood but are soon drowned out by Barbie fiddling with the Dansette. She takes out *Clap Hands, Here Comes Charlie!* and puts on *Bo Diddley is a Lover*. "Wouldn't it be the greatest if we could listen to your collection at the Social?" she asks.

"It would upset Petunia and the entire bridge club," says Sandra-Lee slyly. "That ought to shake things up! We'd probably never get to organize another Social."

"I'm okay with that," I laugh.

"Here."

Sandra-Lee hands me a buttoned blouse with a green tartan pattern. I unhook my overalls and slip off the shirt I put on this morning. From behind me, Barbie shrieks, "What happened?"

I turn to see what she's talking about, for a moment forgetting about my injured back. My sudden twist pulls at the scabby skin which crackles under the gauze pads. Sandra-Lee sucks in a breath, too. I take the blouse from her and yank it roughly over my head.

"It's nothing," I say, wondering if I can get away with telling them I fell on a pitchfork.

"It's *not* nothing!" says Barbie and she lifts up my shirt. "How can you even wear a brassiere right now? It looks painful."

"I fell—" I begin but Sandra-Lee cuts me off.

"It looks like claw marks. Did somebody—" she gasps. "Oh my goodness! Did Purlie do something to you?"

"No! It wasn't Purlie. He didn't do anything." I shake them off of me.

"You can tell us if he did," says Barbie, looking murderous. She slams a fist into an open palm. "If he did you wrong!"

"It wasn't Purlie!" I say again. "Can we just drop it?"

"It *was* somebody though. That's not anything from an accident that I've ever seen," says Sandra-Lee.

"Look, can we just drop it?" My voice shakes and sweat beads on my forehead.

"No, we cannot just drop it! Who hurt you, Delah?" Barbie asks. "We won't stop pestering you until we get an answer."

"Right," says Sandra-Lee. "And if we don't get an answer out of you, Wilma will. She's bound to see it in the changing room. So, you might as well tell us before she can start gossiping."

Sandra-Lee has a point, and I can't see a way outside of this conversation. I've been cornered into a confession by my own forgetfulness. I should have been more careful about undressing in front of them. The day in the stables starts to boil up from the pit of my stomach, urging me to tell them. It is bile and awful in the way it churns and tightens my insides. I hate that I've kept so much from them and the way Barbie looks so determined to do right by me only adds to the unspoken agony. I think of how dangerous Hardy appeared this morning, how it took everything for me to not turn my back on him while that darkness remained behind his eyes. Can I keep the secret of his changing and still be honest about what he did to me? If I don't say anything, will Hardy do the same thing to Barbie? I can't allow that to happen.

They wait for me with expectant faces. With Sandra-Lee tapping her foot, arms crossed, she makes me feel like I've got to explain to her why it isn't my fault. I remind myself that I didn't do anything wrong.

"It was Hardy," I say with a strangled whisper.

"What?" Sandra-Lee nearly gags. Barbie says nothing but her eyes grow.

"He... a few days ago." I did nothing wrong. I didn't encourage him, but I am ashamed. I can't keep looking at my friends and turn my gaze to my toes instead. "We were in the stables, and he grabbed me. I told him to stop. He wouldn't."

"Oh, Delah." Sandra-Lee mirrors my quiet tone.

Barbie steps forward and strikes me across the face. I'm stunned, cheek burning, and fresh tears spring out of me.

"How could you?" she hisses through her teeth. "Why would you say something like that?"

"Barbie! What…" Sandra-Lee looks between us, confused. Barbie doesn't hear her.

"You would ruin what Hardy and I've got going? Are you that petty?" She's not screaming and that makes the situation even worse. I step back because I think she wants to strike me again.

"I'm not! I didn't mean… I don't want to see you hurt!" I stumble over my words, keenly aware of Sandra-Lee's confusion and how my own secret is about to be fully exposed in Barbie's rage.

"Because I'm not *fond* of you? Don't ruin his good name because you're jealous of him, Delah!"

"What on earth?" asks Sandra-Lee.

Barbie throws up her hands. "You know what? Maybe you ought to stay home today. I don't want to see your face if you plan on spreading lies like that."

She marches from the room and moments later, the screen door slams. Sandra-Lee looks from the door to me and back again. "What did I miss? Why would you be jealous of Hardy?"

And then it slowly clicks, and her eyes briefly expand before shrinking into narrow slits. "I'll go talk to her."

I don't say anything. I don't think I can muster the courage. Sandra-Lee hurries out and starts down the steps to the lower levels of the house but I don't hear the front door open again. Instead, she's back in the room, clutching the doorknob, her thinly plucked eyebrows pinched together. "For what it's worth… I believe you."

"Thanks." The word comes out even though I can hardly breathe at all.

"I'll talk to Barbie. I'll make her see sense."

"Not in front of the twins."

"No."

Sandra-Lee disappears again, and I wait for the front door to slam shut again before collapsing. Grief rattles through me like a summer storm. It numbs my face and hands until I become nothing but snot and tears. The room grows dark around me. I pull Kitty's lace pillow tight against my chest, and curl around it. I want to disappear. I want to be dead.

Chapter Twenty-Two

I don't want to be alone while my friends are shopping and having a good time in Abilene without me. The idea of it, and of Barbie telling Sandra-Lee in hushed words about my confession underneath the Lake Sweetwater dock, twists my lungs. Because Purlie knows about this secret of mine, knew without asking and decided not to judge me on it, I call his house. Preacher John answers and I'm tongue tied. Sometimes I wonder if being a man of the cloth means that he can read the inner thoughts of his little congregation. Does he know this sin of mine that I carry? Does he know that I carry Hardy's as well?

"Hi. This is Delah Nix," I say stupidly.

There is a beat before he speaks, and I hear a small, earthly chuckle. "I suppose you want to talk to Purlie... unless there are other matters of the heart you'd like to discuss?"

"No. I'm okay."

"I'll tell you a secret, I'm never sought out at parties either," says Preacher John. "I'll get him."

He must have put the receiver on the table because I can hear him calling out to Purlie. He answers with another distant shout. "I got it in the study, Dad!"

There is a click, followed by another, and I try to think if I already knew about Preacher John having two phones in his house or if that was an added luxury that came with Purlie moving back home. "Hiya, Delah. I thought you were going with the girls today?"

"I... we had a fight. Could you come over?"

"Sure, I can. Give me fifteen." He hangs up.

I place the avocado green receiver back into its cradle and stare out the window, waiting for him. The wind chimes hanging from the porch clank in the light breeze, sunlight dancing through the glass and marbling the floorboards.

Restless, I hike to the stables and check on the ponies. The unnamed foal has started taking turns around the paddock. Navajo Blue and Bonnie Wee Dancer play with him, cantering around the far edge of the field, while Tessie and Ambition stay close to the feed. Tonight, I'll have to braid Nav and Bonnie's manes and tails so they're picture ready for the Church Social. Jeb Barnel promised us the use of his cart so the Mount Olympus theme will be complete.

The foal dances up to me on his wobbly legs, knees pointing in every direction, and presses his muzzle into my face. His hot breath covers the sting of Barbie's handprint. I should've brought him an apple. I lean my head into his and Bonnie pushes him aside, eager for her own affection. They shake their manes and snort at the sound of an approaching car. It's Purlie in his red impala wagon. Bonnie moves her lips against my neck, asking me not to leave them. *Stay forever, Delah. Enjoy the pasture!*

I wave to Purlie and head to the house. Purlie gets out of his car and waves back. In the time it takes me to get from the stables to his car, he's lit a cigarette and eased into that James Dean persona I've always appreciated in him. He hasn't taken off his driving glasses and I decide I like him better with them on.

"So, what happened?" he asks.

"Do you want something to drink? Coke? Coffee?"

"Coffee if you've got it."

"I'll make some."

He follows me inside at a polite distance. In the kitchen, I find an ashtray and place it in front of him. Dad quit smoking a while ago, but we still have a few ashtrays floating around. Kitty and I each made one in Mr. Diggs's art class and hers is the one I offer Purlie. It's shaped like a hand, index and middle fingers raised so the cigarette can rest between them. Mine is not nearly as creative. It's a simple bowl with swirling designs etched in the sides. There is a wooden standing ashtray with an amber glass basin in the living room but it's used to collect bills and unwanted letters now.

"Cute," he says, turning Kitty's handmade ashtray to get a better look at the handiwork. "You okay? You seem distracted."

"I'm just trying to think of where to begin." I turn on the stove and set the percolator down on it once I've filled it with water and grounds.

"Start with why you aren't with them now," he suggests. Lifting his glasses to rest them on his forehead. His eyes are honey lemon and too gentle for a body like that. He belongs on a ship, somewhere in the Indian Ocean, pulling on ropes while embracing a briny wind. If I tell him about the cuts on my back, I'm almost certain he'll respond the same way Barbie and Sandra-Lee did before they found out it was Hardy who did it to me. It's Hardy's jealousy toward Purlie that sparked it and if I mentioned that, too, I can imagine how Purlie will take it. At the same time, I don't think I can hold onto these secrets any longer. I already cracked the dam by telling the girls about Hardy. I might've lost Barbie's friendship forever. Is it worth losing Purlie's, too?

"Remember when we talked about animal-men?" I ask, deciding to go for the boldest of my secrets. If I start Purlie on the most crazy of things, he'll either believe me, or he won't. If he doesn't believe me, then I won't bother him with any of the other stuff that's happened since Kitty's death. If he does believe me, he'll see Hardy's actions are all part of this thing he's becoming, and perhaps, will know how to help us.

"Yeah..." Already, Purlie is tense and cautious. I feel my resolve deflating. His glasses slide back onto his nose. He tucks them into the collar of his shirt. His cigarette butt smolders in the ashtray.

I try again, going for a different angle than what I planned, but still on the same subject. "When Kitty was killed... Hardy tried to save her. He was cut up real good."

"Dad told me," Purlie nods, waiting for the other shoe to drop.

It's a lot harder to talk about it than I thought, and the words are fumbling to make sense in my head. They're stilted on my tongue. I tug at one of my overall straps and fiddle with the brass button at my shoulder. "Don't think I'm crazy."

"What is it?"

"Hardy told me to promise I wouldn't tell. And I haven't... but things are going south quick, and I don't think keeping secrets is so good anymore."

"Go on," he says softly, but the muscles in his forearms tightens.

"Well he... he's been different. He can run fast, faster than light! He can pick up rocks the size of men and throw them great distances! But he's becoming wilder, too."

"Like an animal?"

"Yeah. Like that."

Purlie leans back in his chair, tightened arms uncurling slowly on the tabletop. Behind me the coffee boils over and hisses on the stove.

I turn and grab the percolator with a dish cloth and move it off of the heated surface, glad for something to do. Purlie doesn't say anything.

"You don't believe me."

"It's not that."

"But?"

He leans forward and taps his folded hands thoughtfully on the table. Then he leans back again. I'm reminded of Tessie, uncomfortable and ready to drop the foal. So I tell him, "The other night, Dad heard a ky-ote disrupting the ponies. He says he nicked it, but it ran off before he could kill it."

"The same coyote that everyone's fussed about?" asks Purlie, and I notice how he pronounces coyote in three syllables, like he's trained his tongue to hide his small-town accent.

"That one, yeah. Dad was certain. This morning I went up to Hardy's house and confronted him and I saw his back. It looked like he got clipped."

Purlie utters a curse and the lines around his nose and mouth deepen. Other than this, he has no reaction and I'm about half-way angry. At least Barbie did something. At least Sandra-Lee said something.

Finally, he asks, "So, what's that have to do with you and the girls getting into it?"

"About a week ago, he kissed me. I asked him to stop but he kept on. Barbie thinks I'm blaming it on him because… because I'm jealous. He left marks on me, or I wouldn't have said anything about it."

Purlie's head snaps up at this and the heat in my cheeks rises with the shame of having to admit to this again. His chair legs scrape against the floor and topples over as he stands.

"He violated you?"

"No! No. It was only kissing."

"But you didn't want him to do it?"

"No, I didn't."

"Then he violated you!"

I grab his arm, so he doesn't dash up to Hardy's house and do God only knows. "He's acting animal! Please don't! Please sit down! It's not like him to do this! It wasn't his nature…"

Purlie wrenches his hand free from me but doesn't move towards the door. We stare at each other, eye level. His look has focused inward with intensity.

"I've known him my whole life," I press. "Not once in all the while has he ever laid a finger on me, and I'm scared of this change in him. I just want my friend back."

"Can I see the marks?" Purlie asks.

"No."

"Why the hell not?"

"Because I'm afraid of what you'll do to him!" I shout and he blinks, perplexed by this swell of rage that's come out of me. But it's been there this whole time, since Kitty's murder, boiling, and now I've got a chance to unleash it. "I can't handle any more violence! No more. You can help me by sitting down or getting out. It'll do nobody any good for you to try and beat Hardy into a pulp."

"I can take him," insists Purlie.

"Not the way he is now. I've seen it. You don't stand a chance."

Purlie's fists clench at his sides and he sways to the unspent energy attempting to propel his legs up to the hill and try his luck. He takes a large inhale, nostrils flaring, and sits back down at the kitchen table. "I think I'll take that coffee now."

I fix him a cup and wait for him to talk some more. I'm still unsure if he thinks I've gone crazy in believing Hardy is turning into something less than human. Right now, Purlie is red with the tangle of all this confusion I've laid bare for him and desire to prove he's strong enough to protect me. I think it a sweetheart's foolishness.

"Hardy showed you how he's different?" Purlie asks, once his coffee mug is wrapped between his fingers. He doesn't drink from it but presses his lips against the ceramic and sets it down. "Do you have cream?"

I take a carton out of the icebox for him and watch him under his breath as the ribbon of cream swirls into the mug.

"That's right. I've never seen anyone run so fast and he's stronger than Slick... maybe even you."

"But you haven't seen him in any other form?"

"No... but his eyes do that thing. They glow when the light hits them a certain way."

"But he's only ever had the same body he's always had?"

"What are you getting at?"

I ease into the chair opposite Purlie. Normally, this is where Dad sits at the table, and it is a little odd to see the house from his point of view. Outside, most of the yard is seen through the window above the kitchen sink. The bottom of the stairs and the archway of the living room and part of the couch in there are clearly visible.

Purlie traces his coffee mug with a thumb. "I think Hardy is suffering a shock."

"So, you don't think he's turning into an animal?"

"I think he must believe he's turning into one."

"Explain the super speed and strength?"

"He's doping," shrugs Purlie. "A lot of athletes do it. Turns guys pretty aggressive, too. The doctors at school gave me a few shots to boost me back into fighting shape and it did that. I ended up punching holes in the walls on a regular basis. So, I quit and I lost my scholarship. That's beside the point."

"Are you sure that's it?" I ask, collapsing with relief, nearly giddy at the dark humor of preferring this option to the supernatural horror I've been living with. "It's drugs?"

"It's the only reasonable explanation," says Purlie with a rough exhale. "He got it into his head somehow that the attack and the side effects of doping are related. It's turned into a psychosis and he's acting on it. I bet you he's thinking he's behind all these coyote attacks. It's feeding into his ego."

"What do I do about it?"

"Nothing. Stay away from the bastard. I don't want him hurting you."

"He might hurt Barbie."

"Well, I don't want him hurting Barbie either." Purlie reaches across the table and cups my hand with his. "One of two things will happen. Hardy'll simmer down or I'll whoop his ass in front of the whole town. I won't do it tonight because you asked but I can't guarantee if he pulls shit like that again. Hell, I'll show you the moves so you can whoop his ass yourself."

I smile a little. "Thanks. You know Slick said he'd teach me how to fight, too. I'd like to learn how to whoop ass. But what do I do about Barbie?"

"She'll come around. Hopefully before Hardy tries something with her."

I nod, blushing, and stare at my dark outline in my coffee. I've doctored it with so much cream and sugar, there's hardly any bitter tang left. "I can't believe I was so stupid to think he was turning animal."

"Grief does funny things to the mind. Besides, you weren't told any different. It made sense to you and that's okay. Did you ever read about Plato's cave?"

I shake my head and gulp down a large mouthful of coffee. It's still hot and because the temperature outside is on the rise, sweat breaks across my brow, pressing against the edges of my tight curls.

"The short of it is, all these people lived in a cave and saw shadows against a wall. They assumed they were these big animals and needed to be cautious around them. Then one day, one of these cave dwellers looks for the source of these shadows and sees it's only other men trying to scare them with shapes made in the firelight. He goes and tells his clan they've been had but they don't believe him. They've lived their whole lives seeing these things and so his talk is madness. They cast him out of the cave and go on being afraid of the shadows."

"Hardy's the shadow?"

"Hardy thinks he's the creature. You're the one starting to see what's really making the shadow." Purlie turns in his seat to check the clock hanging on the kitchen wall and sighs. "I told my dad I wouldn't be out long. Maybe call the girls later tonight and hash things out?"

Our chairs scrape out from beneath us and I walk him to his car. I'm much calmer now that I've talked everything out of my system and I'm so relieved he doesn't think I've gone nuts. I'm glad I'm not. It was simply a matter of needing an explanation. Purlie embraces me, pressing his arms tight around my spine and I wince a little. "I'll pick you up tomorrow about six, okay?"

"Okay. Thanks, Purlie."

I cup my hand over my eyes and watch him drive off, mostly making sure that he hooks left, back toward town square and beyond, where Preacher John's house is, and not toward Hardy's. I almost laugh myself into dizziness. This whole thing! This whole time, Hardy's been doping, and it's got nothing to do with witchcraft or Travelers or the full moon.

Chapter Twenty-Three

Sandra-Lee shows up at the house while Dad and I are ushering Navajo Blue and Bonnie Wee Dancer into the trailer to take them to church. It's muggy and dreary out, so she has her hair hidden under a plastic bonnet. It might rain but there are splits in the gray clouds that suggest the storm may pass through.

"Hi, Mr. Nix! Delah!" She whistles and waves, picking her way through the field between house and stables. Her yellow Western Flyer leans next to mine under our wide cedar tree. Ambition huffs from the paddock and watches her with a liquid brown eye. Behind him, Tessie and the new foal plod around, gumming weeds.

"I'll be right back," I say to Dad but he flaps his free hand while the other fits Navajo Blue's harness onto a metal clip. "We're just about done here. Go on and be a kid for a change!"

I don't mind helping Dad, but I don't want him hearing about my fallout with Barbie or the way Hardy forced himself onto me. Between taking the ponies to the Social and picking up a second patrol shift, he has enough to manage without all my drama.

I meet Sandra-Lee halfway and walk back to the porch where we sit and drink ice water from a metal pitcher. It's been sitting out for a few hours, so water rolls down the sides like jewels of sweat.

"How was Abilene?" I ask, trying my best to not sound bitter.

Sandra-Lee shrugs. "It was fine mostly but Martha started to get emotional because none of the dresses were exactly what she wanted. She liked the straps on one but not the sweetheart neckline. The color of another but it didn't come in her size. It didn't help that all Wilma wanted to do was talk about what our dates are wearing and asking if Barbie was going to match Hardy's tie or not."

I pick a speck of dirt off the toe of my shoe and rest my chin on my knee. "Is Barbie still mad at me?"

"I don't think she ever was. I think she just wants to believe Hardy wouldn't do anything like that. It seems unlike him. I believe you though!" she adds, palms lifted in surrender. "It's just so odd."

"Purlie says he's probably doping."

"I'll ask Slick if you want? Maybe he'll make Hardy see sense." She hesitates and sips her water. "But they're not on the best of terms right now."

I glance up, shocked to hear this. "What happened?"

"He won't say. He's trying to keep it casual, but I think something happened at one of their practices." Sandra-Lee adjusts her bonnet with a sigh and sips her water again. "Hardy's making a lot of enemies it seems like."

Dad is finished getting the ponies in order and starts driving out with the pale blue Chevy we only use when we have to transport them. He pulls to a stop in front of the house and cranks down his window. "I'll see you at the Social, okay? Need to make a run to Roscoe first. Save a dance for me?"

"Okay!"

Sandra-Lee and I wave him off. The ponies' braided tails swish to the sway of the trailer.

"Well? What are you wearing tonight? Want help picking it out?"

"Sure."

We head upstairs to the attic room and Sandra-Lee marches over to my wardrobe. She swings open the door with a flourish, then puts one hand on her hip. The other hand drums newly polished fingers across her chapped lips.

"Can I ask you about what Barbie said?" she asks, suddenly taking a pink pleated blouse and slipping it from the wire hanger.

"I guess..."

Sandra-Lee holds up the blouse and closes one eye, picturing me in it. Then she shakes her head and returns it to the hanger. "The way Barbie was talking, it just seemed like she thought you liked her romantically."

I can't hide the blush creeping along my nose and cheeks, but I turn away from Sandra-Lee and pretend to press a bubble of air out from behind my collage of musicians and starlets. There is a shift in the room and the weight of Sandra-Lee's unvoiced thoughts bore into the nape of my neck. I press my index finger into the corners of my eyes, not wanting to cry. If I admitted to this, would I lose her friendship, too?

"How is that possible?" she asks. "Is it... is it all girls or just her?"

"I don't know." I say. "I don't think about kissing her or anything like that."

"That doesn't make any sense," mutters Sandra-Lee. "But I suppose love doesn't have to."

I stop breathing, replaying what she just said, and it hits me in a swirl of emotions.

She studies me, her long fingers tighten around the fabric of a lavender shirt, and her eyes flicker down to the floorboards. In a hushed tone, as though Dad were pressing his ear against my door, she asks, "Do you look at us in the locker room at school? Not just me and Barbie but... all of us?"

I shake my head. "Ugh! No! I'm not a peeper! I just have... I think about being with her. Differently than when you and me are together. Do you mind?"

"I don't know," answers Sandra-Lee and the corners of her eyes begin to water and smear makeup along the curves of her round cheeks. "I know you don't mean to hurt anyone. But I don't know if that's natural... I think it's against God."

"It's against God to sleep with anyone who's not your husband," I counter and there's a harshness in my tone I didn't anticipate.

Sandra-Lee gives a sad nod. "That's true but I wouldn't change it. Is it okay that I don't know what to say? It's a lot to take in. I don't understand it."

"Maybe I'll grow out of it?" I ask, hopefully. It bothers me that Sandra-Lee believes it's wrong but that it's still some type of love. I need her to be decisive for me but she's not shutting me out. I don't think.

"Maybe." She hands me a lavender, nylon shirt with a sweetheart neckline. I loved it when I tried it on in the department store, but I've never worn it to anything. "This with that pencil skirt you never wear... and hose."

"And my church shoes?" I ask. We both looked at the scuffed men's dress shoes and a sigh of disappointment escapes me. If my feet were smaller, I'd have a nice pair of flats or wedges. "Or the tennis shoes?"

"The tennies," agrees Sandra-Lee. "I need to head back home and get ready. I'll see you at the Social?"

She hesitates by the door and then rushes over to me, pinning my arms down in a tight hug. "It'll get better! I promise! You can count on me, okay?"

"Thanks," I mumble, taking in the smell of her lemongrass soap.

I start crying again but this time I don't mind so much that she sees. It's the fact she didn't answer me about Barbie and that she's continuing to be kind to me even though she doesn't understand my secret. It isn't a messy, full out weeping but several tears roll down the edge of my nose and plink onto the floor between my feet. I don't want Sandra-Lee to leave me so soon. I wish she could get ready for the dance here and take the space that belongs to Kitty.

I dress in the clothes she picked for me, hosiery included, even though it makes me itch around the knees. Then I sit at Kitty's vanity and brush my hair so that I can pull it into a bun. Last of all, but the most important thing I must do, I twist open a tube of Kitty's lipstick. My battle armor.

It doesn't take long for me to get ready and now I have a few hours to kill with nothing to do. I sit at the vanity and stare at my reflection without really looking at myself, just through me. Past the irises and into the dark little pupils. Not long ago I stared into Hardy's eyes this way, thinking I was meant to be close to him like that. I thought Hardy might be a fair choice, all things considered, since it's improper for me to pine after a woman the way a man does. But Hardy violated that trust.

Is that why I decided to share his secret with Purlie? Is that why I decided to defame him?

I push myself away from Kitty's vanity and make my way through the house, one floor at a time, trailing my fingers against the walls. They bump along the edge of family photos, little shrines of Kitty's short legacy. There's hardly a picture of our mother and I never minded before. She'd died before either of us understood who she was as a person and all the important photos were kept in a sacred space among Dad's personal effects.

Once outside, I soak in the hot air and patches of sunlight determined to break apart the storm clouds. There's a little box on the porch where we keep some of the garden tools and I go to it. I take a rusty spade and dig up a few irises. Clods of dirt cling to the roots or drop onto my shoes. It isn't a far walk to the old graveyard. I haven't been since the funeral, and I think of how Hardy cried against my shoulder the day he walked me home. The remorse he felt because he couldn't save her still touches me. I wish that Hardy still existed.

Preacher John told Dad the earth wasn't good here but I'm not sure how he meant. Wildflowers of yellow, red, and orange fan out among the tombstones. Every year they thrive and take up more and more space. In spite of this being a go-to make out point for many of my friends, Kitty's grave remains untouched. This is either out of respect or because Dad comes by daily and cleans the space. I'm not sure. Neither would surprise me.

I hesitate and kneel in front of her marker. The permanent one Dad bought, made out of white marble, hasn't arrived yet. Instead, she has a wire stand with a paper note, where the ink has run and blotched because of all the summer rain we've had. Spongy green grass covers the mound of dirt. I take the rusted spade and dig a hole near the wire stand. Dirt shifts through the palms of my hands as I pack it back over the newly planted irises. I pray that heaven is real, and Kitty is happy there.

Purlie's red impala wagon idles in front of the house. He leans against the bumper and smokes a hand rolled cigarette, driving glasses hang from the buttoned collar of his shirt. He isn't wearing a tie or a jacket and I feel more at ease because of this.

"Were you waiting long?" I ask.

He shrugs. "I don't mind. I saw you up there and figured you needed to do stuff."

"Thank you."

"Well, do you want to be on time or fashionably late?"

Before I can answer, the dust kicking up from under a speeding truck approaching distracts me. It's Slick's apple green Chevy. Clods of mug fling out from behind. When he sees us, he honks his horn and pulls to a stop. Sandra-Lee is in the cab with him, her lips pulled into a tight line as she rolls down her window.

Slick leans across her. "Y'all seen Hardy? He's stood up Barbie."

"Nope," says Purlie, evenly and flicks the butt of his cigarette in the direction of the Diggs' Queen Anne.

"Maybe he decided to meet her at the church?"

"That's not what he told Barbie and she's all torn up. She doesn't want to go now," says Sandra-Lee.

"I'll pull him out by the ears if I've got to. Ain't no way to treat a lady," grumbles Slick.

"We'll go with you," says Purlie and he hops into the bed of the Chevy before I can protest. With an agitated sigh, I follow. Slick slams the truck's gears and we bounce over so many potholes, my backside going numb.

"You just need an excuse to punch him, don't you?" I say to Purlie, hanging on the side of the truck, worried I might fall out.

"You don't?"

"I don't want anything to do with him."

We lurch as Slick parks in front of Hardy's house. He's out of the cab and up the three steps before the rest of us can get our bearings. Purlie's a quick second. The two of them look like the thick-necked goon squad only meant for mafia movies. Slick yanks open the screen door and pounds his fist against the half-moon window.

"Hardy?" he calls out. There is no answer. "Hardy, you best open the door and explain yourself or so help me!"

A sticky, rotten odor permeates the hot air. It reminds me of fermented apples thrown into a pile of burning manure. I know Purlie smells it, too, because he places a hand on Slick's shoulder and says, "Wait. Something isn't right."

"You think a coon got into their trash can?" Sandra-Lee asks, sliding primly out of the cab. The skirt of her pink satin dress ruffles up around her thigh. She smooths it flat as she walks around the side of the house with some difficulty because her pointy heels are trying to strike oil.

"It's something awful," I say, pressing my knuckles to my nose. "Slick, how can you not smell it?"

He frowns and inhales. "I'm sort of stopped up. Is it trash? It smells like meat gone bad."

Sandra-Lee and I trek around the side of the house, to the space between the back door and the detached garage. The trashcans aren't turned over and the lids are secured to the tops. We circle the whole house and work our way back to the front.

"Not the trash cans," I tell the others.

Slick presses his face into the door's tiny window and peers inside. Purlie strides over to the nearest window and looks in as well. Sandra-Lee whispers. "I don't hear anything."

"Me either," I say but then the true silence settles on me. No birds in the trees or crickets in the tall grasses. Looking back down the lane I see the breeze working its way through the field, but it seems to die at the edge of the Diggs's property. "Anyone home?" calls Slick. He moves away from the door and starts walking around the house, following the path that Sandra-Lee and I took.

"Maybe they're at the Pharmacy?" I suggest.

"Nope," says Purlie. "I stopped by there to buy you chocolate. It's closed."

We all exchange looks. Mrs. Diggs never closes the store. Even when she's sick, Mr. Diggs or Hardy keeps it running. I open the screen door and test the handle and nudge it open. A swelling, hot stench blasts my face, and coppery undertone reminds me of the school's Ag barn massacre. As my eyes adjust to the darkened rooms, the first thing I see are the dust angels striking the floors in shafts of fading orange light. Sandra-Lee stands close behind me and presses herself to my back.

"Mr. Diggs? Mrs. Diggs?" she calls out, though barely above a horse whisper. Purlie's heavy footsteps veer off to the room on the right and we take the left. I see Slick's face press into the window of the living room. For a comical moment we stare wide eyed at each other. Then his gaze shifts down and he disappears from view as he sprints back to the front of the house.

"Delah!" his voice is quivering and frantic. "Don't!"

There's a foot sticking out from behind the couch. Just a foot.

Strings of sinew and muscle hang free from a mangled ankle as though it's been chewed on. Sandra-Lee lets loose a piercing shriek she turns to run out of the room but slams against Slick just as he enters. Purlie appears at the other end of the room. He gags and leans against the archway for support. Like me, he can't look away. I move forward, numb with a morbid curiosity. Whose foot?

The rest of Mrs. Diggs body is crumpled near where Purlie slumps. A smear of blood takes over the better part of the room and puddles around an open ribcage. She is only half a face on a shredded torso. Her organs are gone. What remains of her clothes are crusted with congealed and blackened blood. Purlie stumbles around the corpse and reaches for me. He pushes my head into his neck, his hand tight around my ear so that I can't turn and look again.

"Oh God." Slick's voice drops like a dime in the room. Sandra-Lee has pushed her way outside. The splatter of her vomit hitting the porch disrupts the titanic wailing that comes from her lungs.

I squirm out of Purlie's grip. "What about Mr. Diggs?"

"Go back to the truck. Be with Sandra-Lee."

He says it with such a resoluteness that I don't protest. Sandra-Lee leans over the porch railing. Her whole body trembles and I half carry her to the truck. Slick has extra paper napkins from trips to drive-ins and diners in the glove compartment. I take one and press it to Sandra-Lee's lips, cleaning up the small gobs of spittle that cling to her lipstick. We sit in silence in the cab of the Chevy, me in numb shock and her gasping for air. I try not to think about what I've just seen but the distorted color of the carpet through the gaps in Mrs. Diggs ribs, but her twisted mouth and eyeless face is seared into memory.

Purlie and Slick sprint down the steps, pale and sweating. Purlie hops into the bed of the Chevy and Slick slams himself behind the wheel. It's dark enough now that he needs the headlights to see down the dirt road but in his frantic state, he forgets to turn them on.

"We gotta get to Barbie!" he shouts over the screeching tires and the gravel that slings against the windows, caught up in the slipstream.

My insides are bubbling. I'm not sure what's happening, and I can't stop the images of Mrs. Diggs's torn body from racing through my head. It's not just her I see, but Kitty and the animals Mr. Hooper loved so much. I remember the shimmering yellow of Hardy's eyes. My fingers shake as I press them to my throat and search for the necklace there. The silver bullet hangs like a raindrop on my breastbone. There is a lonesome howl in the distance, and I twist to look at Purlie riding in the back. He returns my unblinking gaze, and I know he's thinking the same thing I am. Did Hardy do this? Did he do *all* of this?

We stop in front of Barbie's house and Purlie jumps out, tripping as he launches himself to the front door. "Barbie? Mr. Stine? Mrs. Stine?" He bellows their names and presses his face to the windows of each room. "They're not here!" He shouts as he sprints back to the Chevy. "They must be at the Social."

He's barely back into the bed of the Chevy before Slick is off again, peeling through the long, uneven streets toward the church. Slick remembers to turn on his headlights as we near the square. Our church appears like a dark scab against the horizon, silhouetted by the blue of a full moon pushing its light through the persistent clouds. The Chevy's headlights flick across Navajo Blue as she gallops past, her flank covered in a ruby river of blood. My thoughts jump wildly to our ponies back at the stables. Did I hear their familiar whickering as we passed on the way to Hardy's house?

Slick pumps the brakes and skids to a halt. He leaves the truck running and darts up the garden path. Purlie follows and I watch them disappear into the building. I'm not sure what to do. Sandra-Lee leans forward and presses her hands into her face, immobilized by sobs. Nothing happens and then I hear the crack of a pistol. It propels me from the cab, leaving Sandra-Lee behind.

Blue and gold balloons and streamers decorate the open door. Beside it is the abandoned area for couples to take pictures where Navajo Blue managed to escape. Bonnie Wee Dancer was not so lucky. Blood oozes slowly from a gash in her neck. I sink down to stroke the soft bristles between her ears. An involuntary shudder works through me. A body hangs off the side of the wagon. The hem of a torn dress clings to sun kissed knees. I force myself to look at the face even though I know who it is.

Barbie. Her long hair, painstakingly put in a lattice of braids and beads, remains undamaged. The twist of her mouth is frozen in an unrealized horror. Her throat is torn out. Bits of skin and cartilage dribble down the pool of blood that soaks her chest and blue lace of the sash tied around her waist. I reach for her with trembling fingers, touch the soft inside of her wrist. I want to tell her I'm sorry. That I loved her anyway. That she was my best friend. I want to tell her to stitch herself back together and somehow survive.

Another round of shots pulls me away from Barbie's side and I rush blindly around the back of the church. Bodies are everywhere, covered in blood drenched confetti, slung over picnic tables and strewn across the lawn. Martha and Wilma are only tattered faces slumped against the whitewashed side of the building, their matching bodies mangled around each other. Not far from them are their dates, Parker and Albert. The cavity of their stomachs are cracked open like eggs. I spin around. Torn bodies, bits of people I've known all my life. People I'll never see again. Lauren Willoby and Manny are closest to me, half tucked under a table. His body is in a protective curve around hers. Has Hardy killed everyone?

A stray bullet bursts through the stained-glass windows and whizzes by. I duck and thread my way into the church from the back door, which hangs open on broken hinges.

A record player sitting on the punch table scratches out a delicate melody. Preacher John is underneath the piano beside the table. I'm not sure if he's alive but I sink down to my stomach and creep alongside him. I hear Dad scream, "Joe! Watch your six!" and my chest tightens. In all the carnage, I didn't think to look for Dad.

I lift my head up enough to see him at the front end of the church. Slick and Purlie are crouched down, useless, in the pews behind him. But they are alive. Sheriff Muller, standing in the aisle, spins on his heels and shoots up at the rafters. A heavy figure dodges the bullet and jumps from the wooden cross. Dad fires his pistol and the bullet rips through the stomach of the beast but doesn't stop it. It lands on Sheriff Muller and rips out his arm from the socket and flings it across the church. Sheriff Muller bellows for help but his words are minced into a wet gurgle. I see the monster's face, twisted and gore spattered. It's Hardy.

His limbs are stretched into odd angles, hands hooked like daggers, and mouth pulled into a rabid frenzy with teeth that jut through torn lips. But it's unmistakably him. Hardy bends over and tears out a chunk of flesh beneath Sheriff Muller's chin.

Dad pulls the trigger of his pistol again. He has no ammunition left. Only a series of clicking echoes between the crunching of Sheriff Muller's bones.

I freeze. Hardy's dress suit is riddled with bullet holes and his own blood trickles out of the gaps. His muscles and veins are swollen with exertion. His face and hair are smeared red.

"Delah," Dad whispers in a panic, seeing me for the first time. Hardy's head snaps up and he turns in my direction. Both Slick and Purlie vault over the pews and into Hardy's view. He growls and charges at them. Dad bellows, "GET THE GUN!"

He points at Sheriff Muller's arm still holding onto the pistol. Hardy turns toward me again and Purlie punches him with an anvil-like fist in the ear. He dodges a swipe of Hardy's clawed hand. Slick kicks him in the spine and Hardy spins to him, slashing at the air. Slick's stomach splits open and he staggers backward, hands pressed tightly to his wound. Purlie drags Slick between the pews and Dad starts throwing hymnals at Hardy's back, drawing his attention away from the boys. Hardy launches himself toward Dad, but Purlie is quick. He scrambles back to the fight and yanks Hardy down, locking his arms into a half-nelson. For a moment I think he's going to choke

Hardy out but Hardy squirms free. Purlie jumps back and out of the way of another swipe.

I lunge for Sheriff Muller's gun and army crawl back toward the punch table. In my haste, I kick one of the legs and the needle of the record player scratches across the vinyl. Music starts up again and I tense, worried I've just signed my life away on a stupid mistake.

"Get away from my daughter!" Dad hollers and he throws several hymnals at Hardy's head. One of the books bounces off of Purlie's back.

Preacher John stares up at me with his deep-set eyes. His fingers are tacky with blood. They curl around his bible.

"Are you okay?" I whisper.

He blinks and his grip tightens around the leather binding of his book. "I... I... I wet myself."

"It's okay," I tell him.

I feel my veins pumping movement back into my arms and legs. I force my hands to be steady and open the barrel of Sheriff Muller's pistol. I dump out the remaining bullets and yank the silver one free from the braided rope around my neck, then snap the barrel back into place.

Dad lets out a terrible, wordless bellow. I pop up, frightened that Hardy's gutted him, and smack my head against the edge of the table. My hands are shaking too much. I'm worried I'll hit Dad, Purlie, or Slick by mistake.

"Stop! Hardy! Please stop this!" I can't pull the trigger. Slick looks up at me from where he slumps, ashen faced, against a pew. He lets out a pleading moan.

Hardy ignores me and advances on Dad and Purlie. He flings Purlie across the room. Purlie's head smacks against a stained-glass window but he staggers quickly to his feet. Hardy is on top of Dad, tearing at his flesh. Dad's fists are swinging, and he lands a solid punch in Hardy's jaw, another in his bullet-riddled torso. Hardy stumbles backward. Purlie grabs him by the shirt, then slings him in my direction. Hardy's eyes are locked on mine. A shiver runs down my spine. It isn't Hardy. It's something evil wearing his skin.

He's stalking me slowly. No longer hungry for flesh but interested in the game. I'm vaguely aware of the shallow echo of Preacher John's breathing between the beats of The Fleetwoods playing too loudly on the record player. My hand sinks and I think of the first night he was in the bedroom, listening to this album as we talked about what he was becoming. Had I known then that this is what would happen, would I have killed him sooner? Can I do it now?

"Please…" I beg. "It's me."

"NOW, DELAH!" Purlie screams.

The tightly wound muscles of Hardy's brow and jaw shift. For a startling moment I see the fear in him. I see the real and pure humanity of Hardy resurface just as my finger squeezes against the warm trigger.

I don't miss.

Acknowledgements

This book has taken such a journey since its first draft and would not be where it is today without the helping hands of my writing group and friends: Arwyn, Meg, and Kelsey. Your input helped craft a unique story that I kept falling in love with each pass.

Thank you to my mother, who is definitely not the target demographic and will jump at the slightest noise. She stayed up reading through the night in that Memphis loft. She believed that *Maryneal* wouldn't be shelved forever...and if it did? Well, I got to scare at least one person.

For Kate, there is no way to describe the gratitude I have.I gave you an impossible task, cried and complained, and you listened. Also thank you for creating a beautifully amazing cover.

Without Shelby's encouragement to reach out to Wild Ink Publishing, and the amazing team that I found in Abby and Brittany, this book would still be hidden in a dusty drawer, on a thumb drive that no one would ever find. Thank you for giving this book life.

To my friends and elders who were patient with me while I hounded them for details about the sixties and living in tiny towns. There are so many of you. Your patience and grace didn't go unnoticed. Especially when we dived into the sticky politics and how best to navigate the hard(non-supernatural) topics that Delah and her friends face. Although this book deals with the mythical, it was important to me that I stuck close to history and represented life as it was. I wanted to have someone like my grandmother, mixed race and masculine, to be the love interest and the heroine of a story. I could not, then, in good faith, represent a woman like her and not stare at the issues of the times head on.

The inspiration for Maryneal came from several places but the first of which was from a simple question: how does a town stop existing? So, for Nolan County and its unincorporated places, may this book carry your memories even if they aren't true. Even if I made everything up. Even if the land claims you for good. There will always be a little slice of you remaining somehow. Somewhere.

Finally, I must acknowledge Grief. This book would not be where it is today without it. I had lost a friend in one of the most devastating ways imaginable. I found my healing through writing Delah's own process. I hope that others who have lost loved ones through violence have found some connection here. I hope I have given you a safe space to weep and to rage. I hope you stay strong through the day, find a purpose, and never miss.

About the author

Abigail F. Taylor is an award winning Own Voices author from Texas. Her novella, THE NIGHT BEGINS, debuted with Luna Press Publishing Feb 2023. Her short stories and poems can be found in Writer's Digest, Globe Soup, Fractured Lit, Sixfold Magazine, and Illya's Honey, among others. She once spent a year working on the film set for The Dinosaur Experiment, and had a stint in religious studies. When she's not writing, Abigail spends her time out in nature, practicing aikido, and cross stitching. She lives with four cats, a two small dogs, and a sassy rooster.

You can follow her on her website abigailftaylor.wordpress.com